Parker s

He continued to mo... pupils of his eyes, wid... the darkness.

"I collect orchids," he said softly. "Every one of them is more beautiful than the last. I appreciate beauty, but mere beauty doesn't captivate me anymore." He let his gaze sweep over her. "What fascinates me now is the rare and unusual. The unique."

He touched her shoulders, let his hands slide down her arms. "You fascinate me, Bree."

She told herself to step away from him. It would be a mistake to get involved with Parker.

Apparently her body didn't get the memo.

"I'm sorry to disappoint you, but there's nothing especially interesting about me, Professor," she said, trying to ignore the way his hands felt on her skin. "Maybe you're just not used to hearing 'no.'"

His smile was wicked in the dim glow from the porch light. "What exactly are you saying no to, Bree?"

Dear Reader,

So many of us have things in our past that we're not proud of. Things we've done, things we've said, things we've neglected to do. If we're lucky, we pull ourselves together and build a good life for ourselves and our families. But what if you're forced to go back to your hometown and confront your past? And what if that past threatened your future with the man you've fallen in love with?

Bree, the second McInnes triplet, faces this dilemma in *No Place Like Home*. Parker is exactly the wrong man for her—the secrets in her past could destroy his career. How will Parker choose between the woman he loves and the profession he lives for? I loved writing Bree and Parker's story and watching as they figure out how to handle the past and build a future together.

I love to hear from readers! Visit my Web site at www.margaretwatson.com, or e-mail me at mwatson1004@hotmail.com. And look for more from THE McINNES TRIPLETS with Fiona's story in April 2009.

Margaret Watson

No Place Like Home
Margaret Watson

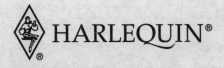

HARLEQUIN®

TORONTO • NEW YORK • LONDON
AMSTERDAM • PARIS • SYDNEY • HAMBURG
STOCKHOLM • ATHENS • TOKYO • MILAN • MADRID
PRAGUE • WARSAW • BUDAPEST • AUCKLAND

Recycling programs
for this product may
not exist in your area.

ISBN-13: 978-0-373-71531-2
ISBN-10:   0-373-71531-5

NO PLACE LIKE HOME

Copyright © 2008 by Margaret Watson.

www.eHarlequin.com

Printed in U.S.A.

ABOUT THE AUTHOR

Margaret Watson has always made up stories in her head. When she started actually writing them down, she realized she'd found exactly what she wanted to do with the rest of her life. Almost twenty years after staring at that first blank page, she's an award-winning, two-time RITA® Award finalist who has written more than twenty books for Silhouette and Harlequin Books.

When she's not writing or spending time with her family, she practices veterinary medicine. She loves everything about her job, other than the "Hey, Dr. Watson, where's Sherlock?" jokes, which she's heard way too many times. She loves pets, but writing is her passion. And that's just elementary, my dear readers.

Margaret lives near Chicago with her husband and three daughters and a menagerie of pets.

Books by Margaret Watson

HARLEQUIN SUPERROMANCE

*The McInnes Triplets

Don't miss any of our special offers. Write to us at the following address for information on our newest releases.

Harlequin Reader Service
U.S.: 3010 Walden Ave., P.O. Box 1325, Buffalo, NY 14269
Canadian: P.O. Box 609, Fort Erie, Ont. L2A 5X3

For my brother Doc,
who's always been a hero to me.

PROLOGUE

Thirteen years ago

BREE MCINNES STORMED INTO her father's office and threw her backpack to the floor. "I hate Shooter Clemmins," she said.

Her dad looked up from his desk and frowned. "What are you talking about, Bree?"

"A boy in my high-school. He said I look like a fire truck." Humiliation made her eyes burn. "He said red hair is b-butt ugly."

"What do you care what some boy named Shooter thinks?" her father demanded. "And what kind of low-class name is that, anyway?"

"Da-ad…!" Bree rolled her eyes. Shooter was the hottest guy in the junior class. "Everyone listens to him."

"You're not everyone, you're a McInnes. My daughter." He leaned forward. "Why are you upset? You're beautiful. Haven't I always told you that you're the prettiest of my triplets?"

"Like what you think counts," Bree muttered.

"What did you say?" He surged to his feet.

"I said, 'Yes, Daddy.'" Bree threw herself into the chair on the other side of his desk. "I wish I had black hair and blue eyes like Zoe and Fiona. No one makes fun of them because of their hair."

"People make fun because they're jealous," he said.

"Yeah, right. Everyone wants butt-ugly red hair."

"Why would you want to look like Zoe and Fiona?" he pressed. He crossed his arms and gave her the smile that made her skin crawl. "You look like me. You should be proud of that. Your mother said I was the most handsome man she knew."

"I don't care what Mom said. Zoe and Fiona are prettier," she said defiantly.

"Why would you say something like that?"

"Because it's true," she said. "They *are*."

"You're the spitting image of me, so I think we both know which of you is more attractive."

"Boys don't like red hair," she muttered, kicking her backpack.

"Why is that important?" her father asked, narrowing his eyes. "What do you care what boys like?"

"Everyone cares what boys think," she said.

"Not my girls. My girls aren't interested in boys," he said sharply.

Yeah, right. "We're sixteen, Daddy. Everyone else in school is allowed to date. Why can't we?"

"You're far too young to date," he said, his voice rising. He stepped around the desk to loom over her. "You're mine and I'm not going to share you with any stupid boys. Besides, who would you want to date from Spruce Lake High? Someone named Shooter, for God's sake?"

Everyone wanted to date Shooter.

"You're so unfair," Bree said, tears spilling from her eyes. "Why won't you let us be normal?"

"Normal? What's normal? Leaving your father alone? Going out with juvenile delinquents and making me sit in that house all by myself? Is that what you want, Bree?"

"Yes," she cried, jumping up. "I want to be like everyone else." She wanted a father who didn't get angry when they wanted to go out with a friend. A father who didn't get mad when guys called them. A father who didn't try to control them every minute of every day.

She wanted her mother. "If Mom hadn't died," Bree sobbed, "she would let us go out. She would understand."

His face dark, he grabbed her arm. "How could you say that to me? Don't you love me? After all I've done for you?"

"Mom was better than you. She loved us. I wish she was here." Bree dashed away her tears.

"Blubbering like that doesn't make you attractive," her father said coldly, letting her go. "No one likes a girl with snot all over her face."

There was a snort of laughter from the door, and Bree looked over to see a tall boy leaning against the jamb. He was a few years older than her, but she knew who he was. Ted Cross. His father was the dean of the college. She'd never realized how cute Ted was, with his dark hair and blue eyes. And she had red, blotchy eyes and snot on her face.

"I hate you, Dad!" she yelled. Grabbing her backpack, she shoved past him and ran out, ignoring her father's shouted order to come back. She clattered down the worn marble steps and burst out the front door. Leaning against the statue of Bernard Collier, she fished in her backpack for a tissue.

She'd barely pulled herself together when she heard someone come up behind her. "He's wrong, you know."

She peered over her shoulder at Ted Cross, then glanced away. "About what?"

"Even when you're crying, you're hot."

She sniffled. "Yeah, right," she muttered, but she felt a tingle of excitement. A college guy thought she was hot?

He sat next to her and pulled out a pack of cigarettes. "Want one?"

She stared at the red-and-white package for a moment, then said, "Sure."

He smelled good when he leaned close to light hers. Like Aramis. The stupid boys in her class weren't sophisticated enough to wear Aramis. He smiled, showing dimples, as he lit his own and took a deep drag. "Fathers can be a real pain in the ass."

Her father would have a cow if he saw her smoking. She inhaled deeply, and the smoke burned her throat and made her eyes water. She coughed so hard her chest hurt, and Ted had to thump her on the back. "First time?"

"I've smoked plenty of cigarettes," she lied.

"What else have you done plenty of times, Bree?"

She studied him out of the corner of her eye. "Lots of things," she said. "Pretty much everything you can think of."

"Is that right?"

She sucked in another lungful of smoke and managed to suppress all but a tiny cough. "Yeah, it is."

CHAPTER ONE

HIS CLASS WAS SCHEDULED to begin in less than ten minutes.

He didn't have time to argue with this bureaucrat.

"What do you mean, I'm not giving you enough lead time?" Parker said into the phone. "I received this invitation to speak two days ago. How could I have given you more time?"

"I'm sorry, Dr. Ellison. The travel department needs at least a week's notice to purchase airline tickets," the prim-voiced woman on the other end of the line said.

"Fine. I'll make the arrangements myself," Parker answered and dropped the phone into its cradle. He turned on his computer, then studied the pictures of orchids covering the walls of his office as he waited for the machine to boot up. How should he frame the speech? The audience would be members of the museum, so there'd be potential donors in the crowd. He'd have to make sure he brought his most arresting and beautiful photos with him.

When the computer chimed its familiar tune, he typed in the Internet address of a travel service, then glanced at the clock and swore. He didn't have time for this right now. And after his class, he had an appointment with the college president.

Marjorie, the department's administrative assistant, could order the ticket for him. Grabbing his lecture notes, Parker hurried out. Voices and laughter drifted through the door of the science department office as he approached. Marjorie's desk had been pushed into a corner, and a cluster of students stood around it. Parker stared. What was going on? Students rarely ventured into the department office.

"Hey," a husky feminine voice said. "One cookie to a customer. Don't be greedy."

"I'm not greedy," a man replied plaintively. "Just hungry."

"Then you shouldn't have skipped breakfast," the woman said.

"Busted, Tennant," another guy hooted. "Get out of here."

"Is there a problem?" Parker stepped into the room.

The group of young men froze. "No, Professor," one of them mumbled. "We're just going."

The students scattered, leaving Parker alone with the woman behind the desk. He'd never seen her before. She had red hair pulled away from her face in a rather severe style, and wore a shapeless beige blouse. Yet her green eyes sparkled with life. She'd clearly been enjoying the attention.

It was obvious what had drawn the students: a large plate holding a few chocolate chip cookies at the edge of her desk.

"You didn't have to scare them off," she said with a grin. "There's plenty left for you."

"Who are you and where's Marjorie?" he asked with a glance at his watch.

Her smile faded and she held out her hand. "I'm Bree, the new administrative assistant. Marjorie took a job in the nursing school. And you are…?"

"Dr. Parker Ellison." He shook her hand and glanced at the cookies. "Marjorie didn't allow eating in the office."

"Is that right?" the new admin said coolly.

"And you moved the desk. Now you can't see who's in the hall."

The woman's eyes flicked toward the door. "I don't want to be distracted."

"Fine. Listen, I need you to do something for me," he said, checking the time. Five minutes. "I need a plane ticket to New York for this Sunday morning, returning on Monday. Whatever airline flies out of Green Bay. Thanks. I'm late for class."

As he turned to leave, she said, "Wait a minute!"

"Just book the ticket," he said without turning around. "I'll be back in an hour."

He ran down the stairs and out the door into the clear June sunshine, then hurried to the redbrick, ivy-covered building next door. He rushed into the lecture hall just as the bell rang, and nodded to the waiting students.

There were almost a hundred of them, he guessed. Boys slouched in their chairs, trying to act cool. A group high up in the back were staring at a laptop—probably looking at porn, he thought with resignation.

Several girls sat in the front row, watching him expectantly, and he quickly memorized their faces. Experience had taught him that female students up front were likely to spend too much time in his office.

One boy sat by himself off to the side. He wasn't a college kid—he couldn't be older than fourteen or fifteen, Parker guessed. He wore a wrinkled brown polo shirt and baggy jeans, and his shoelaces were untied and muddy. The expression on his face was a mixture of wariness and excitement.

Poor kid.

"Welcome to Intro to Biology," Parker said. "I'm Dr. Ellison." He wrote his office hours and room number on the chalkboard. "I like my classes to be informal and interactive. I want you to ask questions, and I'll be asking you questions, too. Let's go over my expectations before we begin."

Most of the students opened their laptops. The kid opened a spiral notebook and picked up a pen.

When the bell rang an hour later, Parker set down the colored chalk and watched the class file out. The young boy gathered his notebook, stuffed it into a dark red backpack, then headed down the stairs. He avoided looking at anyone.

"Hey, there," Parker said when the kid walked past his desk. "What's your name?"

"Charlie," the boy said, his blue eyes wary.

"Welcome to class, Charlie." Parker eased one hip onto the desk. "You look a little young for college."

"I took the AP biology test last spring. I got four out of five."

"That's impressive," Parker said.

He shrugged. "I guess."

"So you like biology?" Parker asked.

"It's okay. I wanted to take herpetology, but Intro to Biology was a prerequisite."

"You going to be a herpetologist?"

Charlie shrugged again. "I'm thinking about it."

"What reptiles are you interested in?"

The backpack hit the floor. "Snakes. I have two ball pythons and a red-tail boa. Ball pythons are called that because they curl into a ball when you pick them up. It's a protective thing. They're really royal pythons."

"You go for the constrictors, huh?" Parker said, smiling. He rarely saw such eagerness in his college students. They'd learned to hide their enthusiasm behind a bored facade.

"Yeah, they're the coolest snakes. Some of them can reach fifteen feet long. Maybe more. That's big enough to eat a pig. I want to get an emerald tree boa, but I have to save up more money. They're kind of expensive."

"I'm a botanist myself," Parker said.

Charlie frowned. "Yeah, I know." He sounded as if he felt sorry for him. "But the guy I talked to said you're a good teacher and I should take your class. Even though you study plants."

Parker bit his lip to keep from grinning. "Plants can be exciting, too."

"I suppose," he said doubtfully.

"You sure you want to spend your summer in a class-room?" Parker asked.

Charlie picked up his backpack, staring at his feet. "I want to study snakes."

"You seem like a smart kid. I bet you could do that on your own."

"I have to take your class if I want to take herpetology."

"So your parents decided you should enroll?"

Charlie fiddled with the zipper on his pack. "I'm the one who wanted to."

The poor schlub. "I hope you enjoy it, Charlie. See you on Wednesday."

"Thanks, Professor Ellison."

Parker watched the boy hurry out. Another kid pushed by his parents, undoubtedly to stroke their own egos. They probably wanted to brag to their friends about their son taking college courses.

It was a hot-button issue for Parker, a reaction from his own forced enrollment in college classes when he was Charlie's age. Maybe he was overreacting, he acknowledged. But what the hell were Charlie's parents thinking? A kid that age should be hanging out with his friends during the summer, not sitting in a lecture hall.

Parker walked outside in time to see Charlie swing his leg over the seat of a battered red bicycle and pedal away. Hope-fully, he had something fun planned for the afternoon.

Parker put the kid out of his mind as he climbed the stairs to the second floor of the science building. When he approached the department office, he heard voices again, just as he had earlier. Chuck Boehmer, the department head, was talking to their new assistant.

"Hey, Parker," Chuck said with a smile, "have you met Bree?"

"I have," he replied. "She's already done some work for me."

The white-haired department head tapped the desk. "Talk to you later, okay?"

"Sure thing, Dr. Boehmer."

Parker looked from Bree to Chuck. What the hell was going on? He hadn't seen this many people in the office on the same day since he'd started teaching here.

After Boehmer disappeared down the hall, Bree's smile faded. "Yes, Dr. Ellison?" Her faint emphasis on his title made him narrow his eyes.

"Did you get that airline ticket for me?" he asked.

"Sorry." She lifted her chin. "The travel office told me I wasn't authorized to make that reservation. They're the only ones who can arrange travel."

"How the hell did they know you were doing it for me?"

She raised her eyebrows. "I had to ask them how to pay for it, of course."

"You don't have a department credit card?"

"I'm the secretary. Why would they give me a credit card, Doctor?" She emphasized his title again as her eyes drilled into his.

"To take care of department business, maybe?" he said impatiently.

"I'm supposed to make appointments, arrange meetings and type up exams and notes for the professors," she said. "Last time I checked, none of those things required a credit card."

Parker glanced at his watch and swore beneath his breath. His appointment with Jonathon Cross was in five minutes. Pulling out his wallet, he tossed one of his credit cards onto her desk. "Look, I don't have time to do this myself. I should already be in a meeting with the college president. Will you please arrange this trip for me? If it's not too much trouble?"

The redhead froze for a moment, then smiled at him. He felt a flicker of unease. "I'll be happy to do that for you, Dr. Ellison. Will you be traveling alone?"

"Yes, I just need one ticket. Thank you."

It was easier to hack his way through a jungle than maneuver through the college bureaucracy, he thought as he walked out of the office. Things were a lot less complicated in the rain forest.

He dumped the papers from his class onto his desk, groaned when he glanced at the clock, then hurried over to the administration building.

"No, THANKS," Parker said, shaking his head, trying to hide his irritation. "I'm honored you thought of me, Jonathon, but I'm too busy right now to serve on a committee of that scope."

"That's why the committee is starting work this summer," Jonathon Cross explained smoothly. "Everyone's teaching load is lighter."

"I have major fund-raising planned for my next expedition," Parker said. "Between that and the papers I'm writing, I can't take on a committee."

"I'm afraid I'm going to have to insist, Parker," Cross said, brushing a hand over his silver hair and straightening his expensive suit jacket. "We need a scholar with your credentials. To give the project high visibility."

"You mean you need a celebrity," Parker said, his irritation growing.

Cross shrugged. "Of course we do. John Henry McInnes was a celebrity himself. Even if the man was…" Cross pressed his lips together. "It doesn't matter what he was. McInnes is dead. But the college needs more press coverage. Celebrating the twentieth anniversary of McInnes's Pulitzer Prize for fiction will shine the spotlight on Collier College. And you have the connections to make that happen."

"There are plenty of other professors at Collier who are media savvy," Parker argued. "Let one of them handle it."

"None of them have your…standing, shall we say, in the popular press." Cross sat up straight in his Aeron chair. "To be blunt, Ellison, you're the only one who can get us the kind of publicity Collier needs. You'll have to talk to the family about his papers, and they're more likely to listen to you."

"What about Ted? He's got a book out now, and he's a hotshot in the history department. Let him schmooze with McInnes's family."

The president clenched his jaw before swinging his chair around to stare at the Henri Cross painting on the wall. If it wasn't an original, it was a damn good imitation. By hanging the Cross, was Jonathon suggesting the artist was a relative?

"Ted wouldn't handle the family as well as you would," Cross finally said. "And he hasn't cultivated the media, either. He doesn't have your connections."

"I'm not interested in playing games with the press," Parker said, gathering himself to leave. "Sorry, Jonathon."

The president spun around to face him again. "It wasn't a request, Ellison." He stood and paced across the Oriental carpet. "This celebration will bring in more donations to assist our scholarship programs for needy students."

Jonathon Cross worrying about needy students would be a first. "I thought this was about publicizing our Pulitzer

Prize-winning professor," Parker said smoothly. "Not fund-raising."

"Don't be naive," the man replied impatiently, reposition-ing the blotter on his otherwise empty desktop. The rich mahogany seemed to glow in the sunlight. "Everything is about fund-raising. This is just another way to draw attention to Collier."

"I think I bring plenty of attention to Collier already." Parker got way too much attention, but it couldn't be helped. "Find someone else."

"Sorry, Ellison. I've let you skate by a lot of assignments in the past, but I need you on this one."

Hell. He could tell from the steely look in the school official's eyes that there was no getting out of it. "Fine. Make sure they put the first meeting into the computer scheduling system so it shows up on my calendar." He stood. "Always a pleasure to meet with you, Jonathon." His voice was a little sharper than necessary.

"Likewise, Ellison." Cross smiled. "I'm looking forward to getting those papers from the McInnes family."

CHAPTER TWO

"What the hell is this?"

Bree heard Ellison down the hall, and she fought back a smile. He must have found the receipt for the plane tickets she'd placed on his desk.

Moments later he rounded the corner and stormed into the office. "What did you do?" he demanded.

"I got you the tickets you ordered," she said, raising her eyebrows. "Did I get the dates wrong?"

"You got the dates right," he said grimly. "It's the times I have a problem with."

"You never mentioned specific times."

He stared at her. "What was your name again?"

"Bree. Bree McInnes."

He did a double take. "McInnes? Are you related to… Never mind. You have me leaving Green Bay at 6:00 a.m. Sunday morning, Ms. McInnes. And I don't arrive in New York until 2:00 p.m. On the return flight, I'm leaving at 6:05 a.m."

"Is there a problem with that?"

"Yes, there's a problem with that! I'd have to get up in the middle of the night to catch the flight. Not to mention I'm getting into New York at two o'clock and have to speak at five."

"It's a fast-paced city," Bree said, fighting even harder to keep a straight face. "I've heard the cabbies can get you places very quickly. You should be fine."

"And then I'm leaving at 6:05 Monday morning."

"That's because you have a long layover in Milwaukee. I think the Brewers are home that day. Maybe you can catch their baseball game."

"What the hell were you thinking?" he said through clenched teeth. Bree noted the fact with satisfaction.

"I was trying to save you some money. You gave me your personal credit card, Dr. Ellison, so I looked for the most inexpensive flights. There were a couple that were cheaper, but I didn't think you'd want to take the red-eye. I'd hate flying all night."

"This is a joke, right?"

"Of course not. I take my job very seriously," she said.

"Why didn't you ask me before you chose these times?" he demanded.

"You tossed your credit card onto my desk and told me to book flights, then you disappeared. When was I supposed to ask you?"

"You must have picked the most inconvenient flights possible."

"Like I said, I was trying to save you some cash. Unless you throw your money around as freely as your orders?"

His cheeks colored. "All right, Ms. McInnes. Point taken. I was a jerk, and I apologize. I don't normally toss orders at our administrative assistants like that, but I was in a hurry and distracted. I'm sorry."

"Apology accepted," Bree said graciously. "Anything else I can do for you?"

He studied her for a moment. Then a dimple flashed in his right cheek and his dark blue eyes twinkled. "Okay, I deserved this. If I promise it won't happen again, can you fix the situation?"

Bree ignored the little flutter inside. She'd always been a sucker for dimples. "Probably. But it'll cost you."

"What?" He glanced down at the empty plate on her desk. "I have to bring the cookies next time?"

Was he *flirting* with her? Did he think that would make her fall in a heap at his feet? She frowned. "No, you have to pay to get the ticket changed. It's at least a hundred dollars each way."

His smile lingered at the corners of his mouth. "Okay. If you'll take care of that, I'll just slink back to my office, properly chastised."

She pulled his credit card out of her locked desk drawer. "What times *would* you like fly?"

"Sunday midmorning, and ditto Monday morning. Later than 6:00 a.m., and with a shorter layover. Thank you." He stood in the office door, watching her, and her heart rate increased. "How long have you been working here, Ms. McInnes?"

"Two days," she answered, suddenly fearful. Was he going to fire her?

"And you've already rearranged the furniture and put me in my place. Welcome to the department," he said. "I predict you're going to handle this job really well."

CHARLIE WAS MAKING a salad for dinner when Bree got home from work that afternoon. With some of the heavy furniture gone and the huge picture of her father removed from the living room wall, she no longer shuddered when she walked into his old house.

"Hey, Mom," Charlie said.

"Hi, honey." She snatched a piece of the cucumber he was slicing and ruffled his shaggy dark hair. "How was your day?"

"Boring." He hunched his shoulders and tossed the cucumber in a bowl.

"Sorry to hear that," Bree said casually. She knew where this was going. "What did you do?"

"Nothing. Not a single thing all day. Because you don't let me do anything."

"Charlie, sulking about it isn't going to make me change my mind. You're not taking that class at the college."

"Because I'm not smart enough. Right?" The carrot he'd begun peeling slipped out of his hand and skidded across the counter.

Bree sank onto a kitchen chair. "Charlie, that's not true. I know you're more than smart enough. That isn't the issue."

"Then what is?" he demanded.

She ran her hands through her hair, pulling out the elastic band and letting him down. "We've already talked about this. We can't afford the tuition."

"That is so bogus," he said. "If you work at the college, you get a discount on tuition. A big discount. I checked, okay?"

Oh, my God. Her kid was *too* smart. "A college campus isn't an appropriate environment for a boy your age," she said, scrambling for excuses.

He threw the carrot in the sink. "Fine. I'll spend every day doing something more *appropriate*. Like play video games. How would that be?"

"Why can't you study snakes on your own?"

"Because I'd have to go to the college library, and that's not an appropriate environment for me."

"Watch your mouth, Charlie," she said, taking him by the shoulders and turning him to face her. "You're getting dangerously close to being grounded."

He snorted. "You already grounded me when you said I couldn't take that class."

"That's it. Go to your room until dinner. I'm tired of your attitude."

"I'm tired of yours, too!" he yelled over his shoulder as he stomped up the stairs.

Bree heard a sigh and turned to see her sister at the back door. "Zo," she said. "Come on in."

Zoe hesitated. "Maybe this isn't a good time," Zoe said.

"It's as good as it's going to get." Bree dropped back into the chair at the kitchen table.

"Why is he so upset?"

"Because I won't let him take a course at the college this summer."

Zoe slid into the chair across from Bree's. "How come? If money's the issue, Fee and I can lend it to you."

"It's not the money, Zo." She sat down again with a sigh. It was put up or shut up time. If she wanted to have a better relationship with her sisters, she had to trust them enough to confide in them. "Charlie's right. With the discount I'd get as an employee, and if I keep my waitressing job, too, we could probably afford the tuition."

"Then why won't you let him take the class?"

Bree glanced at the stairs. "Let's go out to Fee's studio. She should know this, too, and I don't want Charlie to overhear us."

Zoe raised her eyebrows. "Secret stuff, huh?"

"Yes." A secret she'd kept for too long.

When Bree and Fiona arrived in Spruce Lake two months ago, Fiona had turned their father's old garage into a temporary, makeshift jewelry-design studio. A place to keep working while they sorted out his affairs. She wasn't there now, but she'd left her tools scattered on the workbench. Clear plastic boxes holding gemstones in every color of the rainbow dotted the wooden surface.

"What's up?" Zoe asked after Bree had shut the door.

"I can't let Charlie take a class because I can't let him on campus." She took a deep breath. "His father works there."

"What?" Zoe grabbed her hand. "You wouldn't ever say who Charlie's father was, and now you're telling me he works at Collier?"

Bree nodded, both nervous and relieved to unburden herself of her secret. "He's a professor there."

"My God, Bree. A professor at Collier got you pregnant?"

"He wasn't a professor then," Bree retorted. She bit her lip, then said, "It's Ted Cross."

"*Ted Cross* is Charlie's father? You were seventeen! He's five years older than us! That's…that's…" Zoe sucked in a breath. "What a creep, taking advantage of a kid like that."

"He didn't take advantage of me, Zo," Bree said quietly. "It would be easier if I could tell myself that, but I knew what I was doing."

"No seventeen-year-old who gets pregnant knows what she's doing," her sister retorted. "That's how they get pregnant. Ted was old enough to know better. And how come you didn't tell us you were going out with him?"

"The three of us were fighting more than we were talking at that point," Bree said, remembering the tension and stress that had permeated their childhood in this house. "And I was always angry. I wasn't about to tell you."

"I'm sorry," Zoe said softly. "That you had to go through that by yourself. That alone is enough reason for us to hate Dad—he drove you away when you needed us most."

"It wasn't just Dad, although he was part of it. It was Ted's parents, too." Bree stopped. This was every bit as hard as she'd expected it to be.

Zoe watched her with a knowing expression. "They gave you a hard time, didn't they? Sally Cross was very ambitious for Ted. She wouldn't have been happy he got you pregnant."

Bree nodded. "His dad wasn't, either." She stared blindly at Fiona's tools, remembering the day she'd gathered her courage and rung the Crosses' doorbell. "Ted denied it could be his baby. His mother called me…. She said I'd… And his father…" Bree blinked away tears.

Her sister grabbed her hands. "What did he do?"

"Threw a wad of money at me and told me to get rid of the baby. He said that if I didn't, he'd make sure Dad lost his job at the college."

"He couldn't have done that." Zoe shook her head. "Dad was the big celebrity here at Collier, and Jonathon was only a dean at the time. Dad would have wiped the floor with Jonathon Cross. And besides, Dad had tenure. They couldn't have fired him because his kid was pregnant."

Bree sat down on Fiona's stool abruptly. "It sounds silly, doesn't it? But at the time, I was too frightened to think straight." She reached blindly for Zoe's hand. "And I knew how Dad was going to react when he found out. All three of us would have suffered."

"More than Dad had already made us suffer?" Zoe murmured. "You shouldn't have run away."

"I needed to get away from Spruce Lake and everyone in it." Bree closed her eyes and clung to her sister's hand. "I loved Ted. I thought he loved me. When I realized I was pregnant, I figured we'd get married and live happily ever after. I was a fool."

"No, you weren't," Zoe said quietly. "You were a child who shouldn't have had to deal with all of that on your own."

Bree released her grip on Zoe and pushed away from the work table. "So that's why Charlie can't take the class. It has nothing to do with me being a mean mother."

"If you're so afraid of Charlie running into Ted, why did you take a job there?"

"I didn't have a choice—and believe me, I looked everywhere. I couldn't find another job where I'd get health insurance. And it's only for a few months, until I find a full-time teaching job for the fall."

"What if you run into Ted?"

"I'm being careful. I moved my desk into a corner of the office, where no one can see me from the hall. I won't go near the social sciences building. And I'll stay in my office when I'm at work."

"Charlie sounded really upset," Zoe said carefully.

Bree wiped some imaginary dust off the table. "It's a good thing he's not taking the class. The professor who's teaching it is an arrogant jerk."

"Yeah? You met him?"

"He's in my department," Bree said, remembering Parker Ellison's dimple. "He's a big celebrity—he's been featured on *The Tonight Show* and in *People* magazine." She'd run a Google search on Ellison that afternoon and found out just how much of a celebrity he was. The gossip sites were full of pictures of "the Orchid Hunter" with beautiful starlets on his arm. A different starlet in every picture.

She'd only looked because she wanted to find out more about the man she'd be working with.

"So he thinks he's God's gift?"

"Pretty much."

"Charlie wouldn't care about that."

"Charlie's not going to get a chance to care," Bree retorted. "He's not going near that campus."

CHAPTER THREE

"I ONLY HAVE A ten-minute break," Bree said, setting Zoe's soda and Gideon's beer on the table and sliding into the booth next to Zoe at The Lake House Bar and Grill. Zoe let go of her husband Gideon's hand to take a sip of her cola. "I'm training the new waitress and she's handling the tables on her own, but I have to keep an eye on her." Bree rubbed her sore shoulder. "Linda's not picking this up as fast as I thought she would. And I can't quit until she can deal with a Friday or Saturday night."

"You didn't have to stay and train her," Zoe said.

"Yeah, I did." Bree stretched her legs out and flexed her ankles. "Jerry hired me when I was desperate for a job, even though he really didn't need another waitress. I won't leave him in the lurch."

"I'll be glad when you're out of here. The two guys at the table across from us are staring at you," her sister said, giving them a dirty look.

Bree glanced over her shoulder. They smiled and one winked at her. "So what? Do you really think that bothers me?" She smoothed the short skirt she was wearing and grinned. "Compared to stripping, I practically dress like a nun at this place."

"I still can't believe you wanted to work here," Zoe said

under her breath. "Precisely because it's too close to…well, to the kind of place you used to work."

Bree glanced from Zoe to Gideon on the other side of the booth. "I needed money, Zo," she said patiently. She'd already had this argument with Fiona. "I made almost as much money here in tips in two nights as I made in a week while I was substitute teaching."

"Why didn't you say something? Fiona and I would have been glad to help you out."

Gideon covered his wife's hand with his own. "Maybe she didn't want to ask for charity, sweetheart." He rubbed his thumb absently across the back of her fingers.

Bree's throat tightened. "Thank you, Gideon. Not that I don't appreciate the offer, Zo," she added. "But I have to do this myself."

Zoe leaned closer. "What about Charlie's father?" she asked in a low voice. "He's gotten off scot-free for twelve years. I know Charlie's healthy now, but Ted should have to pay a share of his medical bills." She twined her fingers with her husband's. "Gideon can handle the child support suit for you. It's only fair, Bree."

"I'll decide what's fair for Charlie and me. What's right. And bringing Charlie's father into the picture isn't." Anxiety churned her stomach. "Butt out, Zoe."

"We want to help. You're working two jobs and still worrying about money, and it isn't necessary. You have the right to ask for child support."

"Leave it alone, Zo. After arguing with Charlie all week about that stupid class, you think I'm going to turn around and tell Ted about him?"

"Maybe you should. Charlie's not a baby anymore. Maybe he should have a say in whether or not he knows his father."

"Charlie and I have done just fine for twelve years."

"You're being selfish, Bree," Zoe said. "You want to keep Charlie all to yourself."

"That's not it," she said automatically, but she knew there was a grain of truth in what Zoe said. She didn't want to share Charlie. "I have to get back to work. You need anything else right now?"

Zoe frowned. "You're being awfully damn stubborn."

"Guess it runs in the family."

"She has you there, sweetheart," Gideon said, squeezing Zoe's fingers.

She yanked her hand away. "Why are you taking her side?" she demanded.

"I'm trying to see this from Bree's point of view," he said carefully. "Maybe you and Fiona should do the same thing. Would you go to Bree if you needed money? Or Fiona?"

"That's different," Zoe said.

"How?" Bree asked, slapping the table. "How is that different?"

"Because Fiona might think I want her back in my life *because* of her money," Zoe retorted. "But you don't have any."

Gideon looked from one sister to the other. "Does everything have to be a fight with you three?" he asked. "Can't you discuss things like normal people?"

"Old habits," Bree said, picking up the tray. "You sure you knew what you were getting into when you married her, Gideon?"

His eyes gleamed as he looked at Zoe. "Oh, yeah. I can deal with the fighting." He recaptured her hand, brought it to his mouth and kissed her fingers. "There are some upsides to fights, you know."

Gideon's passion was reflected in Zoe's face, and Bree's

throat closed again. "Geez, you two. Get a room," she muttered as she turned away.

She was glad her sister had found Gideon, but seeing their happiness made her feel hollow sometimes. As if she was missing a part of herself. And that was just stupid sentimentality and hormones talking.

An image of Parker Ellison laughing, his dark hair rumpled as if he'd shoved his hand through it too many times, came to her. She realized she was staring into space, and swore at herself. "Get over the dimples, already," she muttered to herself.

"Hey, Bree," someone called, and she dragged her attention back to her job.

"Hey, yourself. What do you need?" she asked the college boy.

He gave her a loopy smile. "How about another round, with a side order of you." The other guys at his table hooted and clapped.

Bree shook her head as she whisked the empty beer mugs off the polished wood surface. "You should be ashamed of yourself, Jasperson. Does your mother know you talk that way to waitresses?"

The boy's smile faded. "How do you know who I am?"

"That's going to be my little secret," she said with a smile. "Benny."

Bree couldn't keep from grinning as she walked away. She'd overheard their conversation—they were loud and getting louder—and filed away their names. She'd learned early in her previous career that that kind of information could come in handy. As she stood at the bar, waiting for her drink order, she saw them whispering to one another. She smiled to herself. She wasn't going to have any more trouble with that group.

"Bree, I just picked up a party of eight." The other waitress, Sandy, wiped a bead of sweat away from her temple and threaded a pencil into her hair. A few strands of the elaborate French braid came loose, and she shoved them impatiently behind her ear. Sliding a drink order to the bartender, she said, "Could you take the two tables against the wall for me? They just sat down, and I'm swamped."

"Sure, Sandy." Her coworker didn't handle stress well at the best of times. Bree glanced at the tables in question. A young couple and a single man.

Parker Ellison.

Her heart sped up. "Um, Sandy? I can take the couple. Why don't you get the guy? He looks like a good tipper."

"Yeah?" Sandy glanced at Parker, her expression calculating, then one of the men from her table of eight waved at her. "Oh, no. They want something else." She hurried toward them, calling over her shoulder, "You can have him, Bree."

She did *not* want Parker Ellison. But it looked as if she was stuck with him. Linda had disappeared, so Bree couldn't even have the new waitress handle Parker's table.

Putting four mugs of beer on a tray, she delivered them to the table of college guys. Benny, she noted, didn't meet her gaze. The other three watched her warily. She hoped they were wondering if she knew their names, too.

Tucking the small, circular tray beneath her arm, she greeted the couple and took their order. Then, steadying herself, she walked over to Parker, who was reading some papers.

"Welcome to The Lake House," she said. "What can I get for you?"

He raised his head, his gaze skimming her skirt and tank top. His gaze lingered on her hair, which she'd left down and curly, then he glanced at her mouth. "I'd love a Guinness."

"Coming right up." She walked away, both amused and irritated. He hadn't recognized her. Granted, her hair was different and she was wearing the Lake House's uniform of short skirt and tank top, but still. He was supposed to be a scientist. A trained observer.

Why did she care if he didn't recognize her? She tossed the drink orders onto the bar. Better if he didn't. Less awkward. Fewer questions. More comfortable for both of them.

Another group signaled her for drinks, then another. She delivered cola and beer to the young couple and the Guinness to Parker. He murmured "Thanks" but didn't look up. She should be relieved, she told herself. One less complication tonight.

By the time she had another chance to catch her breath, a blond woman had joined Parker. Bree strolled over to them. "Another Guinness?" she asked him.

He glanced at her and said, "Thanks." His gaze narrowed, but she smiled blandly and turned to the woman. "Can I get you something?"

"I'd like some wine. What do you have by the glass?"

"We have a nice selection of house wines and—"

The blonde scrunched up her face as if she smelled something bad. "I don't drink house wine."

Bree pulled the drinks menu from the metal holder on the table and handed it to her. "The other wines we offer by the glass are on the back page."

She waited patiently while the woman read. Thoroughly. Bree felt eyes on her back and knew other patrons were looking for her. "How about if I give you a minute and come back?" she asked.

"No, I'm just about ready." The woman looked up with a cool smile. "The service here is very slow."

Of course it would be, if all customers were as rude as this one. Bree willed the smile to stay on her face. Finally, the woman sighed. "I'll have a glass of the pinot noir," she said. "But make sure it's the 2005 vintage."

"Absolutely."

Without looking at Parker, Bree put in the order and checked with her other tables. As she returned with their drinks, the blonde touched Parker's hand and let her fingers linger. When Bree set the glasses down, Parker drew his hand away and thanked her, but the woman only took a sip of wine.

It was a typical Saturday night at The Lake House, and the bar was packed. The jukebox was playing mostly country songs, and a few couples were dancing on the tiny square of hardwood in front of it. People stood two and three deep at the bar, and Bree could barely keep up with the orders.

Sandy had found Linda, the waitress Bree was training, sobbing in the women's washroom, and Jerry had sent her home.

Bree turned Parker's table back over to Sandy once the other waitress had settled down, and she didn't give him another thought.

Well, not many.

She wasn't here to get silly about men, she reminded herself sharply. She was here to make money.

She touched the roll of bills in her pocket, pleased by its thickness. She needed it for Charlie, and that was all that mattered.

PARKER SLID THE ARTICLES he'd been studying about John Henry McInnes into the envelope, and looked around the room. Alicia had left long ago, and now the place was emptying out. He must have stayed longer than he realized.

His first waitress, the one Alicia had been so rude to,

looked familiar. As if he'd seen her before, but not here. He would have remembered that dark red, curly hair.

The other waitress said something to her and she smiled, tucking her hair behind her ear. My God. It was Bree, the department's new admin assistant.

What was she doing, working here?

He watched as she cleaned the salt and pepper shakers and ketchup bottles on each table. Every time she bent over, her short skirt rode up on the back of her thighs.

They were very nice thighs.

Her legs, curvy and toned, went on forever, and the rest of her body was equally curvaceous. He couldn't believe this was the same woman he'd met in the office a few days ago.

That woman had hidden herself in loose, drab clothing. The only reason he'd noticed her was because she stood up to him.

This woman was an exotic blossom among ordinary, everyday flowers. How had he missed that in the office?

Because she'd disguised herself, he realized. Just as his orchids did. To blend in. To be less noticeable. Was this her natural environment? Or was it the office? At which place did she wear a disguise?

And why was she working here? He frowned.

She glanced up from her task and their eyes met. He saw awareness flicker in hers before she looked away.

So she'd recognized him, too.

She'd scrubbed all the tables except the ones around him, he noticed. When she couldn't put it off any longer, she approached his. "Sorry to bother you, but I have to clean up."

"Not a problem. I wanted to talk to you, anyway."

A bottle of ketchup slid out of her hand and landed with a thump. "Did you need something else?"

"Were you fired from your job at the college?"

She jerked back a step. "Of course not."

"Then you must have quit. I'm sorry."

"What?" She seemed confused.

"I gave you a hard time. I assume that's why you quit."

"I didn't quit." She picked up the saltshaker. "I'll be there Monday morning."

His frown deepened. "Then what are you doing here?"

"What are *you* doing, spending your evening in a bar?"

One side of his mouth curled up. "Touché. I guess that was a nosy question."

"Yes, it was."

"I'll show you mine if you show me yours."

The innuendo hung in the air for a long moment as they stared at each other. "Fine," she said, breaking the tension. "You first."

"I had a meeting," he said with a straight face.

She laughed. "Is that what it's called nowadays? I could have sworn they called it a date back in the day."

"Believe me, Alicia isn't my type," he said with an inner shudder. She was everything he tried to avoid—superior, cold and anxious to be seen with a celebrity. However minor.

Bree was going to ask him what his type was; he could see it in her expression. Then she shrugged. "She looked as if she thought she was."

"Doesn't matter what she thinks. We're on a committee. She wanted to talk business."

"A committee meeting? In a bar?" Bree raised her eyebrows. "On a Saturday night? How creative."

"It was the only time she was free."

"Busy schedule," she said with an equally straight face.

"I guess." He leaned back in his chair. "Your turn. Why are you working here?"

"Maybe I enjoy it."

"You're certainly good at it," he said. "That's not the same as liking it."

Bree shrugged. "I enjoy being around people. At The Lake House, I meet lots of people and get paid for it."

"You don't meet people working for the science department?"

"They're a little stuffier at the college," she said. "Not to mention more demanding."

"Ouch," he said, smiling. "Am I ever going to be able to redeem myself?"

"No need for redemption," she said. "You were doing your job, and asking me to do mine."

She turned to go and he grabbed her by the wrist. "Wait."

"Whoa! Hands on the table, pal, not the help."

"Sorry." He held his palms up. "It won't happen again."

She took a deep breath. "Jerry is very protective," she said, her smile strained. "I'd hate to have him toss you out of the bar. It's not very dignified."

"Thanks for warning me."

"No problem. We pride ourselves on our service here at The Lake House."

She walked away, and when the bartender called out that they were closed, she was still working. She didn't look at Parker as he left.

CHAPTER FOUR

SHE KNEW IMMEDIATELY when Parker was in the hall outside her office. It was ridiculous, but ever since the night he'd been at The Lake House, Bree had been too conscious of him. When he walked into the office, she managed to give him an impersonal smile. "Hello, Dr. Ellison."

"Hi, Ms. McInnes. Do you have time to make copies of this test for me?"

"Of course," she said, reaching for the papers. "I'll get them back to you this afternoon."

"I've been meaning to ask you about something," he added. "You have the same last name as a former professor here at Collier, John Henry McInnes. Are you related?"

She laid the test on her desk. "He was my father."

"Really? Your father?"

"Why are you surprised? Spruce Lake is a small town and McInnes isn't a common name."

He studied her. "I guess I wasn't expecting to run into one of John Henry's kids."

"Small world, isn't it?" she said. Her face felt tight from the effort to keep it expressionless.

"I guess it is," he said, then hesitated. "Did you know the college is planning a celebration around your father's Pulitzer Prize? This year will be the twentieth anniversary. We're putting together a display in the library and some literary celebrities are going to read from his works."

She froze as memories bombarded her—her father preening after he'd gotten the call about the award; the never-ending series of interviews he'd given, where he'd dragged out Bree and her sisters and shown off his triplets; his tantrums when he thought he wasn't getting enough attention from his family. That damn Pulitzer had been gasoline on the fire of her father's narcissism. "Why?"

"Because winning the Pulitzer is a huge accomplishment. Because your father was a big deal here at Collier, and we want to honor him."

"Because it's good publicity for the college," Bree said. "Not to mention the money all those readings would bring in."

Parker shrugged. "Can't deny that. But you'll benefit, too. The publicity will sell more of his books. That means more royalty money."

God knew she needed money. But she didn't like the strings that attached it to her father and that damn book. "Fine. Well. Let us know the details." So she could be out of town when the time came.

"You don't seem happy about this," Parker said. "You're shivering."

"That's absurd. The air-conditioning is set too low and it's cold in here," she said, letting her arms drop to her sides.

"Okay," he said after a long moment. "I'll keep you posted."

"You do that." Bree picked up the papers as she stood.

"One more thing," he said. She paused reluctantly. "About the other night—"

"It's fine," she interrupted. "It wasn't important." She'd relived too many times that moment when he'd grabbed her wrist. Because it brought back other bad memories. This time not of her father, but of the strip club.

"It *was* important if I made you uncomfortable," he answered, moving a step closer.

Her pulse picked up. "Uncomfortable? It's part of the job. I'd forgotten all about it." *Liar*.

"Really?" He flashed that dimple. "You mean my charm and charisma didn't knock your socks off?"

Her stomach swooped to her toes. She could dismiss an arrogant Parker Ellison without a second thought. A guy who could make fun of himself was another story. "I read about that charm and charisma somewhere," she said. "Oh yeah, I remember. It was in the checkout line at the grocery store."

"Good one, Ms. McInnes," he said, smiling. What was the matter with her? He was going to think she actually wanted to flirt with him.

She headed for the copy machine. "I'll have these papers for you shortly, Professor."

"No rush," he said. "I'm not going anywhere."

FIFTEEN MINUTES LATER, she rapped on Parker's office door. There was no answer and the light was off. She tried the handle, but the door was locked. Too bad. She could have left the tests on his desk and avoided another encounter with him.

A celebrity professor. She rolled her eyes. *You didn't learn your lesson by living with one for seventeen years?*

She'd barely return to her desk when the celebrity walked in. "Do you have those tests copied? I'll save you a trip."

"Here you go." She handed him the thick sheaf. "Looks like a big class."

"Yeah, a lot of kids want to get the introductory course out of the way in summer school."

"I don't know why." She wrinkled her nose. "I never liked summer school."

"Where did you go to college?"

"A small school near Milwaukee."

"What's your degree?"

"I'm a teacher. High school."

"Really? Then why aren't you teaching?"

"Because it's summer. I don't do summer school, remember?" she said lightly.

She turned to her computer, but Parker lingered in the office. "Can I ask you a question?"

"Sure." She swung around in her chair to face him.

"As a high school teacher, what do you think of fourteen- and fifteen-year-old kids taking college classes?"

Why was he asking her this question? He couldn't possibly know she had a son who wanted to take his class. "I guess it depends on the kid," she said cautiously. "Some can handle it, some can't. Why do you ask?"

"Just curious. I don't think high school kids belong in college."

"Why not, if they can handle the work? What about gifted kids who need the challenge?"

"Let their high school teachers challenge them. Why push them into college early? Let them be kids, for God's sake. They'll have to grow up soon enough." He shoved a hand through his hair. "Not to mention the social problems caused by throwing a kid that young in with nineteen- and twenty-year-olds. High school students should be doing whatever it is kids that age do for fun."

"Don't you know what high school boys do for fun?" she asked, confused.

"It's been a long time since I was that age," he said. He looked away. "I'm sure it's different today."

"Different from what? What did you do when you were in high school?"

"It doesn't matter," he said. "We weren't talking about me. This was a hypothetical discussion."

She tilted her head and studied him. "Were you forced to take college classes as a kid?" she asked softly. "Is that why you're so adamant about it?"

"It doesn't matter," he said, heading for the door. "Thanks for copying these tests for me."

As his footsteps retreated down the hall, Bree replayed their conversation. She suspected it mattered a great deal. And she suddenly wanted to know more about Parker Ellison.

As PARKER HEADED to the administration building, he thought again about the kid in his class. Charlie had answered the questions Parker asked him, he was taking notes every day and he seemed very bright. But he was nervous about something. The poor kid probably felt like a fish out of water.

It wasn't his problem, Parker reminded himself. Although he'd have a few things to say to Charlie's parents if he ever ran into them.

He walked into the president's office and nodded to Marcy, Jonathon's long-time assistant. "I need to see him. Right now."

"I'll see if he's available," she replied, unruffled.

She pressed a button and spoke into the phone, too quietly for him to hear. After a moment, she smiled. "He'll make time for you."

Parker closed the door behind him as he entered. Jonathon ignored him. As he leaned against the wall, the college president continued to read. It was a battle of wills. Parker could almost smell the power and testosterone in the air. As the seconds stretched to a minute, Jonathon finally looked up. "What can I do for you?"

Parker pushed away from the wall. "I know why you put me on this committee about McInnes. It's because his daughter works for my department. That can't be a coincidence."

"Of course not. It's synergy. I was…quite pleased when I saw Bree was a new hire there."

"When you asked me to get her father's papers, did you expect me to screw her for them?"

Jonathon raised his eyebrows. "I had no idea you could be so crude, Ellison, but I doubt such a sacrifice will be necessary. I'm sure she'd be willing to give you anything of John Henry's."

It would be no sacrifice to take Bree to bed. "So I just ask my admin to hand over her father's papers." He narrowed his eyes. "Is there an implied threat here? 'Hand over your father's research for his book or you're fired'?"

"Not at all," the president said. "I'm sure she'll be cooperative. It's to her benefit, remember."

"Why didn't you just ask her for the damn papers yourself?" Parker picked up a blue-and-red glass paperweight and flipped it from one hand to the other. Jonathon's eyes followed the movement. "Was there bad blood between you and John Henry? Were you afraid she'd refuse you?"

"For God's sake, Ellison," the president blustered. "This isn't some cloak-and-dagger affair. The college is honoring her father. Why wouldn't she let us have this work?"

Parker tossed the glass ball into the air and caught it at the last minute on its descent. "Good. You'll ask her, then. How could she refuse the college president?"

"Put that down, Ellison." Jonathon said as Parker lobbed the glass ball into the air again. "One of our board members had that made up in the school colors. I don't want it damaged."

Parker set it in the desk, on the opposite side from where it had been. "So that's settled. We end this farce—quit the committee and concentrate on raising money and the profile of Collier College. You'll ask Bree for the papers." He smiled thinly. "Everyone wins."

"I'm not a micromanager." The president's voice was tight. "I'm not going to waste my time chasing down one of your employees when you work with her every day. I picked you for the committee because I thought you'd get to know the woman. You have established a cordial relationship with her, haven't you? Alicia said she was your waitress at that bar where you met."

Which just confirmed what Parker had suspected—Jonathon had put Alicia on the committee to be his spy. "We have a working relationship."

"I must admit, I wasn't surprised to find out the McInnes woman worked at a bar." Jonathon pursed his lips. "She was always…"

"Always what, Jonathon?"

The president shifted. "She was wild when she was in high school. Caused her father all kinds of problems. There were rumors."

"Is that right? And you knew this because…?"

Now it was the president's turn to smile thinly. "I make it my business to know what's going on at Collier." He pulled the papers in front of him and picked up his pen. "If that's all, Ellison, I have work to do."

So she had been a wild child. He wanted details, but it would be more fun to get the answers from Bree. "Since she works for my department, maybe I shouldn't be on the committee. It might be construed as a conflict of interest."

Jonathon raised his eyebrow. "The only conflict of interest I see is between the amount of money you need for your next expedition and what the college will be able to provide." He nodded at the work in front of him. "I'm going over the figures for the next fiscal year. We have a very lean budget."

"So you'll cut off my funding if I don't get the papers from Bree?" Parker struggled to leash his growing anger.

The other man sighed. "I never said that."

Parker wished he could tell Jonathon to shove his funding, but he couldn't do that. Yet. "Fine. I'll work on getting hold of McInnes's work.

"Good luck, Ellison. I know you'll succeed."

Once Bree got to know him a little better, he'd ask her for the papers. There was no reason for her to refuse.

Then he could concentrate on finding out what kind of wild child she'd been.

CHAPTER FIVE

"I HATE BEING in this room." Bree looked around her father's old study and shuddered. There were too many memories in here, and none of them good ones.

"I know," Fiona said. She rubbed her hands along her legs. "I'm dreading cleaning it out."

"That's why we're doing it together," Zoe said briskly. "Let's do the books first. We can pack them in boxes and find out if anyone wants them."

"I can get boxes from the office," Bree said, desperate to put it off. "Photocopy paper ones are the ideal size for books."

"Perfect." Zoe grabbed a book from a shelf. "But we can start sorting them now. We'll put the ones with notes in the margins in a separate pile." She flipped through the pages, then set it on the floor. "Someone might want the annotations of the famous John Henry McInnes."

Bree reached for a book, paged through it quickly, then dropped it on a chair. No writing, thank goodness. "The college might want some of them," she said. "Ellison told me they're putting on an event to commemorate the twentieth anniversary of Dad's Pulitzer."

"Why would they do that?" Fiona looked at one page of a book and threw it on the floor. "No one cares about that anymore."

Zoe retrieved it and looked through it quickly, then put it in the pile of books that their father had written in. "Of course they do, Fee. It was a big deal when Dad got that Pulitzer. It put Collier on the map."

"They didn't really know him," Fiona said.

"No, they didn't," Zoe agreed, wrapping her arm around Fee's shoulders. "Not like we did. But they're not celebrating the man. They're celebrating his accomplishment."

"Same thing," Fiona retorted.

"Why are you getting your panties in a twist?" Bree asked, tossing another hardcover volume on the chair. "We don't have to get involved. It's Collier's deal. They haven't asked us for anything."

"Do you want to see them talk about what a great writer Dad was?" Fiona said. "Act like he was some great guy?"

"I'm not going to hear a thing. I'm not going anywhere near their 'celebration.'"

Zoe added another volume to her pile, then dropped down next to it. "Hey, guys, he's dead. We have to get past him at some point in our lives. Or are we going to be seventy-five and still whining about Dad?"

"Are you 'past him,' Zoe?" Bree demanded. "Have you been able to forgive and forget?"

"I learned a lot about forgiveness," Zoe said quietly. "I've learned that hatred only poisons your life."

"Easy for you to say," Fiona muttered. "You've got everything you want—a job you love, a great husband. Happiness. That makes it a lot easier to forgive and forget."

'You've gotten what you want out of life, too, Fee," Zoe said. "You always wanted to design jewelry, and now you're famous. Your jewelry is sold everywhere." She laughed. "I had to pretend to be you at an event in Spruce Lake because you were in such demand."

Fiona yanked another volume off the shelf. "Yeah, well, fame isn't everything it's cracked up to be."

"What's wrong?" Bree dropped a book on the desk and peered at her sister. "What's going on?"

Fiona stared out the window. The edge of the garage, her studio, was just barely visible. "My agent and my business manager are pressuring me to keep making the mass market stuff. Pieces that are more *accessible*. Same old, same old. I want to try other things."

"It's your business," Bree said. "Design what you want."

"It's not that simple. There are a lot of people depending on me now. I have artists working for me. The more successful I become, the narrower my options are."

"That's a nice problem to have," Zoe said, shoving books out of the way and perching on the edge of their father's desk. "You can't blame that on Dad."

Fiona spun away. Her back rigid, she said, "I still have nightmares about him. I'm twenty-nine, and all I have is my jewelry. Even that's not making me happy anymore. And what about Bree? Dad drove her out of the house when she was only seventeen. And look where she ended up."

A tiny knife stabbed Bree's heart. "Hey, stripping might not have been the smartest career choice, but it paid the bills. I was able to take care of Charlie."

"You shouldn't have had to do it," Fiona said sharply. "You should have been able to stay here and have Charlie. We should have been able to help you. If Mom hadn't died, you could have stayed home—she could control Dad. Did you ever think about that?"

"All the time." Bree looked down at the book in her hands,

and tears pricked her eyes. It was a colletion of fairy tales their mother used to read to them. The red cover was worn away where tiny hands had held it. She clutched it to her chest. "I can't help thinking about it. If Mom had been alive, I wouldn't have had to face Ted and his parents on my own. I wouldn't have had to run away. I wouldn't have had to strip to earn money for Charlie's operation."

"What do you mean, you wouldn't have had to face Ted?" Fiona stared at her. "Ted who?"

"I was going to tell you," Bree said, ashamed she hadn't made an effort to tell Fiona. She repeated the story of Charlie's father, and why she'd run away.

"Ted Cross is Charlie's father? And he denied it? That bastard." Fiona scowled. "I would have straightened him out."

Bree smiled through her tears. "Oh, Fee, I bet you would have. I can see you taking on Ted and his parents." She swallowed. "But Zoe's right. We can't change what happened when we were kids. We have to get past it."

"How can you do that when you're practically working in Ted's lap?" Fiona asked.

"Ted won't know I'm there." She hoped. "And even if he does he won't find out about Charlie. His office is in a different building. And I'll only be there for a couple of months."

"You're taking a chance, Bree," Fiona warned.

"I know. But I didn't have a choice." She stacked another book on the pile.

"Who's Ellison, by the way?" Zoe asked. "You had a funny tone in your voice when you said his name."

Bree was careful not to meet her sisters' eyes. When they were young, they had been able to read each other too easily. Sometimes she'd felt as if her sisters shared her brain. "He's a professor in the science department," she said, trying to sound casual. "One of the people I work for."

"You haven't mentioned any of the other professors," Fiona said.

Bree shrugged. "He's was a jerk the first time I met him. I guess that's why he sticks in my mind."

Fiona nudged her. "You sure that's the only reason? I looked him up on Google, and he's hot. A total babe."

Bree prayed she wasn't blushing. "Really? I hadn't noticed."

Zoe grinned. "You're going to have to do better than that, Bree."

"Zo's right," Fiona said, also smiling. "I saw that same look on her face when she said there was nothing going on between her and Gideon."

"Trust me, Fee. This is a no-brainer. First of all—" Bree stuck out her index finger "—I work for him. Second of all—" she added her middle finger "—he's a jerk." *Maybe not,* a tiny voice murmured. She tried to ignore it. "And third of all—" she raised her ring finger and closed them together "—he's a professor. A *celebrity* professor. Enough said?"

Fiona's lips twitched. "Sounds like you two are meant for each other."

Bree shook her head. "Trust me. The only thing he wants from me is copies of the tests for his class."

PARKER PAUSED at the door to The Lake House. Maybe he'd been wrong, he told himself. There was probably nothing particularly interesting about Bree McInnes. Chances were good she was as strait-laced, as ordinary as she appeared at the office. Clever, he admitted, remembering what she'd done with his airline tickets, but ordinary.

He was just at The Lake House to have a beer.

He walked in the door and spotted her immediately. She was taking an order from a table of college kids, and a smile lit her face and made her eyes sparkle. She wore bright yellow sneakers and a short skirt that emphasized her long, toned legs, and a tank top that showed just a hint of cleavage. A small apron hung low on her waist.

He stared at her sneakers. Ordinary, strait-laced women didn't wear such flamboyant shoes. They didn't usually work in bars and flirt with all the customers, either. Narrowing his eyes, he watched her with the college kids, who flirted back openly. She laughed as she hurried away to place their order at the bar.

There was an open table next to the college kids, and he sauntered over to it. Only to make sure he was in her section, he told himself.

A couple at another table held up their empty glasses, and she nodded at them. After sliding the order to the bartender, she disappeared into the back room.

At another table, two men shook hands, before one of them pushed away from his chair and headed out. It was Ted Cross, the college president's son. Maybe Ted would have some ideas for dealing with his father.

Parker hurried to catch up. "Hey, Ted," he said, cutting him off before he reached the door. "How's it going? I haven't seen you in a while."

Ted Cross focused on Parker with an effort, as if his thoughts were miles away. "Ellison. What are you doing here?"

"Having a beer. Join me?"

Ted glanced at his watch. "I should get going. My meeting with that student ran late and my wife is expecting me."

"One beer?" Parker said. "The Guinness is exceptional. And I'd like to pick your brain, if I could. College business," he added after a pause.

Ted shrugged. "Okay. I'll give my wife a call and let her know I'll be late."

Parker nodded toward his table. "I'm right over there." He'd known Ted's ambition wouldn't let him walk away. It was no secret he was in line to succeed his father as president of Collier College, so Ted would always play the political game.

He'd become far too cynical, Parker thought wearily as Ted opened his cell phone and stepped outside. No wonder he couldn't wait to get back to the jungle. There were no games being played while you were slapping at mosquitoes and trying to avoid quicksand.

He glanced around the room, but Bree hadn't returned yet. After a few minutes, the other waitress came by. "Bree will be right with you," she said. "Can I get you something in the meantime?"

"Thanks." Parker smiled at the woman. "But I haven't decided yet."

He plucked a menu out of the metal holder in the center of the table and the waitress nodded, looking relieved. "I'll send Bree over as soon as I see her."

"Great," Parker said, pretending to study the list of appetizers.

Bree appeared moments later. "Hello, Professor Ellison," she said warily. "What can I get for you?"

"For starters, you can stop calling me that. My name is Parker."

Her eyebrows rose. "Really? Were you that informal with my predecessor in the science department?"

"Marjorie? God, no. She scared the hell out of me. I think she was a nun in a former life."

Bree's lips twitched and her wariness disappeared. "Maybe I need to work harder at intimidating you."

He leaned closer and caught her scent. She smelled of peaches and rain. "Trust me, Bree. You unnerve me."

Their eyes met for a long moment. Her lips parted. Then one of the boys next to him yelled, "Hey, Bree," and the spell was broken.

"The animals are restless tonight," she said, a bit breathlessly.

Parker glanced at the students, irritated. "What's wrong with those jerks?"

"They're college kids." She looked at them and sighed. "Fortunately, it's not a terminal condition. Can I get you something?"

"Two Guinnesses, please."

Her hand tightened on the order pad as she scribbled his order. "Got it."

"It's not for Alicia," he said without thinking. "A colleague is joining me."

She faced him again, her expression carefully blank. "You don't have to explain anything. It's none of my business who you see. I'll be right back with your drinks." She shoved her order pad into the pocket of her apron and turned to the boys next to him. Instead of looking at the menu, he watched her smile and laugh with them. One reached for her, but she eluded him easily, although her eyes flashed and she spoke sharply to the kid.

As she walked toward the bar, Parker realized that his hand had tightened into a fist.

He fumbled with the menu and stared at the page, but didn't see the words. All he saw was her distaste as she'd dodged the kid's hands. He glanced at the other table again. Did he know any of them?

It didn't matter. It wasn't any of his business.

Even if he couldn't get her image out of his head.

When Bree returned with the two glasses of beer, she set them down on the table and pulled out her order pad. "Anything to eat, Professor?"

He shifted in his chair. "We're back to 'Professor'? Does something about me disturb you, Bree?"

"Very little disturbs me," she said. "Especially not guys in college bars with cheesy lines."

"Ouch," he said, wincing. "You're a hard woman."

"You better believe it."

He closed the menu and slipped it into the holder. "Nothing to eat right now. Maybe later."

"I'll check back." She slipped her order pad into her pocket. "You know where to find me."

As he held her gaze, his grip on the cold glass of beer tightened. "Yeah, I do."

The crowded, noisy bar faded away and all he saw was Bree's mouth. Her cheeks flushed and her tank top rose and fell more quickly. She swallowed. "Good," she finally said.

"Yes, it is," he answered.

She met his eyes for another moment, then turned away, bumping into an empty chair, and murmuring an apology to the couple at the table.

The summer had suddenly become much more interesting.

CHAPTER SIX

PARKER WATCHED BREE WORK the room, taking orders from one table, delivering a pitcher of beer to another, reining in the college kids next to him when they got out of line. She was in constant motion, smiling, friendly, but always just out of reach, both physically and emotionally. It was as if she'd drawn an invisible shield around her personal space, isolating herself in the middle of the crowd. He was trying to figure out how she did it when Ted Cross walked back in and sat down.

"Sorry. Took a while to get hold of my wife." He picked up his beer and sipped from it.

"No problem," Parker said. "You want something to eat?"

"No, thanks," Ted said. "What's up, Ellison?"

"Your father put me on a committee to organize an event to celebrate John Henry McInnes's Pulitzer Prize. Did you know about that?"

Cross laughed. "Yeah, I heard about it. Better you than me."

"How do I get off the committee?"

Cross drank more of his beer. "You don't. When my father wants something, he gets it. He's scary that way." Ted shook his head. "And you've got the star power he needs."

"Damn it," Parker said, without heat. "I was hoping you had the secret to dealing with Jonathon."

"Stay out of his way," Ted said. "Be thankful he hasn't put

you on one of the permanent committees. Do what he wants and get it over with."

"Is that how you handle him?" Parker asked, genuinely curious. He'd never spent much time with Ted, but he didn't seem like a pushover.

The other man sighed. "It's always complicated with fathers, isn't it?"

"Yeah, it is." Parker thought about his own dad, a distant man who'd spent very little time with him. "Did you know that John Henry's daughter is the administrative assistant for the science department?"

Ted frowned. "I thought Zoe worked at that women's shelter."

"Not Zoe." He didn't know Bree had a sister. "It's Bree who works for me."

"What?" Ted paled. "Bree? She's back in Spruce Lake?"

"Yeah." Parker studied his colleague, wondering at his reaction. "She's been working for us for a couple of weeks. Did you used to know her?"

"She was a lot younger than me," he said, lifting his glass as if to take a drink, then setting it back down when he realized it was empty. "I knew about her, of course. Everyone in town knew about the McInnes triplets."

"She's a triplet?" Bree had never mentioned anything about her family.

"Yeah, she has two sisters. Their old man used to call them the 'McInnes Supertwins.'" Ted snorted. "John Henry paraded them around in matching clothes like a traveling freak show. Bree didn't look anything like the other two, but McInnes seemed to like her best."

"Really?" That was a pretty perceptive observation for the kid Ted must've been at the time. "Sounds like they had a rough time."

Ted swirled the dregs of his dark beer around the bottom of his glass. "Who knows what goes on in families?"

"That's for sure," Parker said lightly, remembering his own. "Thanks for the tips about your father."

"Sorry I couldn't be more help." Ted shoved away from the table as if he was suddenly in a hurry. "Good talking to you, Ellison. Catch you later."

He headed for the exit, and Parker saw Bree standing at the bar, staring after him. When the door closed behind him, she looked over at Parker. Even from across the room, it wasn't difficult to read the unease on her face.

Why would Ted Cross make Bree nervous?

WHAT WAS GOING ON?

When had Ted come into the bar? And why hadn't she noticed him?

Why were Parker and he having a conversation? An intense one, if the expressions on their faces were any clue.

It was bad enough to see Ted in the bar. To find him talking to Parker was worse. And as much as she wanted to ignore it, Bree hadn't been able to look away. It was like watching a car wreck unfold in front of you in slow motion, every one of the awful details permanently etched on your brain. Her stomach churned as she watched Ted leave. What had the two men been talking about?

"Bree, your order is up," the bartender said impatiently.

She dragged her attention back to her job and realized she'd been staring at the door, ignoring everything. She forced a smile. "Sorry, Jerry. I must have been daydreaming." More like revisiting a nightmare.

"It's okay, Bree." His voice softened. "I'm getting surly because the drinks are stacking up and we're shorthanded."

He shook his head. "Too bad Linda didn't work out. I'm trying to find another waitress."

"I know." She grabbed the tray and tried to put Ted out of her mind. Parker, too.

But he caught her eye and smiled, and her heart sped up.

She avoided him as she delivered the drinks on her tray and took more orders, but his gaze burned into the back of her neck as she worked.

He's a customer. She knew how to handle bar customers.

"Need another Guinness, Professor?" She smiled brightly as she stopped at his table and picked up the empty glasses.

"Thanks," he said.

His gaze traveled over her slowly from head to toe, as if she was one of his specimens, and an unfamiliar heat crawled through her. She stared back for a moment, then whirled away, slipping on a coaster on the floor as she headed for the bar. Apparently she was still the queen of disastrous choices in men.

When she delivered another round to the table of kids next to him, Parker leaned forward, as if to study her more closely.

She'd had enough. Striding up to his table, she said in a low voice, "What's the matter with you? I'm trying to work. Stop watching me."

He raised his eyebrows. "Am I distracting you, Bree?"

"No. You're pissing me off."

"Am I?" He looked as if he was fighting a smile. "Sorry. I guess I'll just drink my beer and stare at the table all night."

"You're looking at me as if I was one of your damn orchids. Or a science experiment. Stop it."

"Experiments aren't this fascinating. An orchid?" He tilted his head. "They're exotic and unusual. Rare." He let his gaze roam over her again. "Yeah, maybe an orchid."

"That's it," she said, although her pulse had picked up. "Knock it off or you're out of here."

"Really? I've never been thrown out of a bar before. That might be interesting." He sat up straight and his eyes brightened, just like a kid on an adventure.

"Grow up, Professor," she said, but she hid a smile as she walked away.

She didn't catch him watching her again. He talked to several people who stopped by his table—mostly students, she guessed, judging from their ages. One of the girls, a blonde with a low-cut T-shirt and a push-up bra, tried to join him, but he rebuffed her with a smile.

He was still sitting there when Jerry yelled, "Last call!"

A few minutes later Ellison pushed away from the table and strolled out of the bar, and Bree watched the door close behind him. She was relieved, she told herself. He'd been distracting her all evening, and she was glad to see the last of him.

Forcing him out of her mind, she finished her work, talking to Sandy and Jerry while she rolled silverware into napkins and cleaned the plastic menus.

Finally, a half hour after Jerry had locked the door, she walked into the cool summer evening. The faint streetlights of downtown Spruce Lake couldn't disguise the millions of stars that filled the indigo sky, and for a moment she stared up at them. She'd missed the night sky and all its stars when she lived in Milwaukee.

"Amazing, isn't it?"

Parker's voice. Behind her.

"Professor Ellison," she said, spinning around to face him. "Why are you still here?" The breathlessness in her voice both irritated and alarmed her.

He gave her a slow smile. "You noticed when I left. I'm flattered."

"Of course I noticed. I pay extra attention to my problem tables."

"Was I a problem?"

More than she wanted to admit. "What do you want?" she countered.

"I decided to stick around and make sure you got to your car safely." He pushed away from the wall he'd been leaning against. "You can't be too careful at this time of night."

"Oh, for heaven's sake." She shifted her bag to her other shoulder. "This is Spruce Lake."

He raised his eyebrows. "Nothing bad could happen here?"

"I know how to take care of myself." She thought of the club where she'd worked so many years ago, and the men who'd waited by the door. "Thank you for the consideration," she said firmly, dismissing him.

He fell into step beside her. "Where are you parked?"

"I'm not." She stopped. "What are you doing, Professor?"

"That table of fraternity boys was harassing you," he said quietly. "Weren't you afraid they'd hang around?"

The idea had crossed her mind. "I was ready for them," she said. She showed him the pepper spray in her hand, then dropped it into her bag.

He glanced at her purse and nodded. "You were prepared. That's smart."

"I'm always prepared," she said.

"Good to know. How far are we walking?"

"You're not very quick to pick up hints, are you?"

He glanced down at her, his eyes gleaming. "I think I am," he said, his voice low and intimate in the darkness. "That's why I waited for you."

She stopped again. "I was *not* flirting with you."

"Did I say you were?" He shook his head. "You stayed as far away from me tonight as you could."

"You had plenty of company." Including Ted. She didn't dare ask what they had talked about. Maybe if Parker walked her home, he'd let something slip about that. "I was trying not to intrude." As recoveries went, it was pretty lame.

"That was very thoughtful of you, Bree." It sounded as if he was laughing. "You're an excellent waitress," he continued. "Attentive to your tables. Friendly. Efficient. So when you ignored me most of the evening, I had to wonder why."

"Experienced waitresses don't hover."

"Is that it?" he murmured. "I was hoping it was more personal."

"Personal? Of course not. There are guests I avoid for personal reasons, but it's usually because they haven't bathed in a while. You're not offensive at all."

He nodded. "I like smart, clever women who can think on their feet."

"I'm immune to flattery," she said, but her heart fluttered. If he had told her how beautiful she was, it would be easy to ignore him. But no man had ever said she was clever and smart.

"I suppose you would be," he said. "You've probably had people staring at you since the day you were born. I hope I'm not that shallow."

He wasn't. And that was the problem. Parker Ellison wasn't easily dismissed.

They turned the corner onto her street, and she slowed. "I'm just down the block," she said. "You don't have to walk the rest of the way with me."

He looked in that direction, and she saw the scene

through his eyes. One dim streetlight in the distance. Bushes and trees in most of the front yards. Few lights burning in any of the houses.

"I don't think so," he said. He touched the small of her back to guide her down the sidewalk, and she felt it all the way down to her toes.

"Why are you doing this?" she asked, shifting away from his hand. "There must be dozens of gorgeous women in Spruce Lake who would be thrilled to have you walk them home." She stopped in front of her house. "Why did you wait for me?"

He stepped closer, until she could see his pupils, wide in the darkness. "I collect orchids," he said softly. "Every one of them is more beautiful than the last. I appreciate beauty, but mere beauty doesn't captivate me anymore. I'm not awed by a gorgeous flower, and I don't judge women by the way they look. Even one who's exceptionally stunning." His gaze felt as intimate as a caress. "What fascinates me now is the rare and unusual. The unique."

He touched her shoulders, slid his palms down her arms. "You fascinate me."

She told herself to move away from him.

Apparently her body didn't get the memo, because she didn't budge. "I'm sorry to disappoint you, but there's nothing especially interesting about me, Professor," she said, trying to ignore the way his hands felt on her skin. "Maybe you're just not used to hearing 'no.'"

His smile was wicked in the dim glow from the porch light. "What exactly are you saying no to?"

With an effort of will, she pulled away. "To having you wait for me when The Lake House closes. To having you walk me home. To anything else you're thinking about."

"Anything else I'm thinking about?" He traced her lips

with his fingertip, sending a wave of heat through her body. "Does that include kissing you good-night? Because I'm definitely thinking about that."

"Of course it includes kissing." Her voice was breathy and weak. "*Especially* kissing."

"Why?" he asked, tilting his head. As if he was simply curious. "If you're not interested, kissing shouldn't bother you."

"Why would you want to kiss someone who isn't interested in you?" she countered.

"Maybe to find out if she's telling the truth. Or maybe I'm hoping I can change her mind."

"I'm not easily swayed," she said.

"Wrong thing to say, Bree. I love challenges." He lowered his mouth to hers.

CHAPTER SEVEN

SHE BRACED HERSELF for an assault. Experience had taught her that when men tried to kiss her, they didn't waste time. She could have ducked away, of course, but she was curious.

Actually, she was starved for affection. She needed to have someone besides Charlie or her sisters hold her. She would let loose just this once, before she stuffed the need deep down inside her again, where it belonged.

He didn't crush her mouth beneath his or try to force it open. Instead, he brushed her lips lightly, lingering at the corner.

Surprised, she opened her eyes. "Relax, Bree. It's just a kiss," he murmured.

He buried his hands in her hair and nuzzled her neck. "I've been wondering how your hair felt." He let some of the long strands flow through his fingers. "Now that I know, I'll have a hard time keeping my hands away from it." He worked his way across her cheek and back to her mouth, where he settled with a sigh. His lips were soft and undemanding, taking only what she offered. She knew that if she tried to get away, he'd let her go immediately.

She didn't want to get away. She wanted to move closer to him. When he nibbled at her lower lip, her mouth softened. She felt him smile as he tugged her against him.

She had time to notice that his hands were gentle, his chest hard and muscular. Not the chest of a man who spent his days behind a desk or in front of a classroom. Then she didn't think at all. She only felt.

It had been so long since she'd kissed a man. Since she'd wanted to. She'd forgotten that rush of heat, the need that roared through her, the way her bones felt as if they were melting.

She hadn't wanted to remember. It was easier that way.

Before she realized it, her arms were around his neck, her chest was pressed against his and she was kissing him back.

Making up for far too many years of drought.

She felt wild and reckless. As if she wanted to devour him. And wanted him to devour her.

He ran his fingertips over her spine, his thumbs grazing her sides, moving close to her breasts. She wanted to press herself into his hands, give herself up to the need and the heat.

The low rumble of a car engine cut through their desire and reminded her where they were. And what they were doing. She stumbled away from him, bracing her hands against his chest when he tried to draw her close again.

"Stop," she rasped. "Please."

"Are you sure?" His own voice was husky, and his hand shook when he traced her lips.

"Very sure." She stepped out of his reach, away from temptation. "This can't happen again."

His eyes were heavy-lidded and his chest rose and fell too fast. "You were kissing me back."

She couldn't deny it. Wouldn't deny it. "That doesn't matter. I work for you," she said. "This has bad idea written all over it."

"You don't work for me. You work for the college." He tucked a strand of hair behind her ear, let his fingers trace her jaw. "Are you involved with someone else? You seem to know a lot of people at the bar."

"I grew up in this town, Professor. I know a lot of the people who live here. That doesn't mean I'm involved with them."

"I'll take that as a no." He caught her hand and walked with her to the door. "Why won't you call me Parker?"

Because it was too intimate. It made what had just happened feel more important. More significant. If she didn't say his name, she could pretend it didn't mean anything.

Just like at the strip club. She'd never called any of the men by their first names.

Ashamed, she admitted he wasn't like those men. And didn't deserve to be placed in the same category. "All right, Parker. Thank you for walking me home."

"It was my pleasure." He studied her, as if trying to probe beneath the surface. "I'll see you at work on Monday."

"I'll be there," she said lightly as she unlocked the door. "Good night."

"Good night, Bree." He brushed his mouth over hers once more. "Sweet dreams."

After she'd shut the door, she moved the curtain and watched him walk down the sidewalk until he disappeared from sight. She wasn't sure her dreams would be sweet tonight. But she knew she'd dream about him.

"YOU WERE OUT LATE last night." Fiona didn't look up from her newspaper crossword puzzle as Bree walked into the kitchen the next morning.

"I was working." Bree glanced at her sister. "I hate people who do the the *New York Times* crossword in ink."

"Don't change the subject. What's wrong?" Fiona dropped her pen and lounged in her chair, as if she'd wait all day for an answer.

"What makes you think something's wrong?" Bree flicked on the gas beneath the teakettle. "I worked last night. That's why I got home late."

"Is that why you came down to the kitchen twice during the night, tossed and turned in your bed for a few hours and got up so early this morning?"

Bree sank into one of the chairs. "Since when do you pay so much attention to what I do?"

Fiona slid her hand over Bree's. "In spite of all the evidence otherwise, I'm not totally self-absorbed. You hardly slept a wink last night." She grinned. "You never fixed that squeak in your bed. I could always tell when you were awake."

The teakettle whistled. Bree grabbed a pot holder, poured hot water into the teapot and tossed in three tea bags. She needed a big dose of caffeine this morning. "I had a lot of stuff on my mind," she said quietly. "Decisions I have to make."

"You want to talk about it?"

She set the teapot on the table. "You're turning into Ms. Sensitive, Fee. It's beginning to scare me."

"Hey, if you and Zoe can do it, so can I," Fiona said. "Does it have something to do with whoever walked you home last night?"

To gain time, Bree poured herself a cup of tea. Her hand was shaking even before caffeine. Not a good sign.

"How do you know someone walked me home last night?" she finally asked.

"My bedroom is at the front of the house," her sister answered. "I heard you talking."

Bree sipped her tea. "Parker Ellison walked me home. One of the professors I work for."

"Really." Fiona twirled the pen in her fingers. "I thought you said there was nothing going on with him."

She sighed as she set her cup down on the counter. "I don't want there to be anything going on with him. For a lot of reasons. But he was waiting for me after the bar closed. I told him I didn't want him walking me home, but he didn't pay any attention."

"He sounds slick."

"He probably is, but he seems like a nice enough guy."

"Watch yourself, Bree," Fiona said over the rim of her coffee cup.

Before she could frame an answer, she heard Charlie pounding down the stairs. She glanced at the clock, surprised he was up this early, then remembered he was going to Door County with his friends the Grant twins and their father, Jackson.

"Hey, Mom. Aunt Fee," he said, dropping his backpack onto the floor with a thump. "I'm starved."

He opened the refrigerator, and Bree reached down to pull his backpack out of the way. It was much too heavy to hold only a towel and a bathing suit. "What the heck is in your pack?" she said. "It feels like it's full of bricks."

Charlie snatched the bag away from her. "Just a book I want to read."

"Heavy reading, huh?"

"Very funny, Mom," he said, rolling his eyes. "Ha ha ha."

Charlie always used to think she was funny. He wasn't a little boy anymore. "Glad I could make you laugh," she said.

"Are you cleaning today?" he asked. Too casually.

"Isn't that what we always do on Sunday?"

"You want to stay home and help, Charlie?" She nudged him with her elbow. "We can always use another pair of hands."

He gave his aunt a genuine smile. "No thanks, Aunt Fee. I'll be lounging on the beach while you're slaving away."

Bree felt a tiny jab of jealousy at the easy rapport her sister had developed with Charlie. There was none of the tension that seemed to infect her own relationship with her son recently. "We'll save some work for you, Charlie. Don't worry."

"I'll clean my own room when I get home," he said. Too casually again. "Don't go in there, okay? I don't want you scaring the snakes."

"You think I'm going to tap on the glass and make faces at them?"

Charlie scowled. "That is so not funny."

"Apparently I've lost my sense of humor," she said slowly.

A horn honked outside and he grabbed his backpack. "That's Dr. Grant. I'll see you later."

"He's been really surly lately," Bree murmured as she listened to the car pull away.

"He's been fine around me," Fiona said idly as she studied her crossword. "We've been getting along great."

"I noticed." As soon as the words were out of her mouth, she wanted to snatch them back.

Fiona dropped the newspaper. "Are you upset about that?"

"Of course not," Bree said with a sigh. "I knew this was coming. He'll be thirteen pretty soon. But it's as if he's one of the pod people. He looks like my kid, but he doesn't sound like Charlie."

Fiona laughed. "Fun times ahead, Bree."

"Yeah. I can't wait."

THE KNOCK ON HIS office door was tentative, so quiet Parker thought he'd imagined it. When he heard it again, he dragged his attention away from the photograph he was studying on his computer monitor, and with a regretful look at the screen, called, "Come in."

Charlie opened the door and poked his head inside. His knuckles were white as he gripped the edge. "I need to talk to you, Dr. Ellison."

"Of course, Charlie. Come on in."

The boy swung his backpack off his shoulders and stood rigidly in front of Parker's desk, grasping the straps.

"So what can I do for you?" Parker asked. Clearly, it was going to be a while before he could get back to work.

"I have a question," the boy said, shifting from one foot to the other. "About the last test."

He fumbled with his backpack and pulled out a rumpled piece of paper Parker recognized as the most recent quiz he'd given in class. "I think you made a mistake when you graded mine." He put the paper on Parker's desk and smoothed out the wrinkles. "I'm pretty sure number twelve is right. I looked it up."

Parker picked up the test and saw it was true—he had mistakenly marked the answer wrong. He glanced up at the boy, who was biting his lip, as if afraid Parker would snap his head off. "You're *pretty sure* you got it right, Charlie? Or are you positive?"

The boy's Adam's apple bobbed convulsively. "I know I got it right."

Parker nodded. "You did. I screwed up. I must have gotten distracted when I was correcting your paper. And that reminds me, I didn't find your name on the class roster." He'd delayed entering the grades from the first of his quizzes, figuring he'd do two weeks' worth at once. Then had found he didn't have a student named Charlie listed. And he hadn't been able to read Charlie's scrawl on the quiz. "What's your last name?"

He swallowed. "It's McInnes, sir."

Parker stopped still. "Really? Do you belong to one of the McInnes triplets?"

"We're distantly related," he mumbled. "I don't really know them." He added quickly, "I'll go to the office and find out why I'm not on the roster, okay?"

"Thanks. That would save me a trip." Parker pulled up his grade sheet on the computer and added McInnes to the temporary entry he'd made for Charlie. Then he corrected his score. "There you go. A 98 instead of a 96."

The photo he'd been studying came back on his screen when he closed the grade sheet. God, he needed to get back in the field if just the picture of an unidentified orchid had him jonesing for South America. He needed to get away from all the distractions in Spruce Lake.

He should just let Charlie leave, but he heard himself say, "If you know you're right, don't be afraid to say so."

"Some teachers don't like to be corrected," the boy muttered. But he wasn't gripping his backpack so tightly anymore.

"Like who?"

"I didn't mean you," he said quickly.

"Have you taken another course at Collier, then?"

"No." Charlie glanced at his feet. "It was my science teacher. Mrs. Fogarty."

"Yeah?" Parker leaned forward, intrigued in spite of himself. "What happened with Mrs. Fogarty?"

"She doesn't know anything about snakes," Charlie said with disgust.

"Not every science teacher is a reptile expert," Parker said mildly.

"Yeah, but she didn't know *anything*. She said all snakes lay eggs. When I told her that some snakes like boas and garter snakes have live young, she got all mad at me and told me not to make stuff up." He scowled. "I brought in one of my books and showed it to her, but she didn't even care that she'd made a mistake."

"She was probably embarrassed," Parker said.

"Embarrassed?" Charlie wrinkled his nose. "Not Mrs. Fogarty. She thinks she's always right. She doesn't like it when a kid corrects her."

Why was he surprised that Charlie was so perceptive? He was an exceptionally bright kid. Parker had known more than a few teachers who resented having a gifted kid in their class. "Any chance you'll get her next year?"

"Yeah," Charlie answered glumly. "I probably will. There are only two science teachers at the junior high."

"Junior high? I thought you were in high school," he said, shocked.

The kid's chest seemed to puff out. "I'm very mature for my age."

Parker bit his lip, trying not to smile. "You certainly are." He studied Charlie with new interest. He'd been irritated at first about having a young kid in his class, but he'd realized early that Charlie was an exceptional child. He was doing better than any of the college kids.

Just like Parker had done at his age.

"So what are you going to do about Mrs. Fogarty?"

Charlie shrugged. "I don't know."

"Weren't you going to take herpetology this fall?"

His eyes lit up. "I want to."

"Maybe your junior high won't make you take science if you're enrolled in a science class here."

"Yeah?" Charlie stood up straighter. "That would totally rock."

"Have your parents check into it." Parker hesitated. "Do they know about your problem with this teacher?"

"Nah." Charlie picked up a pen from the desk and clicked it several times. "I'm not a baby. It would totally suck if my mom called the school about her."

"I hear you," Parker said. There was nothing more humiliating for a kid in junior high than to have his parents fight his battles. Except not to have his parents around at all.

Charlie gave him a speculative look. "Maybe you could call the school."

"I'm not sure that would be appropriate," Parker said. The last thing he wanted was to get involved with the problems of a kid in junior high school.

Charlie snorted. "Is that, like, an adult's favorite word? *Appropriate?* My mom says it all the time."

"Probably for a good reason," Parker said. A smart kid like Charlie would be a handful.

"It would be so cool if you called the principal," Charlie coaxed. "She'd have to listen to you."

Parker remembered what it was like to be the smart kid in class, one who sometimes knew more than his teacher. And he recalled how humiliating it could be when that teacher resented being corrected. "How about if I write a letter?" he said. He could write one in five minutes and then forget about it. "I could tell your principal how well you did in this course and suggest that you take another science class here next fall."

"That would be great, Dr. Ellison. Thanks," Charlie said happily. He bent down to pick up his backpack and saw the orchid picture on the computer screen. "Cool photo."

The tangled plants were so dense they almost looked like random splashes of green, yellow and brown. "It is," Parker agreed. "One of my friends got this picture from a colleague and he needs help figuring out where it is. He thought I might be able to tell, based on the species in the picture."

"You can do that?" Charlie looked impressed. "That's awesome."

"Yeah." He glanced at the screen. "It's a puzzle, and I like puzzles."

"Me, too." The boy revealed slightly crooked teeth when he grinned. "I like logic puzzles. My aunt Fee does crosswords."

The kid seemed far too serious for a kid his age. "Why do you like logic puzzles?" Parker asked, though he'd liked them himself when he was that age.

The grin disappeared and Charlie shifted nervously again, as if afraid he'd said the wrong thing. "Because you have to think of a lot of stuff at once, I guess. I'm good at that."

"Based on how well you're doing in my class, it looks like you're good at a lot of things."

He shrugged. "What you've talked about had been interesting so far."

"Since I've mostly talked about animals, does that mean you're not going to pay attention when I start to talk about plants?" Parker teased.

Charlie looked at him indignantly. "Of course not," he replied. "I'll study plants."

"I was teasing you, Charlie," he said. "I know you'll work just as hard on the plant section as you have on the animals."

Charlie eyed him doubtfully for a moment. What he saw in Parker's face must have reassured him, because he relaxed. "Yeah, but it won't be as much fun."

"Have to disagree with you there, Charlie. Plants rock."

"They can't even move," he scoffed. "What's so interesting about that?"

Parker pulled up a photograph of a delicate, salmon-colored orchid. "See this? It's from the rain forest in Brazil. The native people who live there use it as a fertility drug."

Charlie peered at the picture. "Is it?"

"I don't know. I haven't done any studies on it." He pulled up another photo, of a white orchid with tiny purple splotches. "See this one? A scientist in New York is studying a compound he extracted from it that he thinks might be useful in treating cancer."

"Really?" Charlie stared.

"Yep. Those are just two plants. There are millions more out there. Probably thousands haven't even been discovered."

Charlie switched his attention to Parker. "Is that what you do? Search for new plants?"

"I study orchids. I look for new species and try to find uses for the ones we know about. Like that cancer treatment I mentioned."

"That's pretty neat," Charlie said. He glanced at the screen again, then back at Parker with more interest. "Do you get to go to other countries to look for orchids?"

"I sure do." He was counting the days until he left Wisconsin again. "I'm going to Peru next winter to study the cloud forest there." He swiveled in his chair and pointed to a large map of Central and South America on the wall. "Those pins show all the places I've been." It was a map of his life.

"Yeah?" Charlie stepped closer. "How come there are different color pins?"

"The green ones are the expeditions I've led. The yellow ones are trips I took when I was younger. They were led by someone else."

"What about this one?" Charlie touched the lone red pin on the map, stuck into Peru.

"That's where I discovered a new species of orchid. The

one the scientist in New York is studying as a treatment for cancer."

"Really? You discovered a new species?" Charlie looked at him with awe. "Did you get to name it?"

"I did," Parker said. "I named it after my father."

"He must have thought that was awesome."

His father hadn't been that impressed; he'd said Parker should have named it after himself. Immortality, he'd told Parker. "Yeah," Parker said quietly. "I think he did."

Charlie devoured the map, touching the pins reverently. "I've read about a lot of these places," he said. "There are a bunch of interesting snakes in South America."

He couldn't disguise the hunger in his eyes, and Parker felt a surge of sympathy. He'd been a kid just like Charlie, longing for adventure, studying the maps every time his parents left on an expedition, dreaming of going along. Always being left behind. "Maybe someday you'll be able to go to South America and study some of those snakes."

Charlie's enthusiasm faded. "Maybe. Thanks for fixing my test, Dr. Ellison."

"I'm glad you caught my mistake." He watched Charlie stuff the quiz paper into his backpack. "You didn't really need those two points, though. You've got a solid A in the class."

"What if I bomb the next test?" Charlie frowned as if what he'd said was stupid. "I'd need the points then."

Parker smiled. "You're awfully competitive, Charlie."

He looked surprised. "What's wrong with that?"

"Not a thing. Competition is good." Parker studied the boy standing in front of him. "Do you play any sports?"

Charlie shifted from one foot to the other. "I, uh, haven't yet. But I'm going to be on the cross-country team this fall. At my school."

"Yeah? That sounds like fun. I like to run."

"You do? My mom hates running," he confided. "Once my aunt tried to get her to go jogging. Mom said she'd rather stick a fork in her eye."

"That's pretty extreme," he said, laughing. "She doesn't know what she's missing, does she?"

"Uh, no." Charlie seemed uncomfortable. "I'll see you in class tomorrow, Dr. Ellison."

"You bet," Parker replied. He stood and held out his hand. Charlie turned red again, then gave it a perfunctory shake.

Someone needed to teach the kid the right way to shake hands. Someone besides Parker. He didn't do kids. He didn't do relationships of any kind.

He had flings. And right now, he was thinking about a fling with his new admin.

CHAPTER EIGHT

As THE COPY MACHINE BEGAN spitting out papers, Bree stood up from her desk, stretched and gazed out the window at the quad. The panes hadn't been washed recently, she noted absently.

A few students were sitting under trees, reading. Two guys were playing Frisbee on the grass. And at the other end, a boy wearing a backpack was riding a red bicycle down the sidewalk.

From a distance, he looked like Charlie. She wiped at the grimy window and squinted, trying to see more clearly, but the dirt was on the outside. What if it had been Charlie? He'd ridden right past the humanities building. What if Ted had happened to look out the window? Charlie looked like a clone of Ted.

The boy on the bike turned a corner and disappeared, and she leaned her head against the glass. She'd sent out ten more résumés last night for teaching jobs. She would send out ten more tonight. She *had* to find another job.

Bree turned back to her desk with a sigh. Until then, she had plenty of work to keep her busy. It seemed as if every professor in the department needed her to type and print something today.

Everyone except Parker. She hadn't seen him all day.

She was disappointed. And that was a bad sign.

She'd spent Sunday sorting through things in her father's study. Looking at his books, his notes, remembering how he'd been, was the best possible way to cool her interest in a celebrity professor.

It hadn't done any good. A humorous book made her think of Parker's smile. A blue book jacket reminded her of the color of his eyes. He crept back into her head whenever she let down her guard.

And when she'd fallen into bed last night, exhausted and longing for sleep, she'd dreamed about him.

"You are pathetic," she muttered as she gathered newly printed exams and stuffed them into the chemistry professor's mailbox.

"You don't look pathetic to me," Parker said from behind her. She spun around to see him smiling. "In fact, you look pretty darn good."

"Hello, Professor Ellison," she said, disgusted once again at her breathlessness.

"What happened to 'Parker'?" he asked. He'd lowered his voice and his question sounded way too intimate for the office.

"We're at work," she said. "I didn't think it was appropriate." *Appropriate?* She'd never thought of herself as prim. But if it helped keep him at a distance, she would be the queen of prim.

"Interesting word choice." He raised his eyebrows. "Even Marjorie called me Parker," he said. "We're pretty informal around here."

"Yeah, right," she said. "I'm sure Dr. Boehmer wants me to call him Chuck." The head of the science department was completely intimidating.

"Maybe not Boehmer," he conceded. He dropped into one of the chairs next to her desk. "I need a favor, Bree."

"What kind of favor?" she asked cautiously.

"I need to send a letter to some of my supporters, explaining my next trip and asking for donations. I'd like to get it out first thing in the morning, because I'm going to be…" He thrust his hand through his hair. "That doesn't matter. I need the donors to get the letter before the end of the week."

"And you just thought of this now?" She glanced at the clock. "I'm supposed to leave at five, and I have a lot of work to do in the next two hours."

"I know it's last minute, but something just came up this afternoon." He fingered the green stone Charlie had given her when he was a toddler—the good luck piece she kept on her desk. He didn't meet her gaze. "I need to talk to you, too."

Her heart plummeted. No wonder he'd been avoiding her all day. "If it's about what happened the other night, don't worry about it. It's already forgotten."

He froze, then let go of the rock. "Really? You've forgotten already?" His eyes turned slumberous. "I haven't been able to think of much else."

Okay, then. She'd guessed wrong. "This isn't the place to discuss that," she said sharply.

"I know. It's something else. And I do need help with the letters."

"So this is strictly work?"

"In a manner of speaking."

Did he expect her to stay late and work for free because he'd kissed her? And because her pulse was still pounding in response to his smile? "Am I going to get paid to do these letters?"

"Of course," he said, surprised. "I wouldn't expect you to do extra work on your own time."

"Dr. Boehmer told me they couldn't afford to pay overtime."

"I'll make sure you get paid."

She needed the money—Charlie had mentioned running cross-country in the fall, and there would be shoes to buy and fees to pay. "Let me call my sister and tell her I won't be home."

"You live with your sister?"

"We're staying in my father's house while we clean it out and get ready to sell it."

"You're getting rid of all your father's stuff?" he asked. His voice sounded casual, but there was a gleam of interest in his eyes.

"Yes, we are. Why? Do you need furniture or something?"

"I don't need any more possessions cluttering up my life. But I'd like to borrow or buy some of your father's papers. That's actually what I wanted to talk about later."

He wanted her father's papers? Bree stiffened. "Let's talk about it now."

Parker frowned. "Did I say something wrong?"

"Why do you want my father's stuff?"

"I told you about that celebration the college is planning, didn't I? Because it's the twentieth anniversary of McInnes's Pulitzer?"

"You did."

He shoved his hands into his pockets, clearly uncomfortable. "It would add a lot to the celebration to exhibit some of the notes he took when he was working on the book."

"Is that what the other night was about?" She was gripping the edge of the desk so tightly her fingers throbbed.

"God, no." He looked so horrified that she relaxed a little. "The papers are college business. They have nothing to do with what happened between us." He'd lowered his voice to a rumble, a husky sound that slid over her nerves like a caress. "That was definitely personal."

"You weren't softening me up before you asked?"

He stepped around the desk and leaned closer. "Oh, I was softening you up. But not for any papers. I have something else in mind entirely."

"Okay. I believe you," she managed to say. Her skin hummed with awareness. She wanted to touch him, but anyone could walk in on them.

He didn't back away. "You sure?" he asked. "Because I can explain in more detail."

Yes. Please. "That's not necessary," she said, swallowing.

He straightened, but was still too close. "Too bad. I'm a detail kind of guy. I examine things closely. That's how I conduct my research."

He wasn't touching her, either, but her skin felt as if it would ignite if he moved any nearer. And they were in the office. In full view.

"Fine," she said hurriedly. "You can have whatever you need."

"Really, Bree?" His eyes darkened. "Whatever I need?"

"The papers and books. My f-father's stuff," she stuttered.

"I'd forgotten all about that."

She was in so much trouble. "That's what this conversation was about, wasn't it?"

"Absolutely." One side of his mouth curled up. "What else would we be talking about?"

"Those letters you want me to type." *Get hold of yourself.*

"Of course. I'll get the letter and my lists." His dimple flashed as he sauntered out of the office. "We'll get into the details later."

Her hands shook as she dialed Fiona. Her sister was working, and sounded vague and distracted. Finally, ten minutes later, Bree hung up with a sigh.

"Problems?" Parker asked from the door. "Do you have to go home?"

"No, it's fine. My sister is a little absentminded."

"Yeah?" He was all business now. Good.

"She's an artist and she's in the middle of a project. She probably won't even remember I called."

"An artist? What does she do?"

"She designs jewelry," Bree said.

He gave her a quizzical look. "Would that be FeeMac Jewelry?"

"How do you know that?" She narrowed her eyes.

"I saw a sign at that frou-frou store in town a while ago about an appearance by the designer of that jewelry line. It wasn't that big a leap."

A reminder not to underestimate Parker. He was smart and quick. "Yeah, that's Fiona."

"Another McInnes celebrity. Quite the family."

"Yeah, we're amazing," she said dryly. She glanced at the papers in his hand. "I'll start these as soon as I finish my work for the day. All right?"

"That's fine. Here's the list of names and addresses for the mail merge." Parker handed her a slender silver flash drive. "The file name is major donors."

She stared at the drive in her hand and something inside her softened. "You could have e-mailed me the information. You don't have to let me poke around in your flash drive."

"I don't have any secrets on it," he said with a shrug. "And the college intranet takes forever to download attachments."

"I won't look at anything else," she promised as she plugged it into her computer.

"I wouldn't have given it to you if I thought you would," he said, heading for the door. "I'm going to compose another letter to send to a different group of donors. Do you have time to work on that one, too?"

How late did he want her to stay? Her heart began to thud as an image of them alone together in the building crept into her mind. "Sure. I'll get started right at five."

"Great." He gave her the smile that always made her feel a little dizzy. "I'll order a pizza later. It seems only fair that I feed you."

Four hours later, Bree pushed away from the desk and worked the kinks out of her neck. Piles of envelopes were neatly stacked in front of her. She would run them through the meter in the morning, then put them in the mail. "Is that all?" she asked when Parker walked back into her office.

"That's it." He dropped into the chair next to her desk. "Thanks. It went a lot faster with two people."

"Not a problem." She sneaked a glance at her watch. Charlie should be calling her any minute. If Fiona had remembered to remind him.

Parker's cell phone rang, and he glanced at the screen. "That's the pizza. I'll run down and get it."

While he was gone, she picked up the phone and called Charlie. "Sorry I had to work late tonight," she said.

"Are you working with that guy Ellison?"

"Yes, I am. How did you know about him?"

"I heard you talking to Aunt Fee. He sounds like a cool dude."

"Hot" was the word she'd choose. "He is. What are you doing tonight?"

"I'm playing video games and drinking a beer," he said with sarcasm. "Because I don't have homework to do. Because you won't let me take that class."

"Why are we talking about that again? I thought you understood why you can't take it."

"No, I don't." His voice turned wheedling. "I can still sign up for it. It's not too late."

"I haven't changed my mind, Charlie. You're not coming to campus."

"Fine. I'll see you later." He hung up.

Bree set the phone down and stared at it for a moment. She hadn't realized he was still thinking about that class. They'd have to talk about it again.

And Charlie had overheard her talking to Fiona about Parker. She'd need to be more careful.

As she tried to reassure herself that her son was a typical adolescent, Parker walked into the office with a square pizza box. "Dinner is served," he said. All thoughts of Charlie disappeared.

Bree began to make room on her desk, but Parker shook his head. "Come into my office," he said. "We'll have more space to spread out."

The words *spread out* put a picture in her head that would have made her blush, if she'd been a blusher.

She wasn't. She'd learned to hide her emotions a long time ago. Emotions made you vulnerable. An easy target. And she was a pro at protecting herself.

But she found herself watching the way he moved as she followed him down the hall. The worn jeans hugged his rear end and long legs. She remembered how he'd felt, wrapped around her the other night.

As he set the pizza on his desk and pushed the door closed, she looked around his office to distract herself. She'd been in here before, but only briefly, to drop things off. She'd never had a chance to really look at it.

Photos of orchids lined the walls. There were white blossoms speckled with burgundy, yellow ones, salmon ones with slashes of purple and others of every imaginable color. Drops of dew glistened on the petals of one deep purple flower. The intricate blooms, with their lips and deep folds, were hauntingly erotic.

She shook her head slightly to clear it. Usually, she was able to ruthlessly shut down any attraction she might feel for a man. So why were a bunch of flower pictures turning her on?

She dragged her attention to a large map of Central and South America on one wall. All the pins stuck in it, a forest of green and yellow, reminded her of her own mundane, pedestrian existence. Milwaukee was the most exotic place she'd been.

A longing stirred inside her. She wanted to visit other countries, other cultures, other continents. She wanted to go someplace that wasn't Spruce Lake, Wisconsin.

"Those pins are all places you've visited, right?"

"Yep." He opened the pizza box. "I'm planning another trip next winter. There are a lot of orchids I haven't found samples of yet." He handed her a napkin and gestured for her to take a slice.

"How often do you go away?" she asked, helping herself to a big piece. Parker did the same.

"Every year," he said, settling into his chair. "I leave after fall semester and stay until late spring. I can't wait to get back there."

He turned his attention to the thick, cheesy pizza, quickly devouring two pieces. *Take notes here, Bree. He's not interested in long term.* Numbly, she nibbled at her own pizza. "From the number of pictures, it looks as if you've been going for a long time," she said at last.

"Since I started college. I've made a lot of trips to South America."

"Your parents must have missed you," she commented lightly.

"Nope." After wiping his fingers on the napkin, he picked up a paperweight that looked like a purple orchid trapped in glass, and tossed it from one hand to another. He didn't meet her gaze. "They weren't around much."

Bree grabbed the paperweight out of the air and set it back on his desk. "What do you mean?" she asked. "Why weren't they around?"

He spun in his chair to stare at the map. "They were archaeologists. They spent most of their time on digs."

"Then who took care of you?"

"I stayed with an aunt when I was younger. Then my parents put me in boarding school."

"You spent your childhood in boarding schools?" she asked. She'd had a less-than-perfect childhood, herself, but at least she'd had sisters. Even the fighting was better than having no one.

He shrugged. "It wasn't that bad."

"And now you run away to foreign countries, just like your parents did."

"Nah," he said, forcing a grin. "I go on my expeditions because chicks dig it."

She glanced again at the photos on the wall. The blossoms were so vivid, she could imagine them dipping in a breeze. "I'll bet they like your photos," she said. One of the white orchids had a slash of deep pink inside its creamy folds.

"Most people think the flowers are pretty. But when I look at them, I see more than their beauty. I see their potential." He pointed to the photo of a yellow orchid. "An enzyme has been isolated from this one that may be able to protect against malaria." He indicated another. "Some scientists are using this one to treat an intestinal parasite."

"Did you discover all these orchids?" she asked.

He smiled and touched a picture of a white orchid with purple splashes on the petals. "Only this one."

Bree studied the photo, wondering what it would be like to come across a species unknown to modern science. To be the first person in the world to see a new species of plant or animal. "It must have been exciting."

"It was." He stared at the photo. "It was like having sex for the first time. Overwhelming and exciting and addictive. It makes you want to do it again. A lot."

She ignored the little zing she felt at his mention of sex. "Is that why you keep going on your expeditions? To feel that rush again?"

"That's part of it." He shrugged. "I get bored easily, and then I get restless. I need a change of pace, a change of scenery. I'd go out of my mind if I had to live in one place year after year."

The map on the wall beckoned like a siren, but she didn't look at it. "It's hard to get away like that when you have a family," she said.

He picked up the orchid paperweight again and rubbed his thumb over it. "People who have jobs like mine shouldn't have families."

"Probably not," she agreed. Those were his boundaries; he wasn't available for happily ever after. "Too hard on everyone."

"Exactly." He studied her for a moment. "What about you? Did you always want to be a teacher?"

No. She wasn't cut out to be a teacher, but it had been a smart choice. "Teaching is a great job," she said. "I have the summers off." Why wasn't she telling him about Charlie?

Because he'd made it clear he wasn't interested in long term. And women with children were usually looking for that. She wasn't. She didn't need a man to complete her life. But a fling…

"That's not what I asked," he said. He leaned closer, still holding the paperweight. "Do you like teaching?"

"It pays the bills."

He let his gaze drift over her. "Turnabout is fair play," he said softly. "I told you about me. Now it's your turn."

"There's not much to tell," she said. Nothing she wanted to reveal. "I moved away from Spruce Lake when I went to college, and now I'm back. End of story."

"Then tell me about growing up in Spruce Lake. About being one of the McInnes Supertwins."

Her stomach twisted, an automatic reaction to the phrase her father had used far too often. "Where did you hear that?"

He shifted in his chair. "You sound upset."

She ran her palms down her thighs and avoided his eyes. "It's been a long time since anyone called us that."

She felt his gaze on her for several heartbeats. "I won't use it again," he finally said. "Sorry."

She shrugged. "Don't worry about it. It was a surprise, that's all."

"You want to talk about it?"

"There's nothing to talk about," she said briskly. "Multiple births higher than twins are called supertwins. My father liked the word."

Parker rolled the paperweight between his hands. "I bet that usually works like a charm to keep men at bay."

"What are you talking about?"

"Your efficient, no-nonsense attitude." He tilted his head. "It's as if you have an invisible force field around you and I'll bounce off it if I get too near."

He was uncomfortably close to the truth. Her invisible force field was the way she'd survived being a stripper. "I have no idea what you're talking about."

"No?" He leaned in, invading her comfort zone. "You're daring me to get more intimate, Bree. And I can never resist a dare."

His voice washed over her, a mix of sin and seduction, and his breath caressed her neck. Blood rushed through her veins and pounded in her ears. With an effort, she drew away from him. "I promise you, my life story is boring. Nothing like yours."

"Boring? I don't think so." He skimmed a finger down her neck and she shivered. "No one who reacts like you do is boring."

"Maybe I'm just ticklish," she managed to say.

"Ticklish? That's an interesting detail. Let's test it."

He ran the paperweight lightly along the groove above her collarbone, barely touching her skin. The glass was warm from his hands and slippery smooth. She swallowed, amazed at the yearning that swelled inside her.

He must have read it in her eyes, because he drew the glass to the hollow at her throat, then slowly downward into the open vee of her blouse. "You don't seem that ticklish to me," he murmured.

"I'm controlling myself."

"Are you?" he asked, a glint in his eye as he moved closer. "Let's see what I can do about that."

CHAPTER NINE

BLOOD ROARED IN Bree's ears as Parker stood in front of her. *Too close.* She could feel the heat from his body, smell the clean tang of the soap he'd used. He slid the warm, smooth glass of the paperweight even lower, and her breasts tightened. "Still controlling yourself?" he murmured.

"Yes," she choked out.

"You're tough, Bree," he whispered as he took her hand and drew her to her feet. "I like that in a woman."

She expected him to pull her into his arms. Her body softened, anticipating the pressure of his hard chest against hers, the feel of his long legs. But he didn't move. Instead, he twined his fingers with hers and, with his other hand, raised the paperweight to her mouth.

He brushed it over her lips, then slid it down her neck again. She couldn't stop the tremor that shivered through her.

"Ticklish there?" He pressed his mouth to the side of her neck and nipped lightly, and she gave a tiny moan. "Yes, I think I found a spot," he murmured, his breath feathering over the place where he'd bitten her. "Let's see if I can find another one."

He rolled the glass ball down her side, barely touching her breast. The fleeting pressure made her gasp. He smiled as he moved the paperweight across her abdomen and up her other side. "Found another spot," he said into her ear.

He moved the globe to the vee of her blouse again, and she glanced down. The purple of the orchid was vivid against her pale skin and the blue of her blouse. She couldn't tear her gaze away as he went lower, then lower still, until it was resting in her cleavage.

Her breasts ached, but he was careful to touch her only with the paperweight. "I know a place where you're probably very ticklish," he said, nibbling her earlobe. "Should we check?"

Her body was crying out for him, for his touch. She hadn't wanted a man's touch for so long. It was as if the desire she'd kept hidden for all these years burst out of its prison, enveloping her with heat and need and want. "Yes," she whispered.

He skimmed the paperweight over the tips of her breasts. She shuddered and cried out at the intensity of the sensation. His hand faltered, then she heard the thud of the glass dropping onto his desk.

He speared his fingers into her hair, pulled her against him and fused his mouth to hers. Their kiss was a blaze of passion and yearning, their mouths open, tongues dancing. He tasted faintly of pizza and a sweet sharp hint of the soft drink he'd had.

He drew her into the vee of his legs. He was as aroused as she was, and she shifted to get closer. To meld her body with his. She felt his hands at her chest, then cool air rushing over her belly. He'd unbuttoned her blouse and pushed it open, and then circled his tanned fingers over the delicate lace of her peach bra. "Look what was hiding beneath that ugly blouse," he murmured against her lips.

Without taking his mouth from hers, he cupped her breasts in his hands, testing their weight, stroking his thumbs over her nipples. She arched against him and groaned.

Parker swung her around and laid her on his desk, then fumbled with the clasp of her bra. It fell open, and he sucked in a breath.

"You're so beautiful," he said, his voice ragged. "Even more beautiful than I imagined."

He stared down at her sprawled on his desk, and a wave of arousal swept over her. She reached for him just as he bent and kissed her, and then they were locked together. His hands moved over her bare breasts, a blind man learning her by touch alone.

The squeak of a cleaning cart coming down the hallway gradually cut through Bree's haze of desire. Then she heard the jingle of a set of keys.

"Professor, you want me to clean your office?" a voice called through the closed door.

Parker froze, his palms cupping her breasts. "No thanks, Justin," he called back. He cleared his throat. "I'm fine tonight."

"Catch you tomorrow, then."

"Okay," he managed to say. She could feel his heart thudding.

She stared up at Parker as her head cleared. Abruptly, she scrambled to tug the edges of her blouse together and get up. He took her elbows and helped her to a sitting position. Then, easing her shaking hands aside, he fastened her bra and began rebuttoning her blouse.

"I think this is the ugliest of all the ugly blouses you wear to work," he said softly. "How do you pick them? By how much of you they hide."

"What do you think I should wear, spandex tube tops? These are perfectly appropriate for work," she said, pushing his hands away and fastening the rest of the buttons herself.

"I like them." She hated them, but they were bland and ordinary. Exactly the image she wanted to portray.

"The only thing I like about this blouse is taking it off you," he said. He played with the top button, absently rubbing it between his fingers. "I'm sorry I didn't get to finish." He brushed a kiss over her mouth. "I didn't even think about where we were."

Neither had she. She'd been lost in the sensations of his hands and his mouth, in the desire he'd stirred in her, in her need for him. It scared the spit out of her.

"I'd better go," she said.

"In a minute. Justin is cleaning the office next door. Let him get a little farther away." Parker ran his hands down her arms to her wrist. "This isn't why I asked you to work late tonight." He nipped at her lower lip. "Although it was a lot more fun than writing letters." He stepped away from her. "I promise this won't happen again."

Disappointment slammed into her, until he added, "At work. The next time I kiss you, I don't want any interruptions. For several hours."

The next time. Did she want there to be a next time?

Yes.

She'd almost forgotten how it felt to want a man and be wanted in return. Forgotten that heady rush of arousal. Now she couldn't think of anything else.

If she decided to throw caution to the wind, she'd need to be very careful. Parker had made it clear he wasn't interested in anything more than an affair. But her body was still humming, and just looking at him made her want to drag his mouth to hers again.

A door closed, and the creak of the janitor's cart moved on down the hall. When the keys jingled again, and another door opened, Bree stepped out of Parker's office. "Good night, Professor."

He smiled at her, a sexy grin that made her stomach flutter. "Good night, Ms. McInnes. I'll see you in the morning."

"So how's it going with the professor?" Fiona asked as she and Bree cleaned up the kitchen after dinner two nights later.

How was it going? Parker had been all business at school since the episode in his office. "We work together, Fee. Nothing's going on."

She raised an eyebrow, her hands immersed in sudsy water. "Really? Didn't sound like nothing last weekend."

Bree's cheeks burned as she slid a plate into the cabinet. "Were you spying on me?"

"Sweetie, I recognized that tone of voice. I know what it means."

Bree slumped against the sink. "He's so wrong for me in so many ways," she whispered, glancing around the corner to make sure Charlie couldn't hear her. "But I can't stop thinking about him."

"That's a good start," her sister said, washing another dish. "And how is he wrong for you? He's not married, is he?"

"No. And he clearly doesn't want to be."

"So what?" Fiona tilted her head. "When was the last time you had a date?"

"A while." A lot longer than a while.

"So what if he isn't husband material? Have some fun with him."

"I'm not sure it's a good idea, Fee." She'd had plenty of time to think in the past two days, while her mind wasn't fogged by lust. She was afraid she'd fall for Parker, hard, if she gave herself half a chance.

"So go find out." Fiona drained the sink and hung up the dishrag. "I'm in the middle of a project and my business manager, Barb, is hounding me to finish it. I'm heading back to my studio."

When she'd gone, Bree wandered into the living room, feeling at loose ends. They'd cleaned out most of the house, except for their father's study. Charlie was in his room, the door firmly closed. Fiona had her jewelry. Bree picked up the romance novel she'd been reading and settled onto the old couch.

The doorbell startled her, and she hurried to answer it. "Parker?" she said, surprised when she saw him slouched against the porch railing.

"Hey, Bree. Is this a bad time?"

"A bad time for what?" Memories of her spread out on his desk like a feast rushed through her.

"Not what you're imagining," he said softly, pushing away from the railing and stepping closer. "Although I like the way you think."

"Come in," she said, shoving the pictures out of her mind and edging aside. Then she frowned. "How did you know where I live?"

"Your job application." He looked around the hall curiously. "I meant to talk to you at work today, but I got held up in a meeting. I was hoping I could take a look at some of those papers of your father's."

She'd forgotten all about his request and couldn't help but feel disappointed. She'd been hoping for something more personal. Which was pathetic. "Sure. Come on into the study. We've been cleaning it out, but we haven't gone through his files yet. Help yourself."

Parker didn't look at the file cabinet. Instead, he cupped his hand around the back of her neck and pulled her in for a kiss. His mouth stayed on hers until she was melting in response. He pulled her closer still and ran his hands restlessly over her back. "Is your sister here?" he whispered.

"She's in her studio out back." Bree drew away reluctantly. "But my son is home."

"You have a son?" He stumbled back as if she'd slapped him.

"Yes. He's twelve." She turned to the file cabinets. Playtime was over. Parker's reaction would have been funny if it didn't hurt so much. "What exactly were you looking for?"

He swung her around. "Why didn't you tell me?"

"It never came up," she said stiffly. "Now you know."

"Do you think it makes a difference?" he asked.

"Sure looks like it does."

"Bree." He grabbed both her hands and held them tightly. "How would you have reacted if I told you I had a kid? Wouldn't you have been surprised?"

"I suppose so," she said. Maybe his reaction had been normal surprise. At least that's what she wanted to believe.

"Should I have asked if you're married?"

"Do you think I would have kissed you if I was?"

"No." He touched her lips. "You wouldn't cheat on anyone."

"How do you know that?"

"I wouldn't be interested in you if I thought you would. And I am. Interested. Okay?"

She drew a deep breath. "Okay." She'd been afraid he'd run out the door if he found about Charlie, she realized. "Do you still want to look through those files?"

"No, I have something else in mind. But this isn't the place for that." He kissed her again, lightly, then let her go. "Let's see what you have." He wriggled his eyebrows. "In the files. We'll save the more interesting revelations for some other time."

"I NEVER REALIZED how much stuff he saved," Bree said a half hour later. "He's got rough drafts of everything he ever wrote in here." She tossed another file folder onto the already cluttered desk.

"Good thing for me," Parker said, glancing through the folder and setting it on the pile he was taking. "This is exactly the kind of material I need. I'm glad your father saved it."

Bree snorted. "He'd love it if he could hear that. He always thought he was the most important writer in the history of the English language." She yanked another folder out of the cabinet and opened it. After scanning the first paper inside, she froze.

"What?" Parker asked quietly.

"Nothing." She closed the folder and set it aside.

He reached for it and flipped through the contents. "These are notes from a conference. What bothered you about them?"

She snatched the file out of his hands and hurled it across the room. "That conference was the day my sisters and I graduated from eighth grade. I gave the graduation speech. I practiced for a month. But he couldn't come. Because being thought of as one of the driving forces in the literary community was more important."

"I'm sorry," Parker murmured. He gently swept her hair away from her face. "Hey, if it makes you feel better, neither of my parents were at *any* of my graduations."

"Stupid to let it bother me now," she muttered. "This is why we've put off cleaning out the office."

"Families are complicated and messy, aren't they?"

"Yes. But worth it." She went over and picked up the folder she'd thrown, straightening the papers, then dropping the file in the box he was taking.

"Worth it? I'm not so sure."

Bree reached for more of her dad's old notes. "Where are your parents now?" she asked.

He shrugged. "Someplace in Asia, I think. We send Christmas cards."

"That's horrible."

"I've never known any other kind of family."

"Now *I'm* sorry." Footsteps clattered on the stairs, and she relaxed. "There's my family now."

"Can I make some popcorn, Mom?" Charlie stuck his head in the office.

"Sure." Bree stepped back, although she wasn't that close to Parker. "Charlie, come in and meet one of my bosses."

"Charlie?" Parker said slowly.

"Dr. Ellison." The boy began backing out of the office. *How did he know Parker?* "Charlie, stop," she ordered. She looked from her son's terrified expression to Parker's confused one. "What's going on?"

"Why didn't you tell me your son was in my class?" Parker asked, puzzled.

"He's not in your class," Bree answered. She looked at Charlie again and saw the guilt. "Charlie. What did you do?"

"Nothing, Mom," he said, his voice cracking. "I can explain."

"Let's hear it."

Charlie's gaze slid from her to Parker and back again. "I was kind of monitoring Dr. Ellison's class. You know, sitting in on it. That's all."

"I told you the campus was off-limits," she said, fear and anger roiling inside her. "But you went there anyway?"

"I only went to class and came home."

"You were riding your bicycle through the quad the other

day, weren't you?" she demanded, remembering the kid who'd reminded her of Charlie. "I saw you."

"Just that once. I had to go to the library to get a book for an assignment." His face was white and pinched as he glanced at Parker again. "Can we talk about this later? Please?"

"You let Dr. Ellison think you were enrolled in his class, didn't you?"

"I didn't tell him I was."

She turned to Parker. "Did he?"

Parker held up his hands. "Hey, I don't want to get involved. This is between you and Charlie."

"You're already involved. He's been…he's been *stealing* that class from you."

"I wouldn't go that far. He's been sitting in on the lectures, doing the homework and taking the tests. It's not like I was giving him private tutoring."

"He's been taking tests? Doing homework?" She heard her voice rise, and struggled to rein in her temper. "How were you doing the homework, Charlie? You don't have any of the books. Have you been going to the library every day?"

"No," he said. He swallowed and rubbed his foot on the carpet. "Aunt Fee bought me the textbook."

"What? You asked Fiona to buy you a book for a class you weren't supposed to be taking? And she agreed?"

"She kind of didn't know it was for the class."

"She just handed you a wad of money?"

"I told her I needed a book." Charlie shrugged. "She said that was cool."

Parker watched Bree's green eyes flash with temper. He wanted to slip from the room and run out of the house. He didn't want to be part of this emotional scene. "Uh, Bree, I think I should leave."

"Not until I have this straight," she said without looking at him. "Charlie, apologize to Dr. Ellison for misleading him. And say goodbye, because you won't be going back."

"Sorry, Dr. Ellison," Charlie mumbled. He spun around and ran up the stairs. Parker heard a door slam above him.

Bree took a deep breath. "I don't know what to say."

"I'd say you have a smart kid," Parker said.

"Too smart for his own good."

"He almost got away with it," Parker said. "He would have, if I hadn't come over here." He shook his head, impressed. "He got the textbook, made me believe he was enrolled, bicycled to class every day. You have to give him credit for that."

"I can't believe you're saying this. You sound as if you admire what he did. What he did was wrong, on so many levels."

"I do admire him. I wish all the kids in my classes wanted to learn that badly." Parker hesitated. "Let him enroll. He's got the highest average in the class so far."

"No! He can't be on campus."

"Why not?"

"Because he's twelve, for God's sake." He watched her struggle to regain her composure. "Twelve-year-olds don't belong in college."

"We talked about this once. You said it depended on the kid, and I agree. Charlie is more than ready to take introductory biology."

"I can't afford to pay his tuition, okay?"

"That's not a problem. I'll arrange for him to get a scholarship."

"No, Parker! He can't take that class." Bree paced the room, her breathing shallow. Panicked.

"What's really wrong?" Parker asked. "There's more going on than you're telling me."

She stopped walking and took a deep breath. Then another. "You're right. There is. But I don't want to discuss it. Leave it alone, please."

"Charlie came to my office," he said. "Last week. Did you know he had trouble with his science teacher last year?"

"Trouble with his science teacher?" Bree repeated. "We didn't move here until April. He was only in the Spruce Lake school for two months. What kind of trouble could he have had in that short a time?"

"Smart kid trouble," Parker said. He began pacing in turn. "His science teacher didn't like the fact that he knew more than she did. The old bat," he added under his breath.

"Charlie told you this?"

Parker already regretted saying anything. "Yeah. He acted like he was scared to tell me I'd made a mistake on his test, and I asked him why. That's when he told me about the teacher."

"Mrs. Fogarty." Bree clamped her lips together. "I didn't like her the one time I met her. She looked down her nose at me the whole time I was talking to her." At the time, Bree had wondered if the woman had heard a rumor about Bree's past.

"Apparently there was a discussion about snakes. She said something that was clearly wrong, and gave Charlie a hard time when he corrected her."

"Thank you for telling me," Bree said stiffly. "But disagreeing with Mrs. Fogarty doesn't excuse what he did."

"No, but it explains it. He doesn't belong in a class with a close-minded teacher who doesn't know how to handle a gifted kid."

Bree's anger faded abruptly. "And you knew exactly what was going on with Charlie because you had the same kind of 'smart kid' problems when you were his age, didn't you?"

He didn't want to answer. Didn't want to let her get that deep inside him.

She took his hand. "You were just like Charlie, weren't you?"

Parker stared at their joined hands for a long time. "Yeah, I was," he finally said. "I was the smartest kid in all of my classes. The other kids thought I was a freak." He smiled wearily when she started to protest. "I *was* a freak, Bree. I was smarter than some of the teachers I had. Way smarter than any of the other students."

"It must have been lonely," she said. "Especially since your parents weren't around."

He pulled his hand away. "I survived. Charlie will, too. But I think it would help if he stayed in my class."

"I don't know if I can allow that," she said.

"At least let him finish the week," Parker coaxed. "We'll be done with the animal section then." He smiled. "I don't think Charlie cares that much about plants, anyway."

Parker heard a door opening upstairs. Was Charlie coming down for another round with his mother? "I should get going," he said quickly. He glanced up the stairs. "Yes, Ms. McInnes, that's a smart kid you have there."

CHAPTER TEN

PARKER HEARD THE DOOR at the back of the lecture hall creak open while he was writing on the chalkboard. Another student sneaking out of class early. He should have expected it—it was sunny and hot, a perfect day to spend at the lake outside of town.

When he turned to explain the equation, he scanned the room, trying to figure out who had ducked out. No one seemed to be missing. But there was another person sitting at the back of the lecture hall, up at the top. He frowned slightly as he recognized Ted Cross.

What was he doing here?

Keeping one eye on the visitor, Parker finished his lecture, ending a few minutes early. As the other students filed out, Charlie McInnes fiddled with his notebook, tied his shoe and took his time stuffing his books back into his backpack. When the lecture hall was almost empty, Charlie slid out of his seat.

"Hey, Professor Ellison," he said.

"Hi, Charlie." Parker glanced at Ted, who was heading his way from the back of the lecture hall. "Does your mom know you're here?"

Charlie's face flushed. "Yeah. She said you convinced her to let me finish this week at least." He shifted from foot to foot, his usual nervous habit. "Thanks, Professor. For making her let me stay."

"I don't think anyone *makes* your mom do anything," Parker said. "But I'm glad she's letting you continue. You're a good student." He propped one hip on the edge of the desk. "What about the rest of the class?"

"She said we would talk about it this weekend." He scowled. "I won't be friggin' doing anything else. I'm grounded for the rest of my life."

More proof that families were messy and complicated, and something to be avoided. But at least Bree seemed to care about what her son was doing. Parker said cautiously, "That seems a little severe."

"She'll forget about it after a while." Charlie shrugged. "I'm going for a run this afternoon."

Parker was relieved they were off the subject of Charlie and his mom. "I'm planning a run, too."

"Yeah?" The boy's eyes lit up. "You want to run together?"

"I don't think so," Parker said hastily. "I'm not sure when I'm going."

Ted had reached the front of the room, and Parker turned to him with relief. "Dr. Cross. How are you?"

"Great," Ted said. He nodded at Charlie. "This one of your students?"

"Yeah, Charlie McInnes, the prodigy in the class. Charlie, this is Dr. Cross. He's in the history department."

"Hi, Dr. Cross," Charlie said, shaking his hand awkwardly.

Ted studied the boy. "You related to the McInnes triplets?" he asked.

"Yeah, they're my aunts."

"All three of them?"

Charlie blushed again. "No. Bree is my mom."

"Really?" Ted's jaw dropped. "I didn't know Bree was married."

"She's not," he said warily as he shouldered his backpack. "See you tomorrow, Professor."

"So long, Charlie." Parker said.

Ted watched the boy walk out, and continued staring until the door clicked shut. Slowly, he turned back to Parker. "Isn't he a little young for college?"

"He's extremely bright. He's more than capable of handling the class."

"How old is he?" Ted's knuckles whitened on the handle of his briefcase.

"Twelve, I think," Parker said, wondering why Ted was so uptight about it. "You must have had kids in your classes before. Charlie wants to be a herpetologist."

The man paled. "That's impossible."

"Yeah, reptiles aren't my thing, either," Parker said with a smile. "But the kid sure knows his snakes." He waited for Ted to mention why he'd come, but he just stood there, staring into space. "So, can I help you with something?"

"Oh, right." Ted opened his briefcase and fumbled inside it. "I was just at my dad's office, and he asked me to drop this off." He pulled out a sheet of paper and handed it to Parker. "A list of the media who have expressed an interest in the McInnes thing. Dad said you can call them."

"Sure." Parker set it on the lecture hall desk. That wasn't going to happen. "He could have sent it through the interoffice mail."

The history professor grimaced. "He wanted you to have it right away. So you could start making contacts."

Ted didn't seem comfortable as Jonathon's errand boy, but that wasn't any of Parker's business. More of those complicated, messy family dynamics. "Well, thanks for dropping it off."

"No problem." Ted glanced at the door again. "Looks like that kid has a bad case of hero worship."

"Nah, he's just happy he can take the class. His mom didn't want him on campus, and I talked her into letting him stay."

Ted's mouth tightened. "Really?"

"I thought it was ridiculous, too. If he can do the work, he's welcome. And believe me, he can do the work. Better than most of the college students."

"Thanks, Ellison." Without another glance at him, Ted hurried through the door.

AN HOUR LATER, Parker was a mile out of town, well into his run, when he became aware of another runner behind him. As he rounded a curve in the road, he recognized Charlie McInnes. "Damn it." The kid had wanted to run with him. Had he followed him?

Parker lengthened his stride until he was over the next hill, then didn't think about Charlie again until he'd turned around and was heading back into town. He hadn't gone far when he saw the boy. He was weaving erratically on the asphalt. As Parker got closer, he noticed that his face was bright red.

As he reached Charlie, Parker slowed and then stopped in front of him. "What's wrong, Charlie?"

The kid bent over, wheezing short breaths in and out. "Nothing," he panted. "Just a little hot."

Parker grabbed his arm. "How long have you been following me?"

"Since you left the science building," he gasped.

"You've run three miles? Where's your water?"

"I didn't bring any."

No wonder the kid was on the verge of heat exhaustion. Parker pulled him into the shade of an oak tree in a field next to the road. "Sit down."

"Why?"

"Because I said so." Parker narrowed his eyes at the boy.

Charlie scowled, but collapsed beneath the tree. "You're not supposed to say that to kids."

"So sue me." He crouched next to him and handed him one of the bottles of water he carried. "Drink this."

"I don't want to take your water," Charlie muttered.

"Either drink it or I'll pour it down your throat. Your choice."

Charlie locked eyes with him for a moment, still panting. When Parker didn't look away, he opened the water and drank it down in thirsty gulps. When he was done, he took a deep, shuddering breath. "Thanks."

Parker sprawled on the grass beside Charlie, who wouldn't meet his gaze. The boy was leaning against the tree, his face less red, but still flushed. His breathing wasn't as ragged now. "Don't you know better than to run without water in this heat?"

Charlie shrugged. "I didn't think about it."

"And look what happened. You overheated."

He touched his face. "I'm just sunburned."

"Don't give me that shit, Charlie."

"You're not supposed to swear in front of kids, either," the boy retorted.

"You trying to distract me? Or make me feel guilty I didn't run with you? It's not going to happen. Those tricks might work with your mom, but here's a news flash, kid—I'm not your mother." He poured half of his second bottle of water over Charlie's head.

"Hey! Why'd you do that?" Charlie wiped water off his face.

"To cool you off." He held out the bottle. "Now drink the rest of it. "What the hell were you thinking?"

"I wanted to run. I need to get in shape for cross-country."

"Why were you following me?"

"I figured you knew the best places to go." Charlie dug the heel of his shoe into the loose dirt.

"You could have asked," Parker said uneasily. Ted was right. Charlie had a bad case of hero worship.

"You were talking to that professor."

"This was a real bone-headed thing to do," Parker muttered, noticing the sweat beading on Charlie's forehead. Thank God. If he was sweating, the danger of heat exhaustion had passed. "Why were you out here during the hottest part of the day? I thought you were smarter than that."

"If this was so stupid, why are you running now?"

"I know what I'm doing," Parker said. He reached for the empty bottles. "I had water with me, for starters."

"I'll bring water next time." Charlie scrambled to his feet.

"Exactly how much running have you done?" Parker asked, already suspecting the answer.

"I've run before." Charlie nudged a twig with the toe of his sneaker and flicked it away.

"When was the last time?"

He shrugged. "I don't remember exactly."

His dark hair was plastered to his head, but the dangerous red flush had almost completely faded from his face, and his breathing sounded normal. "Let's go. We're heading back to town," Parker said, wiping the sweat off his face.

"I'm not done with my run."

"Yeah, you are. I'll walk you home."

"Geez, Professor, I'm not a baby." The boy scowled. "I can get home by myself."

"Really? Your mom would be pretty unhappy if I let you try, and you collapsed on the way."

"What did she tell you?" he demanded, rounding on Parker. "What did she say about me?"

Whoa. What was this about? "What do you think she told me?" Parker asked the kid, whose jaw was clenched as he stepped onto the asphalt road.

"There's nothing to tell," Charlie muttered. "She treats me like a baby, and I'm perfectly okay."

"You're not okay, Charlie. You were getting close to heat exhaustion," Parker said, exasperated yet sympathetic at the same time. "If you hadn't stopped and drunk that water, you might have collapsed. So I'm walking you home. And I don't want any crap about it," he added when the boy opened his mouth.

They trudged along in silence for a few minutes, then Parker said, "I just swore at you again. You going to tattle on me?"

"Who would I tattle to?"

"Your mom."

"Why would I tell my mom?" He looked at Parker out of the corner of his eye. "I don't tell her what happens with the guys."

He was one of "the guys"? At the clear adulation in Charlie's eyes, Parker wiped his suddenly sweaty palms down the sides of his running shorts. He wanted no part of this. What did he know about twelve-year-olds? "Thanks," he said after a moment. "I wouldn't want her to wash my mouth out with soap."

"My mom's pretty cool. She wouldn't do that."

"What would…" No. He was not going to stoop to pumping the kid for information about Bree.

Charlie gave him another sideways glance. "Anyway, it's not like I haven't heard it before. Some guys swear a lot," he said. "Worse than what you said."

"Yeah?" What was he supposed to say to that? "Do you swear?"

The boy dragged a stone with his shoe until it skittered away. "Sometimes. Otherwise, they'll say I'm a dork."

One thing Parker was sure about—Charlie got plenty of grief because of his intelligence. "Ignore them. They're just jealous."

"Of what?"

"Your brains. They know they're not as smart as you."

"No one cares about being smart," he scoffed.

"Trust me, they do."

Charlie hunched his shoulders. "If you say so." It was clear he didn't believe him.

They walked in silence again, Parker steering Charlie under as many shade trees as possible. Finally they reached Bree's street.

At the walk to the front door, Charlie stopped. "Thanks for walking me home, Professor."

"You're welcome, Charlie," he said. "Is there anyone around?"

"My aunt Fee. But she's probably in her studio."

"I'd like to talk to her."

"What for?"

"Maybe I want to meet a famous jewelry designer," Parker said.

Charlie stared at him, clearly suspicious. Parker raised his eyebrows. Finally the boy said, "Her studio is in the garage." He led Parker to the back of the house. "Go on in. I'm going to get more water. I'll see you tomorrow, Professor."

"Right," Parker said. He watched Charlie run up the back stairs and disappear into the house, then he knocked on the door at the side of the garage.

When no one answered, he stuck his head inside. There

were two enormous worktables set at right angles in the open space. Three soldering irons stood on top, along with coils of silver wire in different thicknesses, thin sheets of silver, gold and copper colored metal, and boxes of gems and beads in every possible color. A woman sat on a bench, holding a small tool and a strip of silver. Her black hair was short and spiky, the ends tinged pink, and she wore overalls. She looked nothing like Bree.

"Excuse me," he said when she didn't seem to notice he was there. "Are you Bree's sister?"

The woman dropped her tool and the silver. "Who are you?"

"Parker Ellison. I wanted to talk to you about Charlie."

"I'm Fiona." She stood up, and he saw that the overalls had been raggedly cut into shorts. "Ellison? Aren't you Charlie's teacher? The guy that Bree—" She stopped abruptly and smiled faintly.

Why was that? Parker wondered. *What had Bree said about him?* "Yeah, I'm Charlie's teacher. Did you know he was out running this afternoon?"

"He said something about training for cross-country. I told him to go ahead."

"You need to keep an eye on him this afternoon," Parker warned her. "He didn't take any water with him and he was close to heat exhaustion when I met up with him."

Fiona pushed past him and ran to the back door. "Charlie?" she called into the house.

"He's okay now," Parker said, following her. "But make sure he drinks a lot of water and stays inside. Out of the sun."

"Thanks, Professor Ellison. I will." There was a box sitting on the porch, and she shoved it with her foot. "Aren't you supposed to be taking our father's papers? Here are some more of them."

"You want me to take it now?"

"Yeah. Get it out of my sight. I don't want to look at anything that belonged to the old bastard."

Whoa. What was that about? "Great. I'll take it with me."

Parker headed toward the college, shifting the weighty box from one arm to the other. Fiona sounded as if she hated her dad. And he'd been dead for a while.

Families. Life was much easier without them. And he was proof of that. He'd done fine with parents who were never around.

CHAPTER ELEVEN

BY THE TIME PARKER had dropped the heavy box at his office, it was close to five, and he headed outside to wait for Bree. He wanted to talk to her about Charlie, and the office wasn't the place to do so.

As he waited, he scanned the almost-deserted staff parking lot, trying to decide which car was hers.

He picked out a small, pearly-blue sports car with a lot of attitude. He could picture Bree driving that car. Or maybe the hybrid a few rows over. She must be concerned about the environment; why else would she walk to and from her job at the bar in town?

As he scrutinized the parking lot for more possibilities, he heard footsteps, and turned to see her.

"Parker?" she said, her steps slowing. "What are you doing out here?"

"Waiting for you." She was wearing khaki pants and another shapeless shirt. This one was green. She'd look much better without it.

"Why are you smiling like that?" she asked, stopping several feet away.

"Admiring your shirt."

She smoothed her hands over it. "I thought you didn't like my blouses."

"I'm using my imagination."

Awareness bloomed in her eyes, but instead of trying to hide it, she let her gaze drift over his running shorts and T-shirt. "In public? I'm shocked, Professor."

Desire hit him unexpectedly like a heavy blow to the stomach. "You're a cool one, aren't you?" He'd never met a woman so full of fascinating contradictions. "Do you really want me to kiss you right here in the parking lot?"

Caution replaced her awareness. "I want you to tell me why you were waiting for me."

"I need to talk to you about Charlie."

"What about him?" She started walking again. Past the sports car. Past the hybrid. She finally stopped at a bright blue station wagon that was at least ten years old.

"Is *that* your car?" he asked.

She raised her chin. "Why do you look so surprised?"

He waved toward the sports car. "I thought that was more your style. Or the hybrid."

"In my dreams." She patted the door of the station wagon. "This is reality."

He had no idea how a single mother lived, he realized. He'd been very careful not to date women with kids. Women looking for permanence. "The wagon has a certain flair. Especially that electric-blue color."

"Try telling that to Charlie," she said, opening the door and tossing her purse onto the back seat. "He begs Fiona to drive him places so he won't be seen in this car."

"I met Fiona this afternoon. She doesn't look anything like you."

Her gaze sharpened. "Why were you talking to Fiona?"

"I took Charlie home." He gestured at the car. "If you'll drive me to my house, I'll explain on the way."

"Sure. Hop in." She slid into the driver's seat and reached over to unlock the passenger door. He caught a glimpse of the shadowed valley in the vee of her shirt and his heart began to pound.

By the time he got into the car, she was holding the steering wheel, the green shirt again camouflaging her figure. "Where do you live?"

"Linden Street. Do you know where that is?"

"Of course." She accelerated with a muted roar that sounded like muffler trouble, and pulled out of the parking lot. As she drove toward the other side of town, she said, "Why did you have to take Charlie home? Did something happen in class today?"

"It wasn't in biology. I ran into him out running on Highway H, about a mile outside of town. Probably three miles from your house."

"Charlie was running?" Her knuckles whitened on the steering wheel. "Three miles?" She glanced at him.

"As close as I can figure. Am I right in assuming he's never run before?"

"Yes, other than in gym class. And he didn't even do much of that until…"

"Until what?"

She slid her hands up and down along the steering wheel a couple of times. "Charlie will be upset if I tell you," she finally said.

"Charlie almost got heat exhaustion today. If he's going to act like a knucklehead, people need to know what's going on with him."

"You're not responsible for him, Parker."

"No, I'm not. But he followed me, so I had to deal with it. I found him staggering along the road, trying not to collapse—"

"What?" She slammed on the brakes and pulled to the curb on a residential street. "He almost collapsed?"

"He would have if he'd gone farther. He was seriously dehydrated and he hadn't brought any water with him."

Parker saw a young man walking down the sidewalk, staring curiously at the car. He didn't recognize him, but if the kid was a student at the college, he probably recognized Parker. "Can you keep driving?"

"Sorry," she said, pulling back onto the street. "I didn't realize you were in a hurry to get home."

"I'm not. I just don't want the kids to gossip about me and a hot babe sitting parked in a car."

"You're kidding me."

"About the hot babe? Absolutely not." He ran a finger down her arm and smiled when she shivered. "You're as hot as they come."

"I mean the kids gossiping about you."

"They all read *People* magazine. They know who I am."

"Celebrity is a cruel mistress."

"You think I wanted to be in *People?*" He snorted. "The only good thing was the donations I got because of the publicity. Donors love that kind of stuff."

"You didn't like seeing your face plastered on the magazine rack at every grocery checkout in the country?" she asked. "A lot of people would eat that up with a spoon."

"Not me. But I need to raise a lot of money for my expeditions, and so I have to cultivate donors." He quirked his mouth. "They like it when they can tell their friends they know that geek in *People*."

He had no trouble reading her surprise. Did she really think he was so shallow that he craved publicity? Before he could ask her, she said, "Getting back to Charlie. What happened?"

"Nothing, fortunately. I made him sit in the shade for a while, and gave him some water. Then we walked home. He seemed fine by the time we got there."

Bree saw Parker's discomfort. "It's not your fault," she said.

"I wasn't thinking it was my fault. I was thinking that I don't know a thing about twelve-year-old boys and I need to in case he follows me again."

"He won't," she said grimly. She'd make sure of it.

"How are you going to stop him? Tie him up at home?"

"I'll tell him he *can't*."

"That sure kept him out of my class, didn't it?"

Bree drummed her fingers on the steering wheel. "He wants to try out for the cross-country team at school next fall."

"So he said," Parker agreed. "Exercise will be good for him."

"Not Charlie. I don't want him running cross-country." She thought she'd discouraged his desire to run.

"Why not?"

She turned onto his street, "Which is your house?"

"The white one in the middle of the block on the right. With the black shutters."

The house looked bland and ordinary. There were a few bushes in the front yard, but no flowers. Nothing to give the place any flair or originality. "Home sweet home," she said. "Thanks for telling me about Charlie. I'll see you at work tomorrow."

Instead of climbing out, Parker turned and leaned against the door. "You were going to tell me why you don't want Charlie to be on the cross-country team."

Bree clenched her jaw and stared out the window. She had always cared for Charlie by herself, dealt with his illness alone. She'd never discussed it with anyone besides her sisters. But Parker had rescued her son this afternoon. Maybe she could tell him.

She wanted to share the burden with someone, at least for a few minutes. "Charlie has a heart problem," she said. "He was born with an atrial septal defect—a hole between two of the chambers of his heart. It was repaired when he was five years old, and his doctor said he's as good as new." She bit her lip. "But it makes me nervous to think about him running long distances. My sister Zoe did that in junior high, and I remember how hard she worked. How many miles she had to run every day. What if he gets his heart pumping too fast? I'm really scared that he might have a heart attack."

"Did you talk to the doctor about it?"

"No," she sighed. "Cross-country is a new interest of his."

"Call the doctor. If he says it's okay, why not let Charlie be on the team? It can only be good for him."

"How can you say that? You hardly know him. You have him in class for five hours a week."

"He wants to be like the other kids in his school. He never will be—he's too far beyond them academically. Sports is a way he can be one of the pack. A member of a team. It's a way for him to connect with the other kids. Where he's judged on how fast he is, not how smart he is."

"You sound passionate about it," Bree said.

Parker shifted uncomfortably on the car seat. "I told you I was like Charlie as a kid," he said. "Sports would have helped. A lot."

"You didn't do sports?"

"My parents wouldn't let me."

"I thought they stuck you in a boarding school. How would they have known?"

"They had to sign a waiver if I wanted to be on one of the school teams. They refused."

She stared at him. "I can't believe it. That's really mean."

Parker shook his head. "They thought they were doing what was best for me. They wanted me to concentrate on academics."

"I'm not trying to push Charlie to study all the time. I'm just worried." She sighed. "They found his heart problem a few months after he was born. They thought it might close by itself, but it never did. When he finally had the surgery, it was like a miracle. After five years, he was as healthy as anyone else his age." She turned to Parker, her eyes begging him to understand. "I don't want to take any chances."

"You can't keep him cocooned in Bubble Wrap, Bree," he said. He rubbed her shoulder soothingly, and she wanted to lean into him for comfort. "It must have been really tough to handle that by yourself, and I understand why you're scared. But sometimes you have to let go." He drew back looked her in the eye. "Sometimes I'm afraid to handle my flowers because I don't want to damage them. But they're tougher than they seem. I suspect Charlie's the same." He bent forward and gave her a hug. "If his doctor says it's okay, let him run."

She clung to him awkwardly, grateful for a shoulder to lean on. Even if it was only temporary. Finally, reluctantly, she pulled away. "Thanks for letting me know about the running."

"Thank you for telling me about his heart problem. I promise I won't say anything to Charlie."

"I appreciate that. He's so prickly lately. He probably wouldn't speak to me for a week."

"My lips are sealed." The sun was beating down and the car was getting hot. A bead of sweat rolled down the side of Bree's face, and he wiped it away with one finger. "Would you like to come in? Get a cold drink or something?"

The heat in his eyes had nothing to do with the temperature in the car. "The 'or something' sounds dangerous. Charlie's expecting me at home. Maybe another time?"

"Anytime you like." He touched his mouth to hers. It was supposed to be a casual kiss, a brief goodbye, but wasn't. And when his tongue swept inside her mouth, she wanted to pull him against her.

His chest was rising and falling rapidly when he finally broke away. "Get out of here, Bree. Because in about two seconds I'm going to drag you into my house, and then you'll be really late getting home to Charlie."

She hesitated, aching to go inside with him, then started the engine. "I'll see you tomorrow, Parker."

"Right," he said, easing out of the car.

She glanced in the rearview mirror as she turned the corner. Parker was standing in his driveway, watching her.

BREE WAS TYPING UP A TEST when someone entered the office the next day. Expecting it to be Parker or one of the other professors from the science department, she looked up from her computer. The smile froze on her face. He'd found her.

"Ted. What are you doing here?"

He stood in front of her desk, staring down at her. She had no idea what he was thinking. "Why do you think I'm here?"

Oh, God. She gripped the bottom of her drawer to keep from standing and running away. "I have no idea, and I'm not interested in hearing your reasons. Go away. I'm busy."

"I'm not going anywhere." Ted settled into a chair.

Could he have found out? She'd rehearsed this scene many times since she'd been back in Spruce Lake. She'd thought she was ready, but her hands started to shake. She slid them into her lap.

"I have a lot of work to do," she said.

He leaned across the desk to grab her arm. "Screw your work. Tell me what you've done."

She jerked her arm away. "I don't think so."

"Bree? Cross?" Parker walked into the office. "What's going on?"

"I'm trying to talk to Bree," Ted said. "Privately."

"Yeah?" Parker sauntered over to the desk and parked one hip on the edge, between the two of them. "Do you *want* to talk to him, Bree?"

Parker was trying to protect her. "Thank you," she said, "but I can handle this myself."

"Okay." He didn't move. "Go ahead and talk, Cross."

"What's your problem, Ellison?" Ted scowled. "Why is this your business?"

"She's my administrative assistant. I don't want her upset. Her work might suffer." He showed his teeth in a caricature of a smile.

Bree jumped to her feet. "Oh, for heaven's sake. Get out of here, both of you." They were like a pair of dogs, growling over the same bone. "I'm going to lunch."

She grabbed her purse from the bottom drawer of the desk and walked around Parker, past Ted and out the door.

She didn't take a deep breath until she'd driven out of the parking lot and headed toward Main Street. She went to the drive-up window at the bank, then dropped off some books at the library almost as if she was on autopilot. Finally, when she'd stopped shaking and composed herself, she parked in front of The Lake House and went in.

The bar was nearly deserted; there were only a few people eating an early lunch. "Hey, Jerry," she said. "Do you have our checks yet?"

"Sure do," he said, handing her an envelope. "See you on Friday."

"I'll be here."

She turned to leave just as the door opened and Ted stepped inside, blocking the exit. She wanted to turn and run for the back door, but instead squared her shoulders. She was ready for this. She'd known it could happen since the day she'd come back to Spruce lake.

"Following me, Ted?"

"I spotted your car in front. Hard to miss it."

"What do you want?" She glanced at her watch, pleased that her hand wasn't shaking. She could do this. "I have several other errands to run."

"I want to hear about Charlie. Why didn't you tell me I had a son?"

CHAPTER TWELVE

"HE'S NOT YOUR SON."

Ted scoffed. "Of course he is. You were pregnant with my child when you left Spruce Lake. He would be twelve today. Charlie's age."

"How do you know about Charlie?"

"Ellison introduced us."

Parker had told Ted? She couldn't afford to think about that now.

Ted leaned toward her. "How do you think it felt to have one of my colleagues introduce me to a kid in his class—a kid who turns out to be my son?"

The intensity of her pain surprised her. She thought she'd dealt with Ted's betrayal a long time ago. "That's not what you said when I showed up at your door, pregnant and terrified. You said it wasn't your baby. That I was lying."

Ted rubbed his hand over his eyes. "I was a kid, Bree. I was scared. I didn't know what to do."

"So you denied it was yours. You stood there while your father threatened me, threatened my father and my sisters. While he threw money at me and told me to get rid of your baby. Then you tossed me out of your house and forgot about me. And your child."

Three people sitting at the bar were watching them, but

Bree was too upset to care. Ted took her arm and steered her to an isolated table in the corner. "I'm not the same man I was twelve years ago," he said. "I know I was wrong. I want to make it right."

"How the hell are you going to do that, Ted?" She looked into his eyes. Charlie's eyes. And her hold on her temper unraveled. "It's too late to walk the floor with him all night because he was sick and couldn't sleep. It's too late to sit with him in doctors' offices, trying to keep him entertained when you were terrified what the doctor was going to say. It's too late to stand next to his bed in the hospital, hoping he'd make it through surgery." She closed her eyes and took a deep breath, trying to compose herself. This wasn't going according to the script she'd crafted.

"What are you talking about? What's wrong with him?" He leaned over the table and had the nerve to appear scared.

"Nothing's wrong with him. He's fine now."

"But there was something."

"He had a heart problem. It's been fixed. End of story."

"An atrial septal defect?"

"Yes." She eyed him warily. "How did you know?"

"I had one, too."

She stared at him, at the face she'd found so fascinating thirteen years ago. The face she'd been in love with. She didn't see any trace of the arrogant, brash young man he'd been. What she saw was regret. Genuine sorrow. And guilt.

It didn't matter. Some wrongs couldn't be put right. "It would have helped to have known that, Ted," she said wearily. "To know that you had the same condition and you survived. That you were fine."

"If I could, I would go back and undo all my mistakes. But we can't. We can only go forward." It seemed as if he was going to touch her hand, and she jerked away from him.

"Did you search for me, Ted? Did you wonder what happened to me after I ran away? Did it occur to you that I might have had your baby?" She held his gaze, daring him to lie to her.

He pushed a coaster around on the table, staring at it as if it held all the answers. "You know I didn't," he finally said. "You didn't want a baby, either. I assumed you'd…gone on with your life."

"And you were relieved."

"Of course." He lifted his head. "We were too young to be parents. Too young to get married. It would have ended badly."

"So that justified what you did. You didn't want it to end badly."

"Don't twist my words, Bree. I was twenty-two, for God's sake. I was selfish and self-centered."

"And you're not now?" She couldn't help the bitterness that crept into her voice. "What do you want, Ted?"

"I want to get to know my son. To have a relationship with him."

"He's not your son," she said. "He's mine. Oh, you're his biological father," she admitted when he began to protest. "Half his genes are yours. But that's all of you he has. You're his sperm donor. Nothing else."

"Does he ever ask about his father? About me?"

Ted sounded wistful, and she ignored a twinge of guilt. Charlie had asked about his father constantly when he was younger. "We do just fine on our own. We don't need you."

"Maybe I need him," he said.

"He needed you, too," she told him. "A long time ago." And so had she. "But you weren't there. You were in graduate school, getting your Ph.D. You didn't need him thirteen years ago. What's changed?"

"My wife can't have children," he said quietly. "She was in a car accident when she was a teen, and had to have her uterus removed. I know, now, what I threw away when I turned my back on you. I know how precious children are."

"So Charlie's important to you because you can't have another child." Bree welcomed the renewed anger. She didn't want to feel sorry for Ted.

"He's important to me because I've grown up. I can't tell you how much I regret what I did. I deserve everything you're saying to me, Bree. Every bit of your anger and hatred." He smiled briefly. "You were always tough.

"I want to know Charlie because he's my son. My child." He swallowed. "My wife and I are on the waiting list here to adopt, and we're looking into foreign adoptions, as well. If we're lucky enough to get a baby, he or she will be just as much mine as Charlie is. But I'd like for him or her to have a sibling. An older brother."

Charlie had always wanted a younger brother or sister.

"Forget it, Ted." She didn't want to share her son. Not with the man who'd abandoned them when she needed him most.

"I've changed, Bree."

"Why should I believe that? Why should I trust my son to easy words and blind faith?"

"You're just like your father, aren't you?" he snapped. "Vindictive. Never forgiving any wrongs. Not being able to see beyond your own selfish needs."

"And you're just like *your* father," she retorted, appalled by his accusation. "You think you're in charge of everything. But you're not in charge of me. Or Charlie."

"He's my son and I have a right to meet him." His gaze was implacable. Unwavering.

"What do you think he'd say if I told him his father wants

to meet him?" she demanded. "He's smart. He'd want to know why his dad hasn't been around before now."

"I'll tell him the truth. I wouldn't start our relationship with a lie."

"No."

"What do you want? Money? I owe you back child support," he said.

If she'd had child support, her life might have gone in a very different direction.

"Do you think you can buy him from me?" she asked, her voice rising.

"I don't know, Bree. You're not the woman I remember. I don't know what you want anymore."

"I want you to leave us both alone."

"Not going to happen," he said. "I'm not giving up. I'm not going to walk away and forget that I have a child. A son."

"Don't you dare approach Charlie on your own," she warned.

"I don't want to do that, Bree." He stared at her, and his eyes weren't those of the young man in her memory. These were a man's eyes. With a man's guilt, and a man's determination. "Don't force me to do it."

She shoved her chair back so hard it toppled over. "Stay away from my son, Ted. Stay the hell away." She backed out the door, not caring that everyone in the restaurant was staring at them.

By the time she pulled into her driveway, she was shaking uncontrollably. And cold. So cold, even in the summer heat. The station wagon had barely stopped moving when she jumped out and ran into the house. "Charlie! Where are you?" Her words echoed in the silence. She stuck her head into the living room, but he wasn't there playing video games. She pounded up the stairs. "Charlie! Are you up here?"

Throwing open the door to his room, she could tell with

a glance that it was empty. She skidded down the stairs, barely catching herself when she slipped on the second step from the bottom.

Fiona came out of the library. "Bree! What's wrong?"

"Where's Charlie?" she demanded.

"He's at Jackson Grant's veterinary clinic. His son called this morning. Their kennel person didn't come in and Jackson said he would pay Charlie to clean cages. He rode his bike over to the clinic when he got home from school."

"I need to get him." Bree snatched her keys off the table in the hall, where she'd tossed them, and turned for the door, but Fiona grabbed her by the arm.

"What's going on? What's wrong?"

"We have to leave. Today. Charlie and I. We have to leave Spruce Lake."

Fiona tightened her grip, then pried Bree's keys out of her hand and dropped them in the pocket of her overalls. She slid her arm around Bree's shoulder and drew her into the living room and onto the lumpy old couch. "What happened?"

Bree shoved her hands through her hair, catching her fingers in the tangles. "It's Ted. He knows about Charlie. Knows he's Charlie's father. He wants to meet him." She wrapped her arms around herself. "He wants to be part of Charlie's life."

"How did he find out?"

"Parker introduced them."

"What? The guy you work for? The one who walked you home?"

"Yes." Why had Parker done it? Had he seen Charlie's resemblance to Ted? Or had it been a horrible coincidence?

"It doesn't matter how it happened." Fiona grasped her arm tightly. "You must have thought this was a possibility when you came back to Spruce Lake," she said gently. "Didn't you figure out what you'd do?"

"I did." Bree stared at the faded, threadbare green drapes that hung in the windows. They'd been there since before their mother had died. No one had bothered to get new ones, and now they were falling apart. Just like her life. "I had it all planned out. I'd deny that Charlie was Ted's son, and he would accept that. Ted always assumed the world revolved around him." She rubbed her forehead. "His self-confidence was part of his charm. The old Ted didn't want to take responsibility for anything. I assumed that hadn't changed."

"And it has?"

"Apparently so. He even offered to pay catch-up child support."

Fiona wrapped an arm around her shoulders in a fierce hug. "Bree, that's great. You can pay off those medical bills."

"I told him I didn't want it. I don't want anything from him. I don't want to be obligated to him."

"You wouldn't be," her sister said carefully. "Ted is the one with the obligations. You struggled for twelve years, and it's time he paid what he owes."

"If I take his money, I'll have to let him meet Charlie. Be part of his life. I won't do that."

"Why not? He *is* Charlie's father."

Bree looked at her sister in disbelief. "I told you what happened. How he said he wasn't my baby's father. Now I'm supposed to forget that?"

"Are you thinking about yourself, Bree? Or about Charlie?"

Bree jerked away from her sister. "I'm so out of here."

Fiona covered Bree's keys with one hand and with the other pulled out her cell phone. "Zoe?" she said after punching in a number. "You have to come over here. Right away." She listened for a moment. "No one's hurt, but we need you here."

"You're acting a little dramatic, Fee," Bree said, mentally checking off the things she'd need to find in the house.

"*I'm* acting dramatic?" Fiona snapped the phone closed. "You've been a drama queen since you came out of the womb. Now you're going to run over to the vet clinic and grab Charlie? Scare him to death? Or were you going to tell him the truth? That you're running away from his father?"

"It's the only way I can protect him," Bree said.

"Protect him from what? His dad?"

"His *father* denied that Charlie was his baby. His *father* stood there while Charlie's grandfather told me to get an abortion. Ted doesn't deserve the title."

Fiona wrapped her arms around Bree again and rocked her. "We'll figure it out," she said. "You and me and Zoe. We'll figure out what to do."

Bree breathed in Fiona's familiar smell of citrus and soldering flux, and relaxed against her. She wished it was that easy. She wished her sisters could make this nightmare go away. But she was the only one who could protect Charlie.

She needed to get busy packing, but she allowed herself to hold on to Fiona for another moment. The comfort felt so good. It made her feel as if she wasn't alone. As if a solution was possible.

Maybe the old bonds between her and her sisters had never really broken. Maybe they had just frayed. She hugged her tighter, then let her go. "I have to get our stuff together," she stated.

"Wait until Zoe gets here," Fiona said. She pulled out her

phone again. "I'm going to call your office and tell them you won't be back in today."

She hadn't thought about work at all, Bree realized with a twinge of shame. She would have driven away and not given her job a moment's consideration.

She'd have thought of Parker, though. She'd regret never seeing him again.

But she would still leave. She couldn't risk losing Charlie because of her foolish infatuation with Parker.

"Tell them I'm sick."

Fiona frowned, then spoke into the phone. "Hi, this is Fiona McInnes. Bree McInnes's sister. She can't come in to work this afternoon. She has a family emergency."

"Why did you say that?" Bree demanded, stepping away from her sister. "I told you to say I was sick. Everyone understands illness."

Fiona shook her head. "I'm not going to lie for you, Bree. You're talking about walking away from your job without giving any notice. The least you can do is tell them the truth."

So much for the bonds of sisterhood. "I'm going to pack."

A car door slammed in the driveway. "Zoe's here," Fiona said, appearing relieved. "Maybe she can talk sense into you."

A few moments later, their sister ran into the house. She had a pen stuck behind her ear, and was wearing a man's shirt over her skirt and blouse, covered with what appeared to be finger paint. "What's wrong?" she asked, looking from Bree to Fiona. "What happened?"

Fiona jerked her head at Bree. "The drama queen here is ready to pack her bags and run away. Ted knows about Charlie, and he confronted her today."

"Oh, Bree." Some of the worry faded from Zoe's face, and she enfolded her in a hug. "Was it awful?"

Bree shuddered. "Yes," she said as she hugged her back. "He wants to meet Charlie. He wants to be part of his life."

Zoe slowly eased away and gripped Bree's shoulders. "Maybe that's not such a terrible thing."

"You're as bad as Fiona," Bree cried, yanking away from her. "You two are my sisters. Why aren't you supporting me?"

"Tell me what happened," Zoe said soothingly.

When she finished the story, Zoe sank onto the couch. "That's tough, Bree."

"Of course it's tough. I don't want to have to leave Spruce Lake. I want to help you both finish cleaning out the house."

"That's not what I meant. I meant it's tough because it sounds as if Ted has changed. If he was the same arrogant, thoughtless guy, it would be easy to dismiss him. But he wants to get to know Charlie for all the right reasons. So why do you want to take off?"

Because Ted was a threat to her relationship with Charlie. Having him in the equation would change everything. "What's Charlie going to say when he finds out his father has been here all along? He's going to be upset."

Zoe held her gaze. "Are you afraid that Charlie would be angry at Ted? Or at you?"

Bree's fingernails cut into her palms. "I don't want to share him with…that man," she muttered.

"It's been just you and Charlie up until now," Zoe agreed. "It's hard to let a third person in. But what if you got married? You'd have to share him then."

"That's different." Her voice was barely a whisper.

"It's not," Zoe said, equally quietly. "Ted is Charlie's father, no matter how badly he treated you thirteen years ago. He has a right to see his son. And a twelve-year-old boy needs his father. He needs a man in his life."

Bree had a flashback of Parker, that night in his office. In some deeply buried part of her, had she hoped he would be that man? "Not Ted."

"You can't rewrite history," Zoe said, with a hint of impatience in her voice. "Ted *is* his father. And forget about disappearing. You ran once before, and what did it get you? It's time to stay and face your problems."

Bree had always hated her sister's logic and rationality. It was too hard to argue with her. "That's easy for you to say. He's not your son."

"That's why I can be more objective than you. You need to think about this," Zoe said. "And talk to Charlie. Shouldn't he have a choice about meeting his father?"

"Of course not. He'd say yes."

Fiona smiled. "There's your answer, Bree. You know the right thing to do, even if you don't want to admit it." She took Bree's hands. "Instead of running away, you should be thinking about how to talk to Charlie about this."

The doorbell rang, and Bree stiffened. Was that Ted at her door? Demanding to see his son?

CHAPTER THIRTEEN

PARKER STOOD ON THE front porch of the McInnes house. He had been listening to the voices drifting out the open window. He hadn't been able to hear what they were saying, but he recognized Bree's voice. She'd sounded upset. Scared.

He tried not to let his imagination run away with him. What kind of family emergency could have come up so quickly? Was Charlie sick? Had he stressed his heart too much the day he went running?

Was it one of Bree's sisters? Had Fiona injured herself in her studio?

Parker had raised his hand to ring the bell again when the door opened, and Fiona stood there, wearing a skirt and silk blouse. "Fiona? Is everything all right?"

"I'm Zoe," she said. "I'll get Fee."

"No, wait, I didn't come to see her." Of course this was Zoe. Her features were identical to Fiona's, but her hair was different. Not pink, for one thing. And her expression was less cautious. "I came to see Bree," he admitted.

Zoe moved into the center of the doorway, blocking his path. Protecting Bree? She glanced at his running shorts and shoes. "Who are you and what do you want?"

Apparently, blunt speaking ran in the family. "I work at the college," he finally said. "Parker Ellison." He had no intention of discussing his relationship with Bree with this sister.

"The professor?"

"Yes. Is Bree all right? Is it Charlie?"

Zoe assessed him for a long moment, then nodded as if he'd passed some test. "Come in. I'll get my sister."

When Bree came into the hall a few moments later, her face was ashen. Her eyes were huge and haunted, but when she spotted him, she narrowed them. "Parker. Just the man I wanted to see."

It felt as if he was stepping into a quagmire. "Chuck Boehmer told me you had an emergency," he said cautiously. "I wanted to make sure everything was all right."

"Why did you to it, Parker? Why did you tell Ted?"

"Tell Ted what?" he asked. Had she lost her mind?

"About Charlie. You introduced my son to Ted Cross."

He vaguely remembered Ted coming into his classroom while he'd been talking to Charlie. "So what if I did?"

"Do you have any idea what you've done?" she cried, her hands curling into fists.

"No, I don't. What's going on?" She'd been perfectly fine when she left the office less than two hours ago. It had been no different than any other day, except that Ted had been sitting next to her desk. "What am I missing here?"

Zoe stuck her head out of the room behind Bree. "You all right?" she asked.

Bree spun around. "He introduced Charlie to Ted. And he wants to know what's wrong."

Zoe came out and slipped an arm around Bree's shoulder. A united front against him. What the hell was this about?

"Calm down," Zoe murmured. "He has no idea why you're upset."

Bree drew in a ragged breath, and Parker watched, fascinated, as she composed herself. If he didn't know her, he wouldn't be able to tell there was anything wrong.

"Parker, this isn't a good time for me. I can't deal with you now. I'll talk to you later."

How did she do that? Where had she learned how to protect herself so quickly? And so completely? "No, I want to talk now," he said, beginning to feel angry. "What did I do? And what does Ted have to do with it? I came here because I thought you were hurt. You don't want me here, that's fine. I'll see you later." He'd come running, thinking only about helping her. And she didn't want him here. What the hell was wrong with him? He knew better than this. This was exactly why he didn't get involved.

Zoe was watching him sympathy in her eyes, and it made him squirm. "You going to tell him the truth, Bree?" she murmured. "You're beating up on the poor guy and he doesn't know why."

Poor guy? He was out of here. He reached for the door.

"Wait, Parker."

He turned around. Bree was biting her lip uncertainly. "I'm sorry. I'm upset."

"No kidding." He hesitated, his desire to help her warring with his need to escape.

Zoe patted her sister's arm. "You figure out what to do with Ellison, and Fee and I'll call Helen Cherney. You need a lawyer."

A lawyer? "What the hell is going on?"

Zoe walked away. The protective barrier Bree had erected around herself was cracking, revealing a vulnerable woman he barely recognized.

"You don't have to tell me a thing," he said, giving in to temptation and closing his arms around her. "But whatever is wrong, I want to help."

She was stiff and unyielding against him for a long moment. Then she took a deep, shuddering breath and let go. Her legs trembled against his, and her arms shook as she wound them around his neck.

He brushed his lips over her hair and tightened his grip on her. He had no idea what he was supposed to do, but didn't want to let her go. He didn't want to see that shattered look on her face.

She eased away from him. "Come into the living room," she said quietly.

He walked past two boxes stacked next to the door, and into the room. The furniture was old and uncomfortable looking, the curtains faded and threadbare. There was a large patch on the wall over the fireplace where the beige paint was darker than the rest of the room, as if a picture had recently been removed. Parker had a hard time imagining the legendary John Henry McInnes in this shabby, neglected room.

Bree stood straighter, as if girding herself for battle. "I never told you the reason I didn't want Charlie in your class. Or on campus. It's because of Ted."

"Cross? You know him?"

"Yes, I do."

"This has something to do with why he was in the office this morning, doesn't it?"

"Yes." She paced across the Oriental rug. "He followed me when I left for lunch, and caught up with me at The Lake House. I was picking up my check." She tried to smile. "Hardly seems worth it for thirty-eight bucks. Glad the tips make up for it."

"Why is he harassing you?" Parker asked, stepping closer.

Bree put her hand on his chest. "Ted is Charlie's father," she said. "Until you introduced them, Ted didn't know anything about Charlie."

"Oh, my God." Parker stared at her, not sure he'd heard correctly. "Charlie is Ted's son?"

"Yes."

He pictured her with Ted, and jealousy, hot and poisonous, boiled up inside him. "And he didn't know?"

"Not until you told him."

Parker remembered Ted's stunned expression when he'd introduced them. Recalled Charlie's polite indifference. "How come…why didn't Ted know?"

"It's a long, ugly story and it doesn't really matter. I was going to take Charlie and leave town." She glanced toward the kitchen, where he could hear her sisters talking. "They don't think I should go."

Neither did Parker. He didn't want Bree to disappear. "Does Charlie know who his father is?"

"No. Zoe and Fiona think I should tell him, and let him decide if he wants a relationship with his dad."

Parker felt quicksand beneath his feet, sucking him further and further into the family drama. There was nothing solid to grab hold of, nothing to pull him out of the vortex dragging him down.

Before he could escape, Fiona and Zoe came into the room. Alike, but so different.

"We're going to Helen's office," Zoe said. "She'll be able to look at this objectively."

"I don't need to look at it objectively," Bree said, stalking over to her sisters. "I know what I need to do."

"Yeah, well, you're wrong," Fiona retorted.

Parker watched as the three women all began talking at once. Their voices rose. Bree gestured, her movements jerky. Fiona tried to hug her, but Bree pushed her away. Then threw herself into Fiona's arms. Zoe wrapped her arms around both of them.

So this was what it was like to have siblings. To be a family.

Even when they were fighting, it was clear a bond connected them. He suspected that if he tried to wade into the fray, they'd all turn on him.

He'd always thought families were a burden. A messy, emotional liability. Something to avoid at all costs.

A tiny thread of loneliness wound through him. What would it be like to have someone to count on, no matter what?

To be there for someone else.

Scary. Complicated. Time consuming.

Life was far easier alone.

"Fine," Bree said, her voice rising above those of her sisters. "I'll talk to Helen. But that's all I'm promising."

"That's all we're asking," Zoe replied calmly. "That you take a while and think this through."

He should go. Bree had her sisters. She wasn't alone, and he was too…close. "I'll leave you to work this out," he finally said.

"Thank you for coming over." Bree stepped forward and took his hands. "It means a lot to me."

He held on to her, reluctant to let her go. "Call me if you need anything?"

"I'll do that."

Gravel crunched on the driveway and footsteps pounded on the stairs. "Hey, Aunt Fee. I'm home," Charlie called.

Parker dropped Bree's hands as if they'd suddenly caught fire. All four adults turned toward Charlie.

Charlie stopped abruptly as he saw them. "What's going on?" He frowned when he saw Bree. "Mom? What are you doing home from work so early?"

"Your mom didn't feel well at work," Parker said. "So I volunteered to drive her home."

"Yeah?" His glance landed on his aunts. "Then what's Aunt Zo doing here?"

"I happened to be here when your mom got home," Zoe said. Her smile looked forced. "We were arguing about whether she should go to the doctor."

"Don't waste your time. Mom never goes to see a doctor." Charlie looked at Bree. "What's wrong, Mom?"

"I'm just a little sick to my stomach, Charlie. I'll be fine."

"Okay." He looked at Parker. "Are you going running?"

"Yeah, I'm just on my way out."

"Cool." Charlie rubbed his hands down his shorts, looking at him expectantly. "I'm going to my room," Charlie announced after an awkward moment. He ran up the stairs so fast he tripped on one of the steps. "I'm okay," he yelled, just before a door shut.

"I'll stay with Charlie," Fiona finally said. "You two go see Helen."

Nobody said anything. Nobody moved. Were they waiting for him speak? Offer to watch Charlie? "Let me know if you need anything," Parker said too quickly, edging toward the door. "Good luck getting this unraveled."

"Thanks, Parker," Bree answered.

As he closed the door behind him, voices drifted out the open window. "He was in such a hurry to leave I thought those shorts of his were on fire."

"Stop, Zoe. He's a good guy."

"He sure backed away fast when things got messy."

"It's not his business." Bree's tone was sharp.

You could have stayed.

As he jogged down the street, he tried not to think about what he was leaving behind.

CHAPTER FOURTEEN

"I THOUGHT YOU'D BE ON MY side."

Bree jumped up from the stiff chair and paced Helen Cherney's office. The walls were lined with shelves full of law books, and Helen had a pile of file folders stacked neatly next to her desk calendar. Based on the number of appointments jotted on the calendar, Helen must have scrambled to fit them in. Bree wished she hadn't bothered.

"I'm not on anyone's side, Bree. I'm just giving you legal advice."

"Are you Ted's lawyer, too? Is that why you're siding with him?"

"For heaven's sake, Bree," Helen said. "Get a grip, will you?"

Bree spun around and stared at the blond woman who sat so calmly behind the desk. Zoe wrapped her arm around her shoulder, but Bree yanked away. "*Get a grip?* This is my son we're talking about. You're playing games with his life."

"Not me," Helen said. "*You're* the one who's playing games. You're trying to deny Charlie a relationship with his father. You can't do it legally, and you shouldn't do it morally."

Knowing Helen was right only made Bree angrier. "A lawyer lecturing about morality? Isn't that an oxymoron?" She resisted the temptation to kick the desk.

Helen sighed. "Bree, I get that you're angry. That it doesn't seem fair. But it's the law. Deal with it."

The lawyer was so rational. So dispassionate. Didn't she see that this would screw up Charlie's life?

And Bree's?

Helen had said that unless she could prove he was dangerous to Charlie in some way, Ted had the right to visitation. The right to spend time with her son.

It isn't Helen's fault. Bree had done this to herself. If she hadn't taken the job at the college, if she hadn't gotten involved with Parker...

If she hadn't tried to keep Charlie away from his father, none of this would be happening.

"I'm sorry, Helen," she said.

Zoe reached over and took her hand. "There must be something you can do."

The woman's expression softened. "Get me some dirt on him, and I'll talk to a judge. Until then?" She shrugged. "Fathers have rights. In a case like this, the courts are going to side with Ted. They'll say there's no reason to keep him away from Charlie. My advice? Do it on your terms so you get to make the rules."

"What do you mean?" Bree asked.

"Don't wait for Ted to come to you with a list of demands. You make the first move." Helen leaned forward with a shrewd gleam in her eyes. "Tell him he can meet Charlie, but only with you present. If it goes well, and Charlie agrees, let Ted see Charlie by himself. But you get to decide when and for how long."

"Don't forget, Charlie has a say in this," Zoe said, still clutching Bree's hand. "He may decide he wants nothing to do with Ted."

Charlie could also decide he loved the idea. That he wanted to make up for lost time. Ted was a charming guy, and Charlie was hungry for the influence of a man in his life. Look how he'd glommed on to Parker.

But what if he liked Ted better than her?

That particular demon had been waiting in the wings since they'd arrived back in Spruce Lake. Now it was out in the open.

"There's something else to think about," Zoe added. "Now that Ted knows about Charlie, it's going to be hard to keep it a secret. You know how Spruce Lake is. You spill a glass of milk in your kitchen and the whole town's heard about it twenty minutes later."

"That's not true," Helen said. "It would take at least an hour."

Zoe rolled her eyes, but one side of her mouth curved up. "The point is, if you don't tell Charlie, someone else might. Is that how you want him to find out about Ted?"

"Of course not," Bree muttered.

"I appreciate how hard this must be for you, Bree." The attorney closed the notepad in front of her. "But you can avoid a lot of problems by being proactive. Keep the power in your hands."

"Thanks, Helen. I'll think about what you said."

Bree grabbed her purse and fumbled for the door handle. The room had become claustrophobic, squeezing the breath out of her chest. Pushing her into a box.

"Do you want to go to the A&W and get a root beer?" Zoe asked as they emerged from the old building onto the hot cement sidewalk.

Going to the A&W had always been special when they were kids. Driving up in the car, having the tray attached to the open window, drinking the rich, creamy soda with its heavy foam, was one of the good memories. One of the few good ones.

"No, I'd rather go home."

When they reached the house, Bree headed for the stairs, right past Fiona in the living room. She needed to pull herself together alone. But Zoe caught her by the arm before she could get away.

"You're not going to pack, Bree." It wasn't a question.

She shook her head. "I'm going upstairs to have my nervous breakdown in private."

"You can have your breakdown in front of us," her sister said gently. "We both understand."

"No, Zo. You don't." How could they?

Zoe dropped her hand. "You think you're the only one who's had a hard time, Bree? That you're the only one who got a raw deal?" She jerked her head toward Fiona, who'd jumped up and was watching them. "Fee had to deal with Dad all by herself after you left and I got married. Do you have any idea what that was like?"

"Zoe went through hell with her first husband," Fiona added.

"I'm trying to protect my son."

"You're protecting yourself." Zoe studied her shrewdly. "Ted's going to be the new thing in Charlie's life. A novelty. You're afraid Charlie will like Ted better, aren't you?"

"Damn you, Zoe," she cried. The words touched a painful nerve.

Bree had been their father's favorite. The chosen one, always singled out for praise and admiration.

The one who got the attention.

And it had made her feel horribly guilty whenever she saw her sisters watching her and their dad.

Of course she was afraid Charlie would like Ted better. It would be karma biting her in the butt.

"This is about when we were kids and Dad liked you best," Zoe said, as if she'd read Bree's mind. "Let it go, Bree. We're not seven years old anymore. We're adults. Charlie isn't going to like Ted better than you." Zoe put her arm around Bree's shoulders and steered her into the living room. "Let's sit down and figure out what you're going to say to Charlie."

"So I ENDED UP RUNNING with Dr. Ellison," Charlie said, too casually, as he took a huge bite of his hamburger at dinner that night. A drop of ketchup rolled down his chin and he fidgeted with his napkin after wiping it away.

"What?" Bree dropped her hamburger onto her plate. She glanced at Fiona before asking, "How did that happen?"

He shrugged. "I kind of caught up to him."

"You mean you ran after him," she said, her heart aching. Charlie couldn't have expressed any more clearly that he hungered for a man in his life.

"Whatever. We ran two miles," he told her, picking up a green bean with his fingers.

"Use your fork, Charlie," Bree said automatically. "Did Dr. Ellison ask you to run with him?"

"It's a free country," her son replied. "I can run wherever I want."

Oh, my God. "Were you bugging him?" Bree demanded.

"No." Charlie scowled. "He said I could run with him."

"What did he really say?" she asked quietly.

Charlie dragged a green bean through the ketchup on his plate. "He said it's a free country and I could run wherever I wanted. So I ran with him."

"And…?"

"He was pretty nice after we ran for a while. He was glad I was smart enough to bring water this time. He talked to me about setting up a training program. I'm going to go talk to him tomorrow."

"That was nice of him," Bree said. "I wouldn't know anything about setting up a training program."

"That's 'cause you don't like to run." Charlie's face reflected the utter disgust of an athlete for a couch potato. "Dr. Ellison usually runs five miles, but he took it easy for me." He shoved the last of his mashed potatoes into his mouth. "Can I be excused?" he asked around the mouthful.

"Sure," Bree said, watching as he bounded up the stairs.

"Serious hero worship." Fiona smiled as Charlie's door closed above them. "It's really sweet."

"Yeah." She listened to the sound of him moving around overhead. "I hope he doesn't get too attached to Parker, though."

Fiona's smile faded. "Why not? You're not still planning on sneaking out of town in the middle of the night, are you? Because I'm warning you, I'm a light sleeper, and I will kick your ass if you try."

"Now I'm scared," Bree said, slumping back in the chair. "No, I'm not going to leave. I kind of lost it for a while. Thank goodness you and Zo were here to straighten me out. But, against my better judgment, Charlie's staying in Parker's class. It ends in another few weeks. What then?"

"You don't see a future for you and Parker?" Fiona asked carefully.

"He's leaving to go on an expedition to South America," Bree said, ignoring the desolation she felt at the idea. "And he made it very clear that he doesn't do long term." She smiled, although it hurt to do so. "He's the kind of guy you have a fling with."

"He came here this afternoon when he thought you were in trouble."

"He was reacting to a crisis, that's all." She swallowed. "Do you think what he saw this afternoon is going to make him more interested in me? Get real, Fee. Chaos is exactly what Parker doesn't want."

Bree got up and carried her plate to the sink.

"Are you going to talk to Charlie about Ted tonight?" Fiona asked as she started clearing the rest of the dishes.

"I was." Bree stared out the window at the honeysuckle bushes and the pink and red impatiens Fiona had planted in front of them. "Maybe I should wait. He's in a good mood. I don't want to ruin it."

"Don't make excuses." Her sister used her hip to push Bree away from the sink. "I'll do the dishes. You go up there and talk to him now."

Bree tried to think of another excuse to put it off, but Fiona was right. It wasn't going to get any easier if she waited.

It felt as if she were slogging through mud as she climbed the stairs. Each step was an effort. The closer she got to Charlie's room, the slower she went.

Finally, staring at his door, she took a deep breath and knocked.

"Yeah?"

"It's me, Charlie. Can I come in?"

"Sure."

He was lifting his favorite snake, Beverly, out of her cage as Bree stepped into the room. "Bev doing okay?" she asked.

"She's fine." Charlie coiled the reptile around his arm. "What's wrong?"

"I have something to tell you, Charlie," she said as she sank onto the bed.

"What?" he asked warily.

"I saw someone today I haven't seen for a long time," she began. "For thirteen years."

"Yeah?" He stroked his finger down Beverly's body. "What does that have to do with me?"

"It was…it was…" She jumped up and went to the window. How should she say this? Would Charlie be glad to hear about Ted? Would he be angry? At Ted?

At her?

"It was your father, Charlie."

"My father?" He looked as shocked as if someone had just hit him.

She nodded.

"He lives in Spruce Lake?"

"Yes."

The silence throbbed with questions. "How come you didn't tell me he lived here?" he finally asked.

"I wasn't planning on having you meet him," she said, ashamed of her selfishness. "I didn't think we'd be here this long."

He frowned. "You didn't think we'd be here long enough for me to meet my father? How long does it take?"

"It's complicated, Charlie."

His throat worked. "He didn't want anything to do with me, did he? That's why you never told me."

No, Ted *hadn't* wanted his child. That's why she'd been trying to keep Charlie hidden. She didn't care about Ted's feelings, but she would do whatever she had to do to protect her child. "Your father didn't know you'd been born."

"How come?"

"We were young and we both did stupid things. I ran away when I found out I was pregnant, and I haven't been back to Spruce Lake."

"Why did you run away?"

"Because I was scared. I was seventeen and pregnant and didn't know what to do."

"How come my father didn't look for you?"

"He didn't know where I'd gone." Not the entire truth, but as much as Charlie was going to get. "But he wants to meet you now."

Charlie sat on his bed. "What's his name?"

"Ted. Ted Cross."

He unwound Beverly from his arm and draped her around his neck. "I don't want my name to be Charlie Cross. That's a totally stupid name," he said.

"We're not talking about changing your name," she assured him, watching the snake curl around his neck. "You know I don't like it when you let her do that."

"She's just trying to keep warm," Charlie said. He traced one of the dark splotches on the snake's body with his finger. "How come you never told me about my father before when I asked?"

Had she really thought it was right to keep this from Charlie? "When…when we broke up, I was very sad," she said. "I guess I didn't want to think about it."

"Why did you break up?"

"We were so young, Charlie. Neither of us was thinking straight."

"So why did you change your mind about me meeting him?"

"He found out about you and came to me."

"So if he hadn't found out, you wouldn't have told me?" Charlie set the snake on the floor, in a patch of sunlight, and watched as it glided toward the corner of the room. "Even though we were living in the same town, you wouldn't have told me about him? We would have left and I wouldn't have met him?"

"Charlie, don't let Beverly get so close to the wall."

"Chill, Mom! I'm not going to let her get away," he said, his jaw working.

Was her baby trying not to cry? "I'm sorry, sweetie," she said softly. "I should have told you right away." She edged around the bed, keeping an eye on the snake. "Can you put her away so I can hug you?"

"Beverly isn't going to hurt you," he said. He bit his lip. "All this time I've been living here and I didn't even know about him. Maybe I've already seen him." His voice rose. "I hate you, Mom."

"Calm down, Charlie."

"Why should I? This is a big fricking deal. Why didn't you tell me about him when I asked? I used to ask all the time, and you never said a word."

"Don't swear, Charlie."

"Fricking isn't swearing," he yelled back. "So am I going to meet him or not?"

"Do you want to?"

"Like you care what I want. If you cared, you would have told me about my father when I asked."

She pressed the heels of her hands to her eyes. "I'm sorry. I screwed up."

"Yeah, you did. Get out of my room."

She looked at her son, saw the anger and fear and longing on his face, and knew the distance between her and Charlie was much greater than the length of the bed. And it was her fault.

"I'll tell you anything you want to know," she said.

"It's a little late for that, isn't it?"

With tears pricking her eyes, Bree walked out of his room. And into her own. Fiona was waiting downstairs to hear how it went, but she couldn't face her right now. She couldn't face anyone.

Nothing in her life was ever going to be the same.

CHAPTER FIFTEEN

BREE STOOD ON THE raised slab porch of Parker's house in the darkness and studied the soft yellow glow from behind the shades on his front window. He must be home.

She shouldn't have come here, she thought, wiping her hands on her shorts. She could have waited until tomorrow to tell him what had happened with Charlie.

This has nothing to do with Charlie.

He was just an excuse.

She'd begun to back down the steps when the front door opened. Parker stood there, dressed in navy-blue running shorts and a faded gray Collier College T-shirt. His feet were bare.

"Hey, Bree. I thought I heard someone out here," he said. "The doorbell must be broken." He swung the screen door wide. "Come in."

"I don't want to intrude," she said, reluctant to walk in. Why had this seemed like a good idea? "I just wanted to thank you for letting Charlie run with you this afternoon."

"You can thank me inside," he said, taking her hand and pulling her into the house. He shut the door firmly behind her.

The tiny living room seemed cold in spite of the lush summer heat. It held a couch, two end tables, a lamp and a television. The only pictures she saw were orchids. They were beautiful, but they didn't add much life to the room.

There were no personal effects, not even a magazine sitting on one of the plain pine tables on either side of the plaid couch. His furniture looked like the kind college kids left on the curb at the end of every semester.

It was the home of a ghost, someone passing through and leaving no trace of himself behind.

"Sit down," Parker said. "Can I get you something to drink? A beer? I probably have a couple of cans of soda, too."

"No, thanks," she said, easing onto the edge of the couch. "I don't need anything, Parker." She glanced around the stark room. "You're a minimalist, aren't you?"

"The house?" He shrugged. "It's temporary. A place to crash between trips." He dropped onto the cushion next to her and nudged her with his shoulder. "At least I don't have boxes piled in my hallway like you do."

"We're emptying out that house. Fiona is enjoying getting rid of the stuff. I think it's therapy for her."

"Dumping the memories with the papers?" he said lightly.

"Something like that." Bree cleared her throat. "Anyway, Charlie told me he ran with you this afternoon. I know he followed you. Thanks for…for being kind to him."

"He was like a puppy, wagging his tail. I couldn't bear to kick him." Parker picked up her hand, rubbed his thumb over her wrist. "Is he doing okay? Not too sore?"

"He's fine. Based on the way he talked about you at dinner, you made quite an impression."

"He's a pretty good runner. He'll be a standout in cross-country this fall." He dropped her hand, draped his arm across the back of the couch and started playing with her hair. When his fingers touched her scalp, she shivered.

"Why did you really come over here, Bree? You could have thanked me at work tomorrow."

His voice was a caress that reverberated deep inside her. She jumped up. "I told Charlie about Ted this evening," she said, staring at a photo of an orchid without seeing it. "He was upset." *I hate you.*

"Did you expect him not to be?" Parker came up behind her and put his hands on her shoulders. "You dropped a bomb on him. It had to knock him completely off balance."

"I wasn't going to tell him," she said in a low voice. "About Ted. I didn't want him to know. What kind of woman doesn't tell her child about his father?"

"A woman who's been hurt? A woman who's afraid she's going to be hurt again?" He stroked his palms up and down her arms. "I can think of a lot of reasons."

She turned to face him and he dropped his arms. "I'm not afraid of Ted. And he can't hurt me. I got over him a long time ago." She wanted Parker's hands on her again, wanted to feel that connection to him, so she moved away.

"Why are you beating yourself up, Bree? You can't undo the past."

"Charlie was trying not to cry," she said, shutting her eyes against the memory. "He thought his father didn't want to have anything to do with him."

"And now he knows better," Parker said. "Stop punishing yourself. We all make bad choices when we're young. We learn from them."

Parker pulled her into his arms and she let herself burrow into him. Just for a moment. "Ted said I was exactly like my father," she whispered. "Vindictive and unforgiving."

"I'm guessing Cross needs a lot of forgiving," he murmured into her hair. "So maybe you should call it even."

Parker's heart beat against her ear, strong and steady, and

she put her hand on his chest. Having someone to lean on was different. Nice.

Scary. Especially when that someone was a man with no roots and no ties.

Somehow she found the strength to push herself away from him. "Sorry, Parker. I didn't mean to go all girlie on you."

He drew one finger down her neck to her chest. "You can go girlie on me anytime you like." He bumped her hip, and she felt his erection. "I like girlie."

"I can tell," she said dryly.

He bumped her hip again. "What can I say? It's my default setting when you're around."

Default? The guy was clearly a scientist. "That's so romantic, Parker. I've never been a default before," she said.

"Hey, I'm trying to be respectful here. Give me some credit."

"Who would have thought I'd be smiling at the end of this day?" She wrapped her arms around his neck and pressed her mouth to his. "Thank you," she murmured against his lips.

"Please tell me you don't want respectful tonight." He nibbled at her lower lip, pulling it gently into his mouth.

She didn't, she realized. She wanted heat and passion and mindless need.

She wanted Parker. "Respect is so overrated," she said, leaning into him and nipping at his neck. "Don't you think?"

"I'm not thinking anything," he said, sweeping his hands down her body and cupping her rear end.

He backed her up until she was against the wall, his mouth against hers. Her desire was sharp and all-consuming.

This was why she'd come to him. She'd needed comfort. But she also needed to feel alive. Needed to feel she was more than a mother who'd failed her child.

She wanted to forget everything tonight.

Everything except Parker.

"You've been driving me crazy, Bree," he muttered, running his hands up her sides, framing her face with his palms. "Every time I walk into my office, I picture you there. On my desk. And I want you." He rocked against her, and she arched into him. "Every time I see you in one of those ugly blouses, I remember what you look like without it."

He kissed her through the cotton of her T-shirt, the heat of his mouth making her nipple harden. She couldn't stop the moan that rose from deep inside her.

He shoved the shirt up and cupped her breasts, brushing his thumbs over her aching nipples through the thin, lacy bra, and she moaned again. Afraid he would stop touching her, she put her hands on his and held them in place.

"I want to feel your hands on me, too," he whispered. "Touch me, Bree. Please."

She reached beneath his T-shirt, letting the hair on his chest flow through her fingers as she learned the contours of his muscles. He shuddered when she found the hard nubs of his male nipples, and she shoved his shirt up and licked one. He tasted salty and delicious.

He squeezed her breasts gently, then fumbled for the clasp of her bra. Seconds later, he'd pulled both T-shirt and bra off and tossed them aside. Mimicking her, he licked one of her nipples.

"Anything you can do, I can do better?" she gasped. "Is that the game?"

He smiled and moved up to her mouth. "I like games."

He nibbled at her lip, then soothed it with his tongue. His erection strained against her, and even through their shorts she felt his heat.

Their tongues tangled as she slid her hand into the waistband of his running shorts and closed her fingers around him. He jumped in her hand and his mouth on hers became frantic. He fumbled with the button on her shorts, then shoved them down her legs. His hand swept over her hip, stopping when he touched bare skin and a band of elastic. "A thong," he groaned. "You're killing me."

He traced the strap down the cleft of her hips and she arched into him once more. When he stroked her gently, she wrapped her leg around him, desperate to get closer.

"Bedroom," he managed to say. "Condoms."

He took her hand and led her down the short hall to a darkened room. As she stepped inside, she heard her cell phone buzz.

She wanted to ignore it. She wanted to leap onto the bed with Parker and put his condoms to good use. As she hesitated, he heard it, too.

They stood frozen for a moment, then he walked back to the living room and picked up her purse. "It could be Charlie," he said.

Bree couldn't look at Parker as she fumbled in her bag. The phone was still buzzing when she glanced at the screen. *Charlie.*

"Hi," she said, clearing her throat. Trying to sound normal. "What's up?"

"Where did you go?" he demanded. "You said I could ask you anything, and then you disappeared."

"It was late, honey. I thought you were asleep."

"Where are you? And don't call me honey!" he yelled.

"I'm at a friend's house." She closed her eyes. "I'll be home in a little while. All right?"

"Okay." He hung up.

She stood for a moment, still achingly aroused, then

snapped the phone closed. "Kiddus interruptus. Charlie has questions." She stepped forward and rested her forehead against Parker's. "I'm so sorry."

Taking her in his arms, he stroked his hand down her spine. "Darn it," he said. "Those condoms were getting real excited about being used."

"I hate to disappoint them," she said, holding on to him.

"It'll be tough, but they can wait." He kissed her again, then went to pick her clothes up from the floor.

She tugged them on quickly, a little embarrassed about being naked when he was still completely dressed. She kissed him again regretfully.

"Good night, Parker."

"Wait, Bree. I'm glad you came over," he said.

"Sorry it ended like this."

"I guess that goes along with having kids."

She suspected he hadn't dated many women with children. "Guess so. I'll see you at work tomorrow."

She slipped out of the house before he could say anything else and tempt her to stay.

Remember his house, she told herself as she backed her car out of his driveway. Temporary house, temporary life. No roots…or ties.

IT WAS BUSIER THAN USUAL at The Lake House that Friday evening. Bree stood at the bar, waiting for an order, and scanned the crowded room.

This was midterm week at the college; Charlie had had his exam today. Maybe all the kids were in here celebrating.

She didn't care why it was busy. She touched the thick roll of bills in her pocket. Busy was good. She'd never minded working hard.

The door opened and another couple walked in. They headed for Sandy's station as Jerry put two salty dogs and a martini on Bree's tray. "Those look great, Jerry. Just like downtown."

"Get them delivered and bring me back another order," he said, without looking up from the next drink he was mixing.

"I love you, too, Jer," she said with a grin as she headed toward the booth in the corner.

She was turning away from a group of college kids who wanted a pitcher of Leinenkugel when Sandy came up to her. "One of the tables in my section asked for you," she said. "That one against the wall. The woman in the sleeveless print dress and the man in the black shirt."

Bree's stomach heaved as she spotted the couple. Ted Cross and a woman. His wife? She had a pleasant face and dishwater-blond hair cut short. She looked…nice. Ordinary. Not the kind of person Bree would expect to be with Ted.

She had imagined Ted's wife as someone eye-catching and glamorous. Drop-dead gorgeous. Not a woman who could be her next-door neighbor.

"Thanks, Sandy," she struggled to say. "I'll get them. Do you want to take the next table in my section?"

"No, thanks," the other waitress said with a grimace. "I'm having trouble keeping up with the ones I have."

"Let me know if you change your mind."

She started walking toward the two. Bree didn't have time to prepare herself to face them. Or linger. Thank goodness the bar was so busy.

"Hi, Ted," she said, forcing a cheerful smile. "What can I get you folks?"

"Bree, this is my wife, Melody."

Bree shook the woman's cold, damp hand, feeling a jolt of

sympathy for her. It couldn't be easy to meet your husband's ex-lover, who was also the mother of his child. "Hello, Melody."

"It's good to meet you," she said, hanging on to Bree's hand. She looked as if she wanted to say more.

"Hey, can we get some service over here?" a large, bearded man at the next table bellowed.

Bree extricated her hand. "The natives are thirsty," she said. "Do you know what you want?"

After they'd each ordered a glass of wine, Bree stopped by the next table, carefully staying out of reach of the two patrons. The shorter man, the one who hadn't yelled, looked embarrassed. "I'll tell your waitress you're ready to order," she said.

"About damn time," the other guy said, his voice carrying over the din in the bar. He narrowed his eyes. "I know you."

"You must come in on weekends, then," she said. The man had had too much to drink. Sandy didn't do well with drunks, but Bree had had plenty of experience with them. "How about I bring you a soda?" she said. "On the house."

"I don't want a frigging soda." He shoved the empty pitcher at her. "Fill this up again."

"I don't think so, sir," she said with a smile. "You've had enough beer."

He staggered to his feet with a roar of anger. Bree hooked her foot around his leg and pulled it out from beneath him, and he fell heavily back into his chair. "You don't want me to get Jerry," she said quietly, so only the two could hear her. "Jerry eats little guys like you for breakfast. How about you clear your tab and sleep it off somewhere?"

"That would be fine," the other man said hastily, pulling out his wallet. "How much do we owe you?"

"I'll get your check."

Five minutes later she was back with their change, and Ted and Melody's wine. She watched as the two men departed, the larger one unsteady on his feet. At least they'd left a nice tip for Sandy.

"Sorry about the drama," she said as she set the two glasses of red wine on Ted's table.

"You handled that guy really well, Bree." He paused and leaned forward. "Like a pro."

She froze. He couldn't possibly know. "One of those life skills," she said. "Did you want to order food tonight?"

"Give us more time," Melody said.

By the time they had ordered their meal and eaten it, the bar was beginning to settle down. A lot of college kids had left, probably to go to parties. When Bree picked up the Crosses' empty plates, Melody put her hand on her arm.

"Can I talk to you for a moment?" she said. As if that was a signal, Ted stood and headed in the direction of the restrooms.

"About what?" Bree asked warily.

"About Ted." Melody's gaze followed her husband until he disappeared around a corner. "He's a good man, Bree. He told me about Charlie. About what happened. He genuinely regrets what he did, and I can assure you he's changed in the past twelve years. He's not the same careless, self-centered kid he was back then."

"No? Then why did he demand to meet Charlie without even considering how it would affect my son? That seems pretty self-centered to me."

The woman blushed. "Ted was so excited when he found out about Charlie. So eager to meet him. He probably didn't handle it well."

"I've told Charlie about Ted. I'm leaving it up to him if he wants to meet Ted or not." Charlie's questions on the night he'd interrupted her and Parker had been about his dad—what he did for a living, if he looked like Charlie, if he had any other kids. She'd braced herself to hear how he wanted to proceed, but Charlie hadn't said anything yet. He hadn't said anything to her, period.

"Thank you." Tears filled Melody's eyes. "Thank you so much. You have no idea how much this means to Ted."

"He told me you can't have children," Bree said. "I'm sorry." She wanted to tell the woman she couldn't have Charlie. That she would never be Charlie's mother. But Bree couldn't bring herself to say the words. She couldn't be that cruel.

"Ted knew we would never have biological children when we got married," Melody said. "We're going to adopt." She smiled, but it didn't reach her eyes. "Knowing you can't have children makes you think about what it means to be a family. Ted and I have talked a lot about kids. Believe me, Bree, it's not just vanity or pride that makes him want to know Charlie. Ted wants to be a father to his son."

"I'll let Ted know when Charlie makes a decision," Bree answered.

"Thank you." Melody smiled over her shoulder. "Here's Ted."

"I'll get your check," Bree said. Ted hadn't said anything else to make her think he knew about her past. It had probably been her imagination. But she didn't want to spend any more time than necessary around him.

As she was collecting their money, the door opened. Whoever walked in didn't move past the door, however. She felt someone staring at her, so she glanced over her shoulder. Parker stood there, watching her. Her heart sped up, then she realized he was also watching Ted.

Bree swept Ted's money off the table and walked toward

Parker. Blocking him. "What are you doing here?" she said in a low voice.

"I came to see you and have a beer." He stared past her at Ted. "I'm glad I got here when I did."

"Don't you dare," she said, putting a hand on his chest as he tried to move around her. "Don't make a scene, Parker."

"What does he want?"

"Just to talk. Leave it alone."

"I'd like to talk to him, too."

She stepped in front of him. "I can see the headline in the *Spruce Lake Gazette* now. College Professors Get into Brawl at Local Bar. Throw Out Their Backs Trying to Land a Punch." She tried to herd him away from Ted. "Go sit down, Parker. If you behave yourself, I'll tell you why they're here."

He finally smiled. "All right, smart-ass. I'll go appease my male pride with a Guinness."

"I'll get it." She gave him a tiny shove. "And you're sitting on the other side of the room."

CHAPTER SIXTEEN

"THAT YOUR BOYFRIEND waiting for you, Bree?" Jerry's eyes slid from her to Parker, who was the only customer left.

"He's a friend," she said, slamming down the ketchup bottle she was cleaning. "All right?"

"Whoa!" the bartender raised his hands. "You're Ms. Sensitive tonight."

She sprayed cleaning solution on the table and rubbed it harder than necessary. She wasn't sure what her relationship with Parker was.

He wanted sex.

She did, too. She was a grown-up. She could have a casual relationship with a man. *Casual*. Right.

Tossing the cleaning supplies into the box beneath the bar, she nodded to Jerry and Sandy. "See you next Friday."

"Thanks again for handling that drunk for me," Sandy called. "You sure you don't want part of the tip?"

"It's all yours," Bree answered with a wave. "You did the work. I just showed him out."

Parker met her at the door and held it open for her. As she squeezed past him, he murmured, "You've been busy tonight." His eyes glittered in the darkness, and she could practically smell the testosterone swirling around him.

"What's that supposed to mean?" she asked cautiously.

"All this handling. First Ted, and then a drunk." He slung an arm around her shoulders and pulled her against him. "I watched you all night, wishing I could do a little handling, too."

She shivered despite the warm evening air. "I know," she said, snuggling closer, glad he'd waited for her. She hadn't been alone with him since the night at his house earlier in the week.

She'd been completely professional at work, careful to keep a safe distance from him.

It was driving her insane.

He slid his hand beneath the short sleeve of her blouse and rubbed one finger against her skin. She had to bite her lip to hold back a gasp. They were walking down the sidewalk, in plain view, but his touch was intimate. Private.

She wound her arm around his waist and leaned into him, breathing in the smell of leather jacket and spicy soap. Every time her thigh grazed his, he seemed to tense a little more.

Suddenly he swung her into an alley and out of the glare of the streetlights. In the shadows between buildings, he pushed her against a wall and kissed her with desperation.

They were pressed together from knee to chest as they kissed, the hard planes and muscles of his body sinking into her softness. As his tongue stroked hers, his body moved in time with it and she rocked her hips against him, eager to get closer.

He groaned into her mouth and cupped her rear in his hands, lifting her into him. She wound one leg around his, trying to climb into his skin.

"Hey, Bobby, look who it is. The bitch who threw us out of The Lake House."

Bree jerked away from Parker to see two men standing a couple of feet away, swaying on their feet. It was the drunk from earlier in the evening and his friend.

The first man leered at her. "You know, I figured out where I'd seen you before. I never forget an ass."

She sucked in a breath, afraid of what he would say next. She'd been a stripper so long ago…and it had been nowhere near Spruce Lake. He couldn't possibly recognize her.

"Neither do I, pal," Parker said, and punched him in the mouth.

The guy staggered backward, his hands covering his nose, and bumped into the building. "What'd ya do that for?" he yelped in a muffled voice. "Looks like you like her ass, too."

Parker clenched his fist again, but Bree grabbed his arm. "Don't," she said. "He's not worth the trouble."

His jaw working, Parker stared at the man for a moment, then towed Bree out of the alley and up the street.

Finally he slowed down. "Are you sure you need that job at The Lake House?" he asked, his voice tight.

"I'm sorry," she said quietly. "I wish you hadn't heard that. But I don't take it personally, and you shouldn't, either. It's part of the job." Thank God the drunk hadn't said anything more.

"I shouldn't take it personally when someone is disrespectful to you? Did you really expect me to walk away?"

He turned as if he might go back and punch the jerk again. Unbearably touched, she grabbed the front of his jacket with both hands. "Thank you, Parker." She pressed a kiss to his mouth, sighing when his arms closed around her. "For standing up for me. For punching that guy."

No one had ever stood up for her before. No one had thought she'd needed protecting.

She wanted to stay in Parker's arms forever, savoring his strength. Keeping the world at bay.

He framed her face with his hands, and the glitter in his eyes wasn't outraged anymore. "I think you need to thank me again," he murmured.

She kissed him once more, lingering this time, then grabbed his hand when he flattened it against her belly. "I can see the next headline in the *Gazette*. 'Local Professor Picked Up for Public Indecency,'" she teased as they began walking again. "Wouldn't that look good in your press clippings."

"I don't have press clippings."

"The Orchid Hunter doesn't keep press clippings? Oh, please."

"I'm not a publicity hound, Bree," he insisted. Parker sounded almost sad, as if it hurt that she would think so.

She slowed. "You know, I believe you."

"You seem surprised."

"My father was the king of publicity hounds. It kind of colors your perception."

"Not all men are like your dad."

"Thank God." She tucked her arm into Parker's, letting his closeness warm her inside and out. "You spent a lot of time in The Lake House tonight."

"I wanted to see you." He dropped a kiss on her hair. "I shouldn't have groped you in the alley. That was…out of control."

They were nearing her house. "Do you want to get together tomorrow night?" she suggested.

"I have to go to Chicago tomorrow. I'm giving a presentation at the Field Museum, and schmoozing with donors."

"That should be fun," she said, trying to sound convincing. Would they ever have time alone?

"It's work," he said. "But I could come back early on Sunday." He walked up the stairs with her. "We could have dinner."

"I'd like that."

Fiona had left the porch light on, a warm yellow glow in front of the door. Parker tugged her into the shadows in the corner. "Good night," he murmured.

Aware that Fiona's and Charlie's windows overlooked the front of the house, and that both were open, she whispered, "I'll see you Sunday."

She rose onto her toes to kiss him, and he wrapped his arms around her and met her mouth. Desire reignited instantly and hunger poured through them. Within moments she was aching for him. His erection burned into her and she knew she was trembling.

"Let me come in with you," he whispered. "I can't wait until Sunday. I've been thinking about you all week. About how you taste and how you feel." He rocked his hips against her, and she gasped into his mouth.

"Please, Bree."

When she found herself calculating how she could get him up to her room, trying to remember which was the squeaky stair, she tore herself away. "Parker," she said, panting. "Stop. Charlie is in the room right next to mine. And Fiona is across the hall. Fee's a light sleeper."

"Come back to my house, then."

"If I strolled in tomorrow morning, Charlie would know we'd spent the night together. He's twelve."

She knew the frustration she saw in Parker's eyes was mirrored in her own. But as much as she wanted to go home with him, Charlie had to come first.

"Then come to Chicago with me tomorrow," he said. "We'll have an evening together. Our first date."

They'd have the night, as well. "I'd love to," she said quietly. "But Charlie's still upset with me."

"Maybe he needs some time to himself. And you need time away. So you can both cool off."

"You're being altruistic, right?" she said with a tiny smile.

"Nah. I want you some place where Charlie can't interrupt us. Where nothing can interrupt us."

"I'll talk to him."

"You can help me schmooze the donors at the fund-raiser. Pretend it's part of your job." He sounded as desperate as he'd been in the alley. As desperate as she felt.

She wanted to go with him more than she'd wanted anything for a very long time. Felt a recklessness she'd hidden for too long. "If Charlie's okay with it, I'll see if Fee can watch him."

"Parker kissed her palm. "I won't leave for Chicago until I hear from you."

"I should tell you I don't put out on the first date," she said, leaning into him.

"Is that right?" He kissed her again and she melted against him. "I bet I can change your mind," he growled. After a few more minutes he broke away and pushed her toward the door. "But not tonight. You better get in the house before we're arrested for public indecency."

APPLAUSE FILLED the main hall of Chicago's Field Museum of Natural History as Parker stepped off the podium. Bree had never seen him in a suit before, never seen him address the public, and she couldn't take her eyes off him.

He was beyond charismatic. The elegantly dressed crowd had hung on his every word.

But he hated asking for money, she realized. She saw his distaste.

She didn't think anyone else had noticed. But she'd gotten to know him pretty well in the past few weeks.

Maybe she could help him out with that. After all, she'd learned something from her experience as an exotic dancer.

AS PARKER STEPPED DOWN from the podium, the first person he looked for was Bree. Not his largest donors, he realized uneasily. Not the people he *should* be focusing on.

He spotted her red hair in the middle of a crowd of people standing beneath Sue, the Tyrannosaurus rex skeleton that dominated the north end of the hall. Bree was animated, gesturing with her hands while she spoke, and he watched her for a moment.

She was stunning. There was no trace of the woman who worked in the college office in frumpy shirts and khaki pants. Tonight she wore a black silk tank top and a slim black skirt that showed off her fabulous legs. A green silk jacket clung to her curves and rippled like water when she moved. A diamond pendant nestled above a hint of cleavage.

He heard her low laugh as he edged closer. "It's FeeMac Jewelry," she said to a woman next to her. "Fabulous, isn't it?"

"I love FeeMac," the woman said fervently. "But I don't think I've seen these pieces before."

"They're from her new line," Bree replied. "She's a big supporter of Dr. Ellison's, you know. When she heard I was going to be here tonight, she insisted on lending them to me."

"Really?" another woman murmured. "Fiona McInnes supports Dr. Ellison?"

"She knows what great work he does," Bree said. "If you're interested in donating to his foundation, we have information on the table over here." She shepherded the women toward the display of photos and a description of his next expedition.

The men who'd been standing nearby watched as other

women trailed after her. They weren't looking at their respective partners, however. None of them could take their eyes off Bree.

Even Sue the dinosaur seemed to be watching her.

Two hours later, as another group of guests trickled out of the museum, Parker patted the bulge of checks in the breast pocket of his suit jacket. He'd never gotten so many donations at a fund-raiser before.

He'd never had Bree with him, that's why. She'd worked the crowd like an expert, coaxing donations from almost all of them.

He glanced at Sue. "I bet she got a donation from you, too, didn't she?"

Bree was talking to the Hortons. They regularly donated modest amounts to his expeditions, mostly because Shelley Horton loved his photographs. As Parker joined them, Jack Horton pressed a check into his hand.

"I was fascinated by your explanation of the studies they're doing on that orchid you discovered. Bree was telling us about your funding needs for the next expedition. Go back to South America and find another new one."

Parker glanced at the check and froze. There were a lot more zeroes than he'd expected.

"Thanks, Jack. Shelley. This is very generous."

"Bree is very persuasive," the woman said with a smile. "And our youngest finished college in May, so we're feeling flush."

"I'll have to bring Bree to my events more often," Parker said, tucking her arm through his. He felt her tense.

"You should. She's quite the little rainmaker." Jack winked at Bree. "How about joining us for dinner? Are you two free?"

Parker hesitated. He didn't want to give up a moment of their time alone. But before he could answer, Bree said, "That sounds great, Jack."

"Let's go someplace where there's dancing," Shelley suggested happily.

"So we're set," Parker said lightly. Bree's hand had tightened on his arm. "If it's all right with you, Bree."

"Absolutely," she agreed, though her smile looked a tiny bit forced.

"It's going to take me a while to pack up all my equipment," he said to Jack. "Why don't we pick a club, and you and Shelley go ahead. We'll meet you there as soon as we can."

After a few minutes, they agreed on a popular night spot west of the Loop. As they watched the Hortons leave, Parker asked, "What's wrong?"

"I haven't danced in a long time." She sounded subdued.

"Don't worry about it." He kissed her. "I'm not exactly *Dancing with the Stars* material myself. But tonight we have to celebrate. You were brilliant."

"I enjoyed talking to your donors," she said, her shoulders relaxing. "They were interesting people."

He beat back a tiny, ridiculous spurt of jealousy. "They clearly liked talking to you. They were falling over themselves to donate money."

She nudged him with her elbow. "They all want a piece of the Orchid Hunter."

No, they'd wanted Bree's attention. It was a little disconcerting to be the supporting actor at his own presentation. "They wanted a piece of you."

"You are so full of it," she said with a smile. "Let's get this mess cleaned up and go to dinner. I'm starving."

Clearly, she had no idea how charismatic she was. And the FeeMac diamonds she wore had nothing to do with it. "You don't get it, do you?" he said. "You were the star tonight. I was just the nerd who'd taken the pictures."

"So I'm your lucky charm?" She laughed, but there was a shadow in her eyes.

No wonder. She must be exhausted. Vowing to make it an early evening, he said, "Absolutely. You're permanently in charge of my fund-raising. If you can get my donors to open their wallets like this at every event, I can spend a lot more time in South America. Do a lot more work." He hugged her closely. "I'm so glad I brought you with me tonight."

Bree was far more than a lucky charm. He ignored the niggling thought and draped his arm over her shoulders. "Let's pack up, get some dinner and then see which one of us is the worse dancer."

CHAPTER SEVENTEEN

HE DEFINITELY WON THE worst-dancer contest, Parker thought as he watched Bree on the dance floor. Everyone else was watching her, too. She'd taken off the green silk jacket and her shoes, and had abandoned herself to the music.

She was both graceful and sensual, her body flowing from side to side, her hips swaying. Full of joy. She'd said it had been a long time since she'd danced, but she clearly hadn't forgotten a thing. She moved as if every atom in her body felt the music and responded to it.

She'd been reluctant to step onto the hardwood floor at first, but Jack Horton had insisted. Finally, with an apologetic grimace at Parker, she'd let Jack lead her out.

Parker had politely asked Shelley to dance, but hardly glanced at his partner, training all his attention on Bree. He wanted to be dancing with her. Touching the smooth skin of her back. Feeling the slide of her silk skirt against her hip.

"She's amazing," Shelley said into his ear. "And you should be dancing with her yourself." She smiled. "Jack's only good for one dance, anyway. If he doesn't go willingly, I'll drag the old hound dog off the floor after this one."

"I don't think I'm in the same class as Bree," Parker said.

"None of us are," she agreed. "She's a lovely young woman, Parker. You're very fortunate."

"I know." He watched Bree laugh as Jack spun her around. The older man put one hand on her waist, and the sudden urge to rip Jack Horton's head off shocked Parker. Their dance was harmless and innocent, but he couldn't bear the sight of another man's hands on Bree.

What did that say about him? He'd never been a jealous man.

"Oh, dear," Shelley murmured, swallowing a laugh. "You have it bad, don't you? Would you like me to cut in on Jack?"

"Don't be silly, Shelley," Parker said, feeling like an idiot as he dragged his attention back to his partner. He forced himself to grin. "I'm enjoying dancing with you."

"You're a sweet man, Parker, but if you were any more full of it, your eyes would be brown." She sighed as the song ended. "Thank God." She waded into the crowd, grabbed Jack and towed him back to their table.

Parker edged through the other couples and slid his arm around Bree's waist. "I think you just hustled me. You said you weren't much of a dancer."

"I said I hadn't danced in a long time," she corrected. "There's a difference."

"Looks like you're making up for it now."

"I've always loved to dance," she said. The music started again, a number with a pounding rhythm, and she grabbed him. "Dance with me, Parker."

They danced close together, their bodies brushing as they moved with the music. Bree bumped his hip gently with hers, then moved behind him and wriggled her rear against his. That brief stroke of her body, the tiny signal that she wanted him, too, was enough to demolish the last scrap of his control.

They were close to the edge of the dance floor, and he pulled her away from the other dancers. Backing her into a shadowy corner, he kissed her long and slow.

The music was too loud to hear over, but her moan vibrated in his mouth. When he stroked her tongue, her hands tightened on his shoulders. And when he pressed closer, she trembled against him.

"Let's get out of here," he said, his lips at her neck.

"The Hortons," she panted. "We can't just leave them."

"Watch me," he said, nibbling her lower lip. She tasted like the wine she'd been drinking, tart and sweet at the same time. He eased away from her only enough to pull her close to his side.

Minutes later, after he'd told the Hortons he'd exhausted himself with all the dancing, they stepped onto the sidewalk outside the club. A lake breeze cooled the evening air, although the smell of hot asphalt and car exhaust remained from the day.

"What are Jack and Shelley going to think?" Bree asked as the two of them slid into a cab. Her face was still red, and he wasn't sure if it was from their earlier kiss or embarrassment at what he'd said to the Hortons.

"That you've bewitched me," he said, dropping a kiss on her hair. "It doesn't take a rocket scientist to see that."

She leaned into him. "You're just saying that to make me change my 'no putting out on the first date' rule."

"Is that still your official position?" He bit down gently on the tendon in her neck, smiling against her skin when she shivered.

"Are you going to give me a reason to change it?" she asked, her breath tickling his ear.

"I'm going to try." He glanced at the cabdriver, who was talking animatedly into a cell phone attached to his right ear. He wasn't going to be paying any attention to his passengers.

"Give it your best shot, big guy." Bree pressed her thigh against Parker's.

He wanted to lay her down on the seat and pour himself

into her. He closed his eyes to block out her tousled hair and face, shiny with sweat from their dance. No one had ever made him lose control, and the fact that he was so close to the edge was frightening.

He couldn't make love to her in a cab.

But he could do other things.

Exhaling slowly to steady himself, he draped one arm casually over her shoulder, letting his fingers dangle just above her breast. When the cab turned a corner, his fingertips skimmed over her. Almost as if it was an accident.

When he heard her suck in a breath, he smiled to himself. She should have known what he would do when she threw down the gauntlet.

Bree snuggled closer, brushing the side of her breast against his arm, and he shifted on the seat, even more uncomfortable. Maybe she *had* known what he would do.

"You like playing with fire, don't you?" he murmured, nipping her neck.

"I have no idea what you're talking about," she answered, dropping her hand on his thigh. With one finger, she began to draw small, lazy circles.

"Is that right?" He forced his body to relax, tried to ignore what she was doing to him. He eased her over so that they were directly behind the driver, and slid his hand beneath the hem of her skirt.

She froze, her fingers digging into his thigh.

"This isn't my best shot, by the way," he whispered into her ear. He shifted his palm a few inches higher over her smooth, silky skin. "I haven't gotten there yet."

She turned toward him, kissing him with a hunger he could taste. He smiled against her mouth and reached higher on her thigh, until his fingers touched lace.

She jerked against him. "Parker," she said. Her voice was low and throaty, and she grasped his jacket in one fist.

He stroked her through the lace and she shuddered. The El train rumbled on the tracks overhead, its lights flickering. He glanced at the driver, who was still talking on his phone, and stroked her again. Parker felt her body clench and knew she was on the verge of release. He leaned over her, shielding her in case the cabbie glanced in his rearview mirror, and touched her one more time.

Bree climaxed around his hand and he wrapped his other arm around her, holding her while she shook. As he kissed her, savoring the tiny noises she made, the taxi screeched to the curb.

They'd reached the Palmer House. Without letting Bree go, Parker smoothed her dress over her legs. He pulled a bill out of his pocket and handed it to the driver, then eased her out the door. Clamping his arm around her waist, he walked her to the door, trying to ignore the discomfort in his groin. His legs were wobbling as much as hers.

No one else got into their elevator, and he pressed the button for their floor before gathering her close and devouring her mouth. "There are probably cameras in here," he said. "Want to dare me again?"

She held his hands against her belly as she kissed him. He tried to tug one free, but she wouldn't let go. He smiled against her mouth. "Chicken."

"You're going to be so sorry you did that," she said softly.

"Promise?" The elevator stopped and he pulled her into the dimly lit hall and to their room.

Bree stood in the corridor, dazed, as Parker swiped the key through the lock. Her legs felt like water and she was still vibrating from her climax in the cab. Parker didn't bother to turn on the lights as he drew her inside the room. The door was barely closed when he shoved her against it.

His fingers fumbled at her waist, then her skirt dropped to the floor. Her silk jacket followed, and he cupped her bare cheeks in his hands. "Good thing I didn't realize this was a thong while we were in that cab," he muttered. "I barely managed to control myself as it was."

Her arms felt like lead as she tried to strip away his jacket. Shrugging it off impatiently, he pulled the thong down her legs and took in her body. She was leaning against the door, her legs almost too shaky to support herself, naked except for the tank top.

"You. Too many clothes," she managed to gasp.

Stepping slowly away, he began to unbutton his shirt. "Does that mean you've abandoned your first-date rule?"

She couldn't suppress a smile. "Bite me, Parker."

"I thought you'd never ask." He tossed the shirt away and began to unbuckle his belt as he leaned in and lightly bit her earlobe. Moments later he yanked the thin silk top and strapless black bra off her and devoured her with his gaze as he tore open a foil packet.

Then he surprised her. He took the time to lead her into the bedroom. Ripping the duvet off the bed, he eased her onto the cool sheets.

"I'm not going to slam you against the wall the first time we make love," he said, sweeping his hand down her body to her waist. "I want to make this special."

She wound her arms around his neck as the last of her defenses crumbled. "You already have," she murmured.

She couldn't wait to feel him inside her, to join with him. And he shuddered above her, all his muscles clenched with the effort to go slow. But he slid into her gently, kissing her as he moved. She wrapped her legs around his hips and drew him deeper, his care and tenderness overwhelming her.

Moving with him, she moaned his name, pouring herself into their kiss. Each stroke brought her closer to the edge, until finally she arched and cried out. As spasms of pleasure poured through her, she felt him tremble with his own release.

She wasn't sure if it was minutes or hours later when their breathing finally slowed to normal. He rolled over so that she sprawled on top of him, and started caressing her back. "Much better than the wall," he said into her ear.

"Mmm," she agreed. "Except that wasn't exactly how I'd planned to get even with you for the cab."

"No?" He smoothed the hair away from her face. "What did you have in mind?"

"I think I'd rather surprise you. Sometime when you least expect it." She wriggled against him, the rough hair on his chest making her breasts tighten. Concentrating on every sensation, she felt him respond to her touch.

"I don't expect anything right *now*." He lifted his hips and pressed closer. "I'd be totally surprised."

"Is that so?" She undulated against him and smiled when his hands tightened on her. "Well, in that case…" She trailed her mouth down his neck to his chest, then moved lower. His hips lifted off the bed and he groaned her name. When he finally dragged her back up his body and slid into her, she wasn't thinking about anything but Parker.

THE DISTANT BLARE of a horn slowly penetrated the haze of sleep. As Bree surfaced, she realized a warm body was curled around her, and the night came rushing back.

Parker. She nestled closer. They'd made love for hours, falling asleep only when the sky began to lighten. They would have to leave for Spruce Lake soon, but she wanted a few more minutes to luxuriate in the sensation of having his body against hers. To think about nothing but the things they'd done together the night before.

She drank in the scent of his skin, the way he felt snugged up against her, the sight of his rumpled hair and dark eyelashes fanned out against his face. She was so in love with Parker that the mere sight of his unshaven, bristly jaw made her dizzy.

She'd deal with the pain later. Right now, the sun was shining and they were cocooned together in bed. She didn't want to waste a minute of the time they had.

"It wasn't a dream," he murmured. His arms tightened around her. "You really are here." He opened his eyes and smoothed her hair away from her face. "I don't want to leave this room."

"Me, neither," she confessed.

"Let's stay another night." He put his hand on her breast and kissed her neck. "We'll leave in the morning, early enough so you get to work and I make it to my class."

She closed her eyes, battling her body's response. "I want to say yes," she said, nipping at his lower lip. "But I need to get home. I can't ask Fiona to watch Charlie for another day."

He sat up, and the sheet dropped to his hips. "We have time to take a shower before we leave, don't we?"

"Of course," she said, her heart expanding. He might be disappointed by her refusal to stay, but he'd given in grace-fully.

His eyes gleamed. "The shower is huge," he said. "More than enough room for both of us. Can I wash your back?"

"Only if I can wash my favorite parts of you."

He stood and held out his hand. "Let's go negotiate."

Six hours later, he pulled into the driveway of her father's house in Spruce Lake. Parker had spent a good part of the trip home telling her what a wonderful job she'd done at the fundraiser and what he was going to do with the money she'd raised. She'd grown more and more quiet, but he hadn't seemed to notice.

Bree's dad had used his daughters to get attention for himself, by parading them around Spruce Lake and dragging them to press conferences.

Isn't that what Parker just did?

He kissed the palm of her hand. "When can we do this again?"

"We can't spend the night together in Spruce Lake," she said. "But we can have very late dates."

"I like waking up with you," he argued, twining one of her curls around his finger. "Seeing you in the morning, kissing you before I get out of bed."

"Me, too. But I have a son who doesn't need to know his mom is sleeping with his teacher."

"Then we should go away again. Soon." Parker shifted in the seat so he was facing her. "I'll make you my official fundraiser. You can come with me to all my donor presentations."

Her stomach curled into a cold fist. "So I can be your rainmaker?" she asked.

"You made a thunderstorm last night." He leaned forward and kissed her. "In more ways than one. And the donors loved you. I can't wait for you to do it again. It means I'll have you to myself for another whole night."

"That sounds lovely," she said, swallowing hard and fumbling for the door handle. "I'll see you at work tomorrow, okay?"

"Bree?" He put his hand on her arm, stopping her. "Is something wrong?"

"Only that everything about last night was wonderful, and I'm sorry it's over," she said, grabbing her bag and closing the car door before he could get out and help.

She watched him drive away, then let herself into the house. What was over? The weekend? Their romance?

She would stay away from Parker until she'd sorted out her feelings, she resolved. Give herself a little distance in order to be more objective.

Objective. About Parker? She wasn't sure that was possible.

CHAPTER EIGHTEEN

PARKER IMMEDIATELY LOST interest in the application he was filling out when he heard footsteps coming down the hall.

Bree.

Everything about her was burned into his brain—the flame of her hair and the green of her eyes, the shape and feel of her hand when she touched him, the scent of her skin. Even the rhythm of her steps on the hardwood floor outside his office.

He half rose to greet her, but she passed his door. He heard her talking to Chuck Boehmer in the next office, and he slowly sat back down.

In the two days since they'd returned from Chicago, she'd avoided him. She was probably right to be cautious. He couldn't trust himself around her. Every time he caught a glimpse of her, he wanted to sweep her into his arms and devour her.

He would ask her to stay late and do some work for him, he decided. Once the building emptied, they could relax around each other.

Away from her family.

"ELLISON?" The college president's voice crackled over the phone a half hour later. "Get over to my office. Right away."

"What's up, Jonathon?" Parker asked, leaning back in his chair.

"We'll discuss it when you get here."

Parker dropped the phone into its cradle and turned back to his computer. This grant application was his priority right now. And after learning what the Crosses had done to Bree, he was in no mood to jump to Jonathon's commands.

When he walked into Jonathon's office an hour later, the man glared at him. "I said right away, Ellison. What part of that didn't you understand?"

"I was finishing up a grant request, and I knew you wouldn't mind waiting," he said. "Every penny I get from another source is one penny less that Collier needs to contribute to my expedition."

He read the irritation in the president's eyes. The man didn't like being second. "There's something we need to discuss."

Parker dropped into a chair. "What? Did you get a parent complaint that I wasn't fair to their little darling?"

"This has nothing to do with the students. It's about your personal life." He pushed a tabloid newspaper across the desk, and Parker picked it up, puzzled.

"'Party-girl Starlet Pregnant with Alien's Baby'?" He read the headline, then tossed the paper onto the desk. "I'm not an alien, and I've never even met this young woman."

Jonathon's lips thinned. "Look at page 34."

Parker thumbed through the paper to a picture of Bree dancing with him at the club on Saturday night. The photographer was damn good, he acknowledged silently. He'd caught the naked lust Parker knew had been in his eyes all evening.

"She went with me to the Field Museum that evening, and

we had dinner with some of the donors afterward," Parker said evenly. "What's the problem?"

Jonathon closed the paper. "She'll be fired immediately, of course. We can't have her associated with you in people's minds. And you won't be introducing her to any more of your donors. What if they found out about her past?" he asked. "Do you think they'd be so eager to socialize with her then?"

A rush of anger made Parker jump to his feet. "You're worried they'll find out about Charlie?" His hands shook with the urge to wrap them around Jonathon's neck. "Your grandchild? Yeah, she told me all about Charlie's father," he spat when the older man paled. "And what you and Ted did when she found out she was pregnant. So you can take your sanctimonious crap and shove it up your ass."

He headed for the door as Jonathon said, "I'm not finished, Ellison."

"Yeah, you are," Parker said without turning around. He slammed the door behind him.

"WHAT WERE YOU THINKING, Bree?" Ted asked, striding into her office.

"What are you talking about?" She swung around in her chair to face him, puzzled.

He tossed a tabloid on her desk. The headline was about starlets and alien babies. "What's that?" she asked.

Ted thumbed through the paper quickly, turning it around so she could see the picture of her and Parker. Dancing on Saturday night. Dancing way too close.

Her stomach churning, she picked it up. "Why is this in the paper?"

"Ellison is a big deal," Ted said impatiently. "He's photographed whenever he's out in public with a woman. This time it happened to be you."

This time? "I went to a donor presentation with him," she said, unable to tear her gaze away from the photo. She and Parker looked so happy. So involved.

"That's what I mean. You can't associate with him in public. If his donors find out what you used to do, they'll drop him like he was on fire."

Bree clutched the paper, crumpling it. After a moment, she opened her fist and smoothed out the page. So Ted's remark at The Lake House the other night hadn't just been a shot in the dark. "How did you find out?"

"I have a son. I wanted to know everything I could about him. The private investigator I hired was thorough."

"So you found out I was an exotic dancer," she said quietly.

Ted snorted. "You were a stripper. You took your clothes off for money. If you're seen in public with Parker, have your picture show up in rags like this, someone will eventually recognize you." He leaned closer. "Does Charlie know?"

"Of course not. He was just a baby."

"Do you want him to find out?"

She caught a movement out of the corner of her eye, but when she looked at the door, no one was there. She turned to Ted. "Are you threatening me?"

"I'm worried about my son."

"I'm not going to tell him. Are you?" Despite her outward calm, she was seized with fear. Ted knew. How long before everyone else did, too?

Including Parker.

"Do you think I'd tell my son something like that about his mother?"

"You're making it sound so dirty," she said, gripping the

edge of her desk. Her fear was turning into anger. Ted wasn't the only one who could play hardball. "And it's not making me feel kindly toward your request to meet Charlie."

"Are *you* threatening *me?*" Ted asked incredulously.

"You threw out the first ugly insinuation."

He stared at her for a moment, then dropped into the chair next to her desk. "How did this turn into a fight? I came here because I wanted to warn you to be careful."

"It didn't sound that way."

He sighed. "I have no idea how you feel about Ellison," he said. "Although, based on that picture, I can guess. I was trying to do you a favor."

"This is all to protect me, right?" She raised her eyebrows.

"Believe it or not, it was supposed to be. If you care about Ellison, keep a low profile."

"I should hide because he'd be ashamed of me."

Ted picked up the picture of Charlie on her desk and gazed at it, not meeting her eyes. "If that's the way you want to put it."

"Thank you, Ted," she said, snatching the photo away from him. "I appreciate your good wishes. I'll talk to Charlie tonight and ask him again if he wants to meet you."

"This wasn't blackmail," he said quietly.

"Yes, it was. Go away." Bree sank back in her chair and stared at the image of Charlie. He had a smile on his face and was holding Beverly. She didn't put the picture down until she heard Ted walk away.

Moments later, Parker stepped into the office. "Bree?"

She heaved a sigh, still too shaken by Ted to deal with Parker.

"I heard you and Ted talking."

Oh, God. How much had he heard? "About what?" she asked cautiously.

"About something Charlie shouldn't know about you." He

shoved his hands into his pockets. "I just came from a meeting with Jonathon. He tried to tell me something about you, too, but I didn't give him a chance. What's going on?"

She stared at him, feeling as if her body were made out of glass and someone had just taken a hammer to her. The cracks were spreading, and any moment she'd crumble into shards.

"It sounds as if it's been a day for revelations." She stood and walked past Parker, heading for his office. "This is something I'd rather discuss in private."

He hurried to catch up with her. "What the hell is wrong? You look as if someone just died."

Not someone. Something. She should have known he'd find out. *Maybe he'll understand.*

She didn't think it was likely.

When he'd closed his office door, she crossed her arms in front of her. Holding herself together. "Ted was talking about what I did for a living shortly after Charlie was born. He didn't think your donors would like it if they found out."

"What?" he asked. "You make it sound like it's the end of the world."

It might be. "I was a dancer."

"Ballet?" He sounded puzzled.

"No, Parker." She closed her eyes, then forced herself to look at him. "I was an exotic dancer."

His perplexed expression turned to disbelief. "You were a *stripper?*"

"We prefer the other term."

"You took your clothes off in front of men?"

"That's why people call it stripping."

"I don't understand," he said. "Why were you a stripper?"

"I needed money, and dancing pays well. Very well," she said flatly.

He shoved his hands through his hair. "My God." He scanned her from head to toe, and suddenly she felt cold. "What did…how…?"

She knew what that meant—she'd gotten the same response when her principal at the school in Milwaukee found out about her past and confronted her. Emily Ralston had been more blunt; she'd asked Bree directly.

She refused to let him see how badly his reaction affected her. "I didn't do anything but dance," she said. "Since you asked." He hadn't, but she knew he'd been thinking it.

"I wasn't asking if you were a prostitute."

"But you were wondering."

"Don't put words in my mouth," he said sharply. "You have no idea what I'm thinking."

"Tell me, then. Are you okay with knowing that I took off my clothes so men could look at my body? Are you okay with your donors finding out about it?"

He backed away and sat heavily in his chair. Putting the solid expanse of his desk between them. "Why didn't you tell me?"

She stood rigidly. "Because we don't have that kind of relationship," she said. She'd been trying to make herself believe that they did. But you couldn't fit a square peg into a round hole. It was about as easy as turning a globe-trotting celebrity into family material. "You don't do families. You've made it a point to avoid Charlie and my sisters. You and I had sex, Parker. That's all. You've made it more than clear that your upcoming expedition—your work—is what's important to you."

"You're wrong, Bree. *You're* important to me."

"I'm important because we had great sex. Because I was attractive arm candy for you at the fund-raiser. Because I was able to convince your donors to open their wallets. Are you going to tell them about me?"

He rubbed his hand over his eyes. "I can deal with it personally. But I can't tell donors something like that."

"You can 'deal with it personally'? Am I supposed to be grateful? Get down on my knees to thank you?" She stood straighter. "I don't get down on my knees. And no, I didn't do it when I was a stripper, either."

"For God's sake, Bree. I didn't say that. I didn't even imply it. I just want to know why you did it."

"If you have to ask, Parker, there's no reason to tell you." She wasn't going to justify what she's done by telling him about Charlie's medical bills. She was *not* going to beg Parker to love her. To accept her the way she was.

She'd done that with her father, and it hadn't worked. Maybe she should have paid more attention to that lesson, she thought bitterly. Men loved women conditionally. They loved you only as long as you did what they wanted you to do.

And they were never there when you needed them.

Her father had never forgiven her when he found out about Charlie.

She'd thought Parker was different.

"I can't change the past," she told him. "I can't go back and erase that part of my life for you." She swallowed. "It's probably just as well this came out now. It would have been a lot harder to say goodbye a few months from now."

"Why would you be saying goodbye to me in a few months?"

"When you left on your expedition."

"Wait a minute, Bree," he said, but she opened the door and slipped into the hall. He didn't come after her.

CHAPTER NINETEEN

"YOU DON'T HAVE TO come in with me, Mom," Charlie said as they stood on the porch of Ted's house. He shuffled his feet and adjusted the belt of his baggy shorts. "It's okay if you want to wait in the car."

"Of course I'm coming in," she exclaimed, controlling the impulse to ruffle his hair. Charlie had spent longer than usual combing it before they left the house. His shoes were tied, and he'd made an effort to wear a clean shirt, which he'd tucked into his khaki shorts. He put on a show of bravado, but he was as nervous about this as she was. "I wouldn't let you face this alone." And she'd be there in case Ted did or said anything inappropriate.

"Thanks," he muttered, just as the door opened.

Ted stood there in dress pants and shirt, and drank in the sight of his son. Apparently Charlie wasn't the only one who'd groomed himself carefully.

"Charlie, this is your father," she said. The words stuck in her throat. "Ted Cross."

Ted extended his hand slowly. "Hello, Charlie. I'm so glad to meet you."

"Uh, yeah." He gave Ted's hand a perfunctory shake, then let go quickly as he studied his face. "We met before. In Professor Ellison's class."

"Yes, we did. I'm surprised you remembered." The man smiled tentatively. "You're very observant."

Charlie shrugged. "Whatever."

Ted cleared his throat in the uncomfortable silence. "Come in."

Bree followed Charlie into a home that was formally decorated and spotlessly clean. The wall-to-wall carpeting was off-white, the couch and chairs light blue. The end tables held a collection of delicate figurines. Not a house decorated with children in mind.

"Would you like a soda, Charlie? Or iced tea?"

"Can I have a Coke, please?" he asked as he studied the house and its furnishings.

"Sure. Bree?"

"Iced tea is fine. Why don't we sit in the kitchen, Ted?" she suggested. Charlie was eyeing that fragile, feminine living room apprehensively. He'd be a lot more comfortable in a less formal setting.

"Sure," Ted said. "It's in the back of the house."

It was a cheerful kitchen, decorated in yellow and red, and obviously well used. Pots and pans hung from a rack above the island. A bright blue spoon rest sat next to the stove. There was a calendar stuck to the refrigerator.

Ted busied himself with the drinks as Bree and Charlie settled at the table. She took one end, leaving the two males across from each other. Ted took a long drink of his cola, then laced his hands together in front of him.

"I'm sorry we're meeting for the first time today, Charlie," he said, and Bree tensed, ready to pounce if he tried to blame her. "I hope you didn't blame your mother, because it's my fault we never met."

Bree studied Ted's face and saw nothing but sincerity. She let out the breath she hadn't realized she'd been holding.

"Mom told me you guys had a fight and she ran away before I was born," Charlie said, staring at the cola can as he twisted it around. "So how come you didn't look for her?"

"For the same reason we had the fight." Ted's knuckles were white as he gripped his own can. "I'm guessing your mother didn't tell you the details."

"That's not necessary, Ted," Bree interrupted. "He doesn't have to know what we fought about." No matter what she thought of Ted, Charlie deserved to make his own decisions about his father. Telling him the ugly particulars of their last confrontation all those years ago wouldn't help anyone.

With a tiny nod in her direction, Ted said, "Charlie, when your mom said you wanted to meet me, I promised myself I wouldn't lie to you. You should know that we fought because I was immature and selfish. I wasn't thinking about you and your mother. I was thinking of myself and my own plans. That's why I never looked for her." He swallowed as he stared at his son. "I've regretted what happened ever since."

"Yeah?" Charlie shrugged, but Bree saw his knee jiggling beneath the table.

"You probably have questions you want to ask me," Ted said. "Shoot."

Charlie took a long drink of his soda and set the can on the table with a bump. "Why did you get my mom pregnant? Didn't you guys have sex ed back then? Didn't you know about condoms?"

Oh, my God. "I don't think that's an appropriate question, Charlie," Bree said quickly.

"It's fine," Ted said. "We did use condoms. One of them

failed. And that proved we were too young to be having sex, since we made such a hash of your life."

"There's nothing wrong with my life," Charlie said. He squeezed the can so hard he left a dent in the side. "Me and Mom are fine by ourselves."

Surprisingly, Ted smiled. "I can see that. Your mother has done a great job raising you, and I'm not trying to take her place. I'd just like a chance to get to know you. To spend time with you. Is that okay with you?"

Charlie raised one shoulder. "I'm here, aren't I?"

"Yes, you are." Ted looked as if he was about to reach across the table to touch him, but didn't. "Tell me about yourself," he said. "What do you like to do?"

"I'm going to try out for the cross-country team at school," Charlie said. "And, well, you know I'm taking a biology class at the college. I'm probably going to take herpetology there this fall."

"I understand you're pretty smart," Ted said.

The same shoulder went up. "I guess," Charlie muttered.

Bree sat stiffly in the chair, listening as the man asked questions and her son gave stilted, uncomfortable answers. She wasn't sure what she'd expected, but it wasn't this painful exchange of information. She'd done this to Charlie.

And to Ted. How horrible to be a stranger to your own child.

She had to make this better. As Ted and Charlie's conversation dwindled, she said, "I think you two should spend some time together alone. Charlie, how about if your father takes you to that reptile show in Green Bay next weekend?"

"I thought you wanted to go with me," Charlie protested.

"I do." She hoped he couldn't detect the white lie. "But Ted hasn't been to one of those shows with you. I bet he'd think it was pretty interesting."

Charlie glanced at him. "Would you?"

"I'd love to take you," he said, clearing his throat. "Since you're into reptiles, I'd like to learn something about them, too. I can't make up for the years I wasn't around, but I'd like to have a relationship with you now."

"What if we move back to Milwaukee after we finish with my grandfather's house?" Charlie asked, a challenge in his voice. "That's a long way from here."

"It's not that far," Ted said. "Even if you're a few hours away, I wouldn't forget about you. I want to be part of your life, no matter where you live." He looked at Bree. "But what about Parker?"

"Dr. Ellison?" Charlie asked. He glanced from Bree to Ted. "What about him?"

She'd been so careful to make sure Charlie didn't find out she and Parker were involved. Or had been, she thought with a stab of pain. Clenching her teeth, she said, "He's your teacher, Charlie. That's what Ted meant."

"Right."

It was clear Charlie didn't believe her, and she didn't blame him. He was much too smart to accept such a lame answer. "Charlie, would you wait outside? There are some things I need to arrange with your father."

"Sure." He stood up and set his soda can on the counter. "Uh, so long, Mr. Cross. I guess you and Mom will figure out next weekend."

"It's okay to call me Ted," he said. Bree saw the pain in his eyes. "It seems kind of silly to call me Mr. Cross."

"Okay, Ted." Charlie headed toward the front door.

She waited until she heard it slam behind him. "Please don't say anything more about me and Parker. He's Charlie's teacher."

"Sorry," Ted said. "I wasn't thinking." He stood and threw

out the empty soda cans. "Thank you, Bree. You're being really decent about this."

"I wouldn't do anything to hurt my son," she answered.

"You could have told him what I did. I appreciate that you didn't."

"I could have told you about him a long time ago, and I didn't do that, either. I'm trying to make up for it."

"Maybe we could both put the past behind us," Ted said. "Or at least try."

"I'm willing to try. For Charlie's sake."

"Good. I want you to know I've arranged to pay Charlie's tuition at the college for the class he took this summer, and any more classes he takes there. The bursar will be sending you a refund check." She'd paid the discounted tuition when she decided to let Charlie stay in the class. She hadn't wanted to be indebted to Parker. "And I'm setting up a college account for him."

"That's not necessary," she said automatically. But it would make her life so much easier. She's already begun to worry about money for college. Now she wouldn't have to feel so guilty about quitting her job at The Lake House.

She'd have her weekends free.

That didn't matter anymore, she reminded herself. She didn't have Parker to spend them with. She stood up abruptly and put her glass in the sink.

"I know it's not necessary, but I'm doing it anyway. And later, we're going to talk about back child support."

"Ted," she began, but he held up his hand.

"Not now, Bree. Okay? We can fight about it some other time."

"Fine." She ran her fingertips over the cool granite of the counter. "Where's Melody?"

"Shopping. She thought it would be better if I met Charlie by myself, at least for now. When you think he's ready, I'll introduce them." He rinsed her glass under the tap. "We'll talk about my father later, too."

"A long time later," Bree said.

"Yeah, I'm pretty pissed off at him myself. He should never have gotten Parker involved in that business with your father's work," Ted said. "And I've told him so."

"What do you mean?"

"Why do you think my father put Parker on that committee? He needed someone who could pry your old man's research out of you. He knew damn well he couldn't ask you himself."

"Did he know I worked for Parker when he put him on the committee?"

"My father knows everything that's going on at Collier, Bree. Haven't you figured that out?"

"Are you saying that he put Parker on that committee so he could seduce my father's papers out of me?"

"No, he probably just implied it," Ted said. "Do whatever you have to do to get those papers or we'll cut your funding. That would be more his style."

She hadn't realized her heart could break into any more pieces than it already had. "No. Parker wouldn't do that."

"Are you sure?" Ted sighed. "Look, I hope Ellison is on the up-and-up. That he's an honorable guy. But I don't want you to get hurt again. Okay? I'm just trying to help you here."

"You think this is helpful?"

"I'm being straight with you. My attempt to make up for what I did, I guess."

"So you're telling me that everything that happened between me and Parker was staged? That it was all a big game?" Parker had told her more than once he liked games.

She muffled a sob. "Is this supposed to make me feel better? Because I have to tell you, Ted, it's not working."

He studied her for a long, uncomfortable minute. "I shouldn't have said anything," he finally murmured. "Your relationship with him is a lot more serious than you're letting on, isn't it?"

She had no relationship with Parker, and never would. If she'd harbored any hope of working things out with him, Ted had just sunk it.

BREE POUNDED ON THE DOOR to Parker's office, then stormed inside without waiting for an invitation. He was sitting at his desk, a pile of yellowing paper in front of him. Next to his desk sat a cardboard box with the logo of an egg company on it. A box she'd given him.

"Bree," he said, straightening the stack of papers. "What are you doing here?"

"You bastard." She picked up the glass paperweight from his desk and flung it at the map. Pins scattered on the floor.

"What's wrong? What are you upset about?"

"It was all a lie, wasn't it? Jonathon told you to get my father's papers, or he wouldn't fund your expedition. Did he ask you to sleep with me if you had to? Pretend as if you cared about me?"

"It wasn't like that, Bree," Parker said, squirming in his chair. "Jonathon didn't tell me to get involved with you. Your father's papers have nothing to do with how I feel about you."

"Is that right? So you chased me and seduced me because you fell madly in love with me? The funding for your expedition had nothing to do with it." She kicked the box on the floor, but only hurt her foot. "No wonder you freaked out when you found out about me stripping. You introduced me to your donors, and the relationship wasn't even real. It would be pretty ironic if they found out about my past and cut off their support, wouldn't it?

"That's crazy. Why would I use you to get hold of your father's papers? All I had to do was ask you. Anyone could have asked you."

"Not just anyone. I would have burned them if Jonathon had asked me, and he knew it. So he sent you to sweet-talk me. Did he think I'd just fall into the Orchid Hunter's hands, swooning over your attention?" She picked up the paper-weight again and threw it at his head. He ducked. "He was right, wasn't he? I did." She was trapped in a carnival fun house, surrounded by distorting mirrors that reflected her nightmare back at her. "No wonder you didn't want anything to do with Charlie or my sisters. Why bother with them when you were only here for business?"

"I ran with Charlie."

"After he followed you and begged you to let him tag along. You never made any effort to get to know him. Most guys at least fake an interest in their girlfriend's kids. Oh, wait. I wasn't really your girlfriend, was I?"

"That's not true, Bree. You were my…"

"You can't even say it, can you?" She pulled herself together. She wouldn't let him see how shattered she was. How deeply his deception had cut. "I should have listened to you at the beginning," she muttered. "You said you liked games, but I didn't pay attention. You said you were only interested in a fling, but I stupidly thought we were different.

"Calm down, Bree," Parker ordered. He reached for her, but she shoved his hand away. "You're angry and upset, but you know it wasn't like that. I was never using you."

"No?" She took a step toward the desk. "You told me you wanted to use me to coax money from your big donors. I should have figured it out then—that I was helping you raise money so you could leave Spruce Lake. And here I was thinking you and I had something going that might keep you here. That you might want to stay.

"Then you used me to get those papers." She shoved the pile off the desk, and yellowed pages fluttered to the floor. "And then you used me for sex."

"My God, Bree! How can you say that?" His expression hardened. "You wanted me as much as I wanted you. Remember? You were as into it as I was."

Of course she was. She'd thought she was in love with Parker. "That's because I didn't know the agenda. And you had the nerve to judge me because I was a stripper when I was nineteen and twenty years old? Yes, I took my clothes off for money. But at least I was honest about what I was doing. I didn't try to pretend it was anything else. You're whoring yourself to Jonathon Cross, and for what? For money for your important expeditions."

"That's enough, Bree," he said.

"Yes. It is." Her foot slipped on some pages, but she kept walking to the door. She opened it, turned, and managed to say, "Goodbye, Parker."

CHAPTER TWENTY

BREE SAT IN HER CAR on the driveway and tried to calm down. Charlie wasn't home; she'd called Fiona and checked on that. She hadn't wanted him to see her like this. But now she had to face her sister, when all she wanted to do was curl into a ball and let the tears fall.

She didn't cry over men. She'd cried rivers of tears when she'd been pregnant, alone and afraid, and had sworn she'd never do it again.

No man would matter enough to make her cry.

She'd been foolish enough to break her own rule. She just wished the penalty wasn't so steep.

When she walked into the house, she found Zoe there, too. Both sisters hurried out of the kitchen to meet her, their faces pinched and anxious. Zoe gathered her into her arms. "Bree," she murmured, rocking her back and forth. "What happened, babe?"

Bree couldn't get the words out of her suddenly swollen throat. She just clung to her, blinking furiously to keep the tears from falling.

"What are you doing here?" she said after a moment. "You're supposed to be working."

"Fee called me. She said you sounded bad."

As if it was the most natural thing in the world for Zoe

to drop everything and run to help her, and Bree held on more tightly.

Finally she stepped away. "Fee, thank you."

"For calling Zoe?" She shrugged, but Bree saw her concern. "It sounded as if you needed a shrink."

"A shrink?" She shook her head. "What I need is a hit man."

Fiona grabbed her by the shoulders. "What did Mr. Orchid Hunting rat bastard do to you?"

"Why do you assume it's Parker?" she asked, appalled she'd been so easy to read. "Maybe it's Ted. Or one of the other professors at work."

"You don't care enough about Ted for him to put that look on your face. Same goes for the job."

Bree rubbed her eyes. "You're right," she said quietly. "It's Parker."

"Do you want to talk about it?" Zoe asked, herding her into the living room.

"No. Yes. I don't know." Bree threw herself onto the couch, shifting when one of the springs poked her. "Parker and I…" She closed her eyes. "He found out about the stripping a few days ago. He was horrified. He said he couldn't let his donors find out about me. Then today, when Charlie and I were at Ted's, I discovered something else."

She took a broken breath and told them about the committee and her fight with Parker. "He didn't even try to defend himself."

"What a slimy asshole." Fiona clenched her fists. "Why couldn't he have just asked for them?"

"He did. And I was fool enough to believe that the flirting, the kisses…" *Me falling in love with him.* "Had nothing to do with Dad's research."

"He doesn't deserve you, Bree," Zoe declared, reaching out

to tuck a strand of hair behind her ear. "As much as it hurts, it's better that you found out now."

"Thanks, Zo. That makes me feel so much better," she said bitterly.

Fiona dropped onto the other end of the couch. "I hope he comes sniffing around here, looking for more of Dad's things. I'll be waiting for him."

Bree rested her head back. "He won't," she said. "He's too smart for that." She dredged up a smile as she glanced at Fiona. "But I'd pay money to see that confrontation."

"What are you going to do about your job?" Zoe said.

"I haven't even thought about the job." Could she go back to the science department office, knowing she'd see Parker almost daily?

"Are you going to run away again, Bree?"

"No." She shook her head slowly. "I'm not going to let him drive me away."

"You have a home here," Zoe said. "If you want it."

"Charlie seems happy here," Fiona interjected. "He's making friends and he can take courses at the college. Instead of quitting, why not transfer to another department? Fight for what you want, Bree."

"I'm not going to beg him to love me." She got up and stared out the window. "I did enough of that with Dad to last a lifetime."

"Ellison's a fool to choose his job over you. But you're going to have to figure out how to deal with him if you stay," Zoe said. "Because you're going to run into him."

Could she stay?

Bree stared through the glass, looking at the impatiens and begonias Fiona had planted, the lush grass she'd nurtured. From the outside, this house looked cheerful and happy. Welcoming. Like a home.

Maybe she *could* stay here in Spruce Lake and make a life for herself and Charlie. She ignored the voice inside her that begged for adventure.

Women with twelve-year-old sons had enough adventure without looking for more.

Maybe, if she and Charlie stayed, they could get rid of the ghosts in this house and make the inside match the outside.

"I'll think about staying. What about you, Fee?" she asked. "Are you going to stay in Spruce Lake?"

"I can't," Fiona said, not meeting her eyes. "I have a business in New York. Five employees who count on me. Friends. A life. But we don't have to sell the house. Right, Zoe?" Fiona glanced at their sister, who nodded. "Ted can help you pay off Charlie's doctor bills. Then you and Charlie can live here. We'll fix it up, get a new couch and chairs for the living room, new drapes, paint the walls. We'll redo the kitchen. We'll make this place a real home."

"You have it all figured out," Bree murmured.

Fiona glanced at the bare spot above the fireplace where their father's picture had hung. "Not all of it," she said. "I don't know how to make things right for you."

Bree managed a tiny smile. "That's not your job, Fee. But I appreciate the thought."

"We're both here for you, Bree," Zoe told her. "At least for a while," she added under her breath, elbowing Fiona. "Just tell us what you want us to do."

"Yeah," Fiona added. "I have lots of tools out in my workshop. I'll personally take apart anyone who hurts you. Or Charlie."

"Wow, Fee," Bree said. "You're going to make me cry, and I swore I wouldn't do that."

Zoe squeezed her hand. "Go ahead and cry, babe. We're

here to wipe your tears away. And talk a little smack about that pond-scum-sucking lowlife."

PARKER SAT IN HIS OFFICE, staring at nothing. He'd been there ever since Bree had blown out of the room.

He hadn't seduced her for the papers. It was crazy for her to think that. He'd asked her for the papers, and she'd said yes. That was it. Done. Hadn't she seen he was attracted to her? That he wanted her?

Maybe not, after his reaction to the revelation about her stripping, he thought uneasily. And she was right about Charlie and her sisters. Parker had tried to pretend the kid didn't exist. He'd avoided her sisters. He'd wanted Bree, not her baggage.

He pushed aside the neat stack of papers, stood and kicked the cardboard box out of his way. His paperweight had a star-shaped crack where it had hit the floor earlier, and he replaced it carefully on his desk. He had fond memories of that piece of glass.

Then he crouched to retrieve the pins that had been jarred loose from his map. As he replaced them, he thought about the trips each pin represented. Hiking through the mountains. Paddling canoes down brown, sluggish rivers. Camping in clearings hacked out of the jungle, the hot, humid air pressing down on the tent every night.

The incredible, heady rush of realizing he'd found a new species of orchid.

The exhilaration of knowing it might yield new medicines, new treatments for intractable diseases.

How could Bree expect him to give that up? He'd shrivel and die if he had to live a sedentary life in Spruce Lake, teaching classes full of bored undergraduates for the next thirty years.

How could he choose between them?

"Doesn't matter now, buddy." Bree had made it very clear she was through with him.

He could concentrate on his plans for next winter's expedition. Once he finished teaching this class, he'd devote all his time to fund-raising and research.

The fund-raising wouldn't be nearly as much fun without Bree.

Throwing himself back in his chair, he closed his eyes and thought about the night at the museum. He stirred uneasily. He'd been really impressed about what she'd done. Enthusiastic about how much money she'd raised for him, how she'd wowed his donors.

Maybe too enthusiastic.

He'd said he wanted her to attend all future fund-raising events with him.

He'd wanted her to come with him so they could spend time together. Alone. But he'd never said that, specifically. So it wasn't a reach for her to assume he'd just been using her to help him raise money. Especially since she now didn't believe anything about their relationship was real.

He'd screwed up. Badly. He'd made one mistake on top of another.

He'd hurt someone he cared about a lot. When she left, she'd looked as though he'd cut her heart out.

Parker was dumping the papers back in the box when someone knocked on the door. Bree?

"Come in," he called.

Charlie stuck his head in. "Are you busy, Professor Ellison?"

"Not at all," he said, pushing the box into a corner. "What's up?"

Charlie was dressed in shorts and new white-and-red running shoes.

"How's it going, Professor?" he said, shuffling his feet.

"Good," Parker said cautiously. "How 'bout you?"

"I'm okay." Charlie cleared his throat. "I, uh, know about you and my mom."

Parker froze. "What about us?"

"I know you have something going on with her." He leaned against the door casually, but Parker saw his foot twitching. "That you're, like, going out with her."

"You do?"

"Yeah." The boy pushed himself away from the door and wandered over to the map on the wall. "Ted said something when we were over there, but I had already figured it out." He glanced sideways at Parker. "That's why she went with you to Chicago, wasn't it?"

"Um, she went to help me raise money for my expedition," he answered.

Charlie grunted. "Right."

"It's the truth. Turns out your mother…" *Is amazing. A miracle. The woman I…* "She's a great fund-raiser."

"Whatever. I'm down with it."

"You are?"

"Why wouldn't I be?" Charlie shrugged one shoulder, his typical gesture. "You're okay."

Parker suspected that was the ultimate approval from a twelve-year-old. "Thanks, Charlie." He cleared his throat. "How did it.go with your dad?"

"Ted?" He focused on the map. "It was weird meeting him. Talking to him, when I'd wondered about him for so…"

He hitched up the baggy shorts, which were sliding down his skinny butt. "I never thought I'd meet him, you know? Never thought I'd have a dad. It might be okay. He's taking me to a reptile show in Green Bay next weekend."

Parker was very sure the use of "Ted" was deliberate. Charlie wasn't going to claim the man as a father yet.

Good. Good? What was that about? Was he jealous of Ted Cross? Envious?

Parker had never wanted kids. He'd had no interest in having a family. So why was he suddenly unhappy that Charlie had connected with his father?

Don't think about it now. "That'll give you a chance to get to know him," he said.

"I guess." Charlie touched one of the pins in the map, just as he had the first time he'd been in Parker's office. "It'll be better for my mom, though."

"Really?" Parker tensed. "How so?" Ted was married. Was he going to get a divorce?

"He has a nice house, so he probably has some money. Maybe he'll help Mom pay my medical bills." The boy faced Parker. "She owes a lot of money. I had a heart thing when I was a kid. She never said anything to me, but I heard her talking to my aunts. It cost a lot to get it fixed."

Parker relaxed his fists as the proverbial lightbulb came on. Was that why Bree started stripping? To pay for Charlie's medical bills? "She didn't have insurance?"

"Nope. It was before she started teaching. And when she left her job in Milwaukee, we didn't have it again. That's why she started working here. So we could get it." He grinned at Parker. "I heard her tell my aunts that, too."

"You do a lot of eavesdropping, kid."

Charlie shrugged again. "That's the way you find out

what's going on. Mom won't tell me stuff." He kicked at one of the boxes behind Parker's desk. A box that held his grandfather's papers. "She thinks I'm still a baby."

"Your mom doesn't tell you stuff because she doesn't want you to worry."

"I could help her if she told me what was going on."

"Maybe you should tell her that."

"Maybe I will." He lifted his chin. "But right now I'm going running. You want to come with me?"

"I'd love to, Charlie." And he would, he realized. Even though he'd been exasperated when the kid had followed him, he'd enjoyed running with him. Seeing him struggle and succeed. Watching his enjoyment of the sport grow.

And now Charlie had confided in him about his heart problem. Who knew being the recipient of a kid's secrets could make a man feel so good? He smiled at him.

"Yeah?" Charlie's eyes lit up. "Really?"

"Sure. We'll head out of town on a different road. There's a spot on County U where I've seen a snake sunning itself on the asphalt. I'm not sure what kind it is, though."

"I'll know," Charlie said eagerly. "I know all the snakes around here."

"But I'll have to change my clothes. Can't run in sandals."

"You got that right," Charlie said with a snort. Parker saw the grin lurking behind his preteen cool. "Man, kids would laugh at me if they saw me running with a dork wearing sandals."

"God forbid," Parker said as he grabbed his briefcase. He was reaching for the door when his phone rang. He hesitated for a moment, then reluctantly answered it. "Yes?"

"Parker? This is Shelley Horton. Do you have a minute? I had an idea for a fund-raising event."

Damn it. "Hold on a second, Shelley." He put his hand over the phone. "I have to take this call, Charlie. Can I take a rain check on our run?"

"Sure," he answered, but his smile no longer reached his eyes. "No sweat, Professor."

"I'll try to catch up to you if I can. Maybe tomorrow we can try that road where I've seen the snake."

"Whatever," Charlie said. "See you later."

The door closed behind him and Parker felt a sense of loss. He should have told Shelley he'd call her back. That he was busy.

That's what Bree would have done.

Charlie and Bree were a family. They put each other first. Bree wouldn't have brushed Charlie off for a conversation about fund-raising.

Parker yanked open his office door, to find the corridor empty.

He'd never really been part of a family, and a knife-sharp longing swept through him. He was beginning to understand what he had missed.

CHAPTER TWENTY-ONE

"WHAT DO YOU MEAN, Parker couldn't run with you?" Bree said as she threw a load of laundry in the dryer. "Did you actually ask him to?"

"Yeah. I've run with him before," Charlie said impatiently. "Why wouldn't I ask him?"

Okay, she had to handle this carefully. "You never asked him those other times," she said. "You just followed him. He probably doesn't want to run with a kid who's just starting out." She searched frantically for a reason Charlie would believe. "He's probably a lot faster than you."

"He said he would," Charlie said. "He was going to go with me, until he got a phone call."

"From who?" Bree asked, then winced. How could she stoop so low?

"Someone named Shelley. He said he had to talk to her, but that we could run tomorrow."

Shelley Horton? Parker wouldn't hesitate to brush Charlie off to take a call from one of his donors.

"I'm not sure I want you running with him," she said abruptly. "He shouldn't be responsible for you."

"He isn't. We're just going together, that's all."

Parker was going to hurt Charlie, and she hated him for that. "Don't ask him to run with you anymore. Okay?"

"How come?" Charlie demanded.

"Because…" Bree stopped herself just in time. The old "because I said so" wasn't appropriate for a twelve-year-old. "Because I'm not working for him anymore, and you're almost finished with his class."

"What does that have to do with anything?"

"Let it go, Charlie. Okay?"

Her son gave her a shrewd look. "You guys have a fight or something?"

"Why would we fight? As I said, we don't work in the same building anymore."

"Yeah, what's up with that? How come you're working in another department?"

"Because they had an opening and it sounded interesting."

Charlie rolled his eyes. "Give me a break. You're doing the same thing you were doing in the science department, Mom." He studied her, and she avoided his gaze as she set the dryer temperature. "You *did* have a fight. Aren't you going out anymore?"

"What makes you think I was going out with him?"

"You went to Chicago together. And I'll bet you didn't have separate hotel rooms."

"Charlie McInnes." She dropped the laundry basket with a thud. "That's none… Why would you think…" She picked it up again and pushed past him. "We're not having this conversation."

"Why not?" Charlie asked, following her. "You gave me the whole 'use condoms, wait until you're twenty-five to have sex, don't do what I did' speech. So why can't I ask you about *your* sex life?" he needled. "Did you like having sex with Professor Ellison?"

"Charlie!" She whirled to face him. Her throat was tight and she prayed she wouldn't cry in front of her son. "That's a rude question. My sex life is none of your business."

"Then can I ask him to go running with me?"

"No! If you need someone to run with, call your aunt Zoe. She runs almost every day. She'd be happy to go with you."

"I don't *need* anyone to run with," he said, scowling. "I can go by myself. I *want* to go with Professor Ellison. We talk about guy stuff."

"I'm sorry, pal. Parker is off-limits." She forced a smile. "If you want to talk about stuff while you run, maybe I'll go with you."

"Forget it," he said scornfully. "You wouldn't make it to the end of the block, anyway."

"Charlie, come back," she called as he slammed out the door. The only answer was the sound of his feet hitting the gravel on the driveway.

Okay, that went well.

Damn it, why did Parker have to get involved with Charlie? It was one thing for her to get hurt.

Hurting her kid was something else entirely.

Maybe Zoe and Fiona could help her figure out a way to keep Charlie occupied and not focused on Parker. She wandered into the kitchen for a drink of water. Leaning against the counter as she gulped it down, she studied the cracked cabinets and stained Formica countertop. Maybe she could put Charlie to work on the kitchen.

Boys loved to tear things apart. She and Charlie could rip everything out and update the room completely. New cabinets, new appliances, a new floor. They could start with the money she'd gotten back from Charlie's tuition. She grew excited as she visualized the new room. The kitchen was the center of a house and it was the first place she'd make her own.

An hour later, Bree was folding laundry upstairs on

Charlie's bed when she heard the doorbell ring. She ran down the stairs and threw open the door.

Jamie Evans, a Spruce Lake police officer, stood on the porch. "Hey, Jamie. What are you doing here?" She held open the door. "Come in."

"Hello, Bree," he said as he stepped inside.

"Hey, I met Helen the other day," Bree said with a smile. "Zoe told me you were seeing her."

Jamie didn't smile back. "This isn't a social call, Bree."

He stayed near the door, and her heart began to race. She gripped the doorknob fearfully. "What's wrong, Jamie?" she asked.

"I'm sorry, Bree," he said. "There's been an accident."

PARKER DROPPED THE PHONE into its cradle. He'd cut Shelley off, but she'd just laughed and asked if Bree was waiting for him. Her question reverberated painfully in his head. He'd only realized he wanted Bree waiting for him after Shelley said it. And after it was too late.

He was hurrying down the hall, hoping he could catch Charlie, when Ted Cross rounded the corner. "Hey, Ellison. Just the person I was looking for."

"Can it wait?" Parker asked. "I'm in a hurry."

"It's up to you," he answered. "It's about Bree."

"What about her?"

"I don't think you want to do this in the hall," Ted said. "Your office?"

"Fine." Parker retraced his steps and unlocked his door. He threw himself into his chair and waited.

Ted looked at his hand. "You sure you want to do this now?"

Parker realized he'd been drumming his fingers on the desk. He put his hands behind his head and said, "Yeah. What's up?"

"I need to tell you some things about Bree," Ted said. He crossed his legs and smoothed the crease of his pants.

Parker's heart thundered. "Are you getting together with her? Because if you are, I don't want to hear about that."

"Me and Bree?" his colleague asked incredulously. "I'm married, you idiot. I love Melody."

"Then what did you come here to tell me?"

Ted studied him for a moment. "You love her, don't you?"

"How I feel about Bree is none of your damn business."

The man smiled. "Yeah, I thought so. I came here to tell you about her father, and what it was like for her growing up."

"John Henry was an asshole. I got that. She had a rough time. I got that, too. And you were an asshole to her. Does that about sum it up?" Parker didn't need Ted to tell him anything about Bree.

"Pretty much," Ted said quietly. "Believe me, Ellison, you can't say anything worse about me than I've been saying myself. But maybe I can make it up to Bree, just a little, by helping to make things right for the two of you."

"How do you know we've got a problem?"

"She applied to be the admin assistant in the humanities department," Ted retorted. "That was my first clue. I figured if everything was sunshine and roses between the two of you, she'd still be in your office."

What? "I don't believe you."

Ted shrugged. "Your choice." He stood and headed for the door. "I guess I was wrong. But if you just wanted to get laid, you should have picked a different woman." His expression hardened. "Bree doesn't deserve to be treated like that, no matter what you've heard about her."

"Hold on, Cross," he said. "How do you know so much about Bree? Are you buddies now?"

Ted turned slowly. His scornful appraisal had Parker squirming in his chair.

"Forget it, Ellison," he finally said. "I don't need crap from you. I've got plenty of other people standing in line to give me grief. Including my kid."

The door was almost closed when Parker yanked it open. "Sorry, Ted. Come back. Please," he added when the man didn't comply.

Parker had never been controlled by jealousy and guilt, and he didn't like the way it made him act—small and petty. He waited until Ted returned and sat down again.

"I'm being a jerk," Parker admitted.

"You think?"

"I'd like to hear what you have to say."

Ted leaned back in the chair. "You sure?"

"Yes." Parker turned his back and plucked a pin off his map, blindly driving it into the corkboard. "Yes, I want to know."

"Bree's father was the most selfish man I've ever known," Ted said unemotionally, as if he was announcing the title of a seminar. "He wanted to possess those girls completely. No, not in a sexual way," he said quickly. "Emotionally. And it was the worst for Bree, because she was his favorite. Not because he loved her more. The bastard didn't love any of them. Because she looked like him. She was a reflection of him."

Parker felt ill. Hadn't he done the same thing when he'd acted as if her revelation would hurt his career?

"Are you hung up on the stripping?" Ted asked. "Are you worried about what all your donors are going to say?"

Parker touched a few other pins, then swiveled to face Ted. He wanted to hear what the man had to say, but he wasn't about to discuss his feelings for Bree with her former lover. "It was a long time ago."

"Yes, it was. She was eighteen, alone, and the mother of a sick child. Her father had made a public exhibit of her and her sisters her whole life. The stripping was a natural extension of that." Ted sighed. "Plus, it was the only way an eighteen-year-old could earn the kind of money she needed for Charlie."

"If you're so positive about her stripping experience, why did you threaten to expose her if she didn't give you access to Charlie?"

"That's not how it was," Ted said. "At least not much.

"I was pissed off because she'd kept my son from me. I wanted to hurt her." He looked away. "I'd like to think I'm a better man than that."

"She was letting Charlie make the decision himself, you know," Parker said. She'd told him that the night she'd come to his house. Needing comfort. And he'd jumped her bones.

"I know that now."

Parker studied the man sitting in front of him. "Why are you bothering with this, Ted? Weren't you afraid that if I loved Bree, the way you seem to think, I'd take a swing at you?"

"Two reasons. The first is selfish. She's the mother of my son, and I don't want him to be miserable. And if Bree is unhappy, it's not going to be fun living in that house."

"I guess I can buy that," Parker said grudgingly.

"The other reason is atonement. I didn't stand up for her when I should have. I wasn't there for her when she needed me. I thought if I could make you understand Bree better, it might be the first step in making amends to her." He smiled faintly. "You want to take a swing at me now, Ellison, go ahead. I have to tell you, though, I did some boxing in college."

"Forget it, Cross. I'm not going to waste my time on you."

"Smart man." He stood. "If you want her, you're going to have to work for her. Bree knows how to hold a grudge. Something else she learned from her old man."

"Thanks for the words of encouragement."

"She's not easy, Ellison. But she's definitely worth it."

The last of Parker's resentment died. Bree's old lover was trying to do him a favor, and he'd been acting like a fool. "Thanks, Ted."

"Make her happy, and we'll call it even."

CHAPTER TWENTY-TWO

DAMN IT, he was too late.

Parker slowed to a jog, then to a walk. County H stretched out in front of him, flat and deserted. Nothing moved besides a few cows in a weedy pasture. He was at least five miles from Spruce Lake. Maybe six.

There was no sign of Charlie.

The scene he'd pictured in his mind, of Charlie excited to see him and forgiving Parker for blowing him off, vanished. The two of them weren't going to jog back to Spruce Lake together and grab a soda at The Lake House.

Not today, anyway.

Maybe tomorrow. Parker had acted like an ass with Ted Cross, but was glad he'd listened to him. Glad Ted had told him about Bree's childhood and the reasons she'd become a stripper.

It shouldn't have mattered, though. Guilt slid through him again. His first reaction should have been about Bree, not about his donors.

Parker scanned the horizon one more time, but Charlie wasn't there.

As he headed to town, the thoughts of Bree he'd been trying to hold at bay rushed back. Without the excuse of looking for her son, he had nothing else to fill his head but her.

After Ted told him she'd applied for a job with the humanities department, he'd run up to her office, sure his colleague must be mistaken.

There was nothing on her desk except the computer keyboard and monitor. The picture of Charlie was gone and the drawers were empty.

She'd left, and it was clear she wasn't coming back.

She'd slipped out of his life so easily. Almost as if she'd never been there at all.

In the past, that was exactly what he'd wanted—relationships that were quick, disposable and forgettable.

Bree wasn't Kleenex. But he'd treated her that way.

Parker ran faster. It was almost six o'clock. Bree would be home by now. He'd stop by her house.

He'd beg her to forgive him, both for screwing up in the first place, then handling everything so badly. He'd plead for another chance. Try to make her see how important she was to him.

But when he got to the house, there were no cars in the driveway and the front door stood open.

Hurrying up the steps, he rang the doorbell several times. "Bree?" he called. "Fiona? Charlie?"

There was no answer, and he began to feel uneasy. Where were they? Why was the door open?

He stuck his head inside, but the silence was complete. No one was there.

Or in Fiona's workshop, either. The garage was unlocked, leaving the green, red and blue gems scattered on her workbench unprotected, along with coils of gold and silver wire.

Something was wrong.

He locked the garage on his way out, then stared at the house. Something had happened, and they hadn't called him.

Why would they?

He'd let Bree walk away.

Parker's legs felt stiff and heavy, but he ran home. There was no message on his answering machine. Bree didn't answer her cell phone.

His sweat dried as he paced the house, leaving him itchy and uncomfortable. Finally he took a quick shower, then threw on jeans and a T-shirt.

An hour later, he tossed down the botany journal he'd been trying to read. As he roamed from one room to the other, he noticed the light blinking on his answering machine. "Damn it!" He punched the button. Someone must have called while he showered.

"Parker, this is Zoe. Charlie was hit by a car, and we're at the Spruce Lake hospital with him." She hesitated. "I thought you might want to know."

The dial tone hummed as Parker stared at the machine. Then he turned and ran for the door.

Fifteen minutes later, he stood in front of a gray-haired woman at the hospital information desk. "Charlie McInnes. I need to know where he is."

"Surely," she said with a smile. "Let me look him up. How do you spell his last name?"

Parker told her and watched her scroll through a list. "There he is." He pointed to Charlie's name.

"He was admitted to the emergency room," the woman said. "But it doesn't say whether he's still there."

"Then where is he?" Parker didn't want to think about the possibilities.

"I don't know." She frowned as she studied the screen. "If you'll have a seat, I'll check."

She walked toward a double door labeled Emergency, and

Parker followed her. Once he was through it, a nurse intercepted him. "Can I help you, sir?"

"I'm looking for Charlie McInnes. He was hit by a car."

Saying the words made him ill with dread. The nurse's expression softened. "Are you a family member?"

"Yes." He answered without thinking, and the woman nodded.

"He's in cubicle 3."

"Is he…?" Parker couldn't make his mouth form the words.

"I don't know his condition," she said. "Sorry."

A blue curtain billowed out in front of the cubicle, and Parker slowed as he approached. It wasn't pulled shut completely, leaving a ten-inch gap between it and the wall. Charlie lay on the bed, motionless and pale, except for an angry scrape on the left side of his face. Bree stood next to him, gripping his hand. Fiona and Zoe clustered around her, and a tall, dark-haired man stood next to Zoe, his arm around her shoulder.

Ted Cross stood on the other side of the bed, his fingers wrapped around the rail. Even from here, Parker could see his white knuckles.

Charlie was alive. Parker saw the slow rise and fall of the blanket covering his chest. He took a deep breath and let go of his worst fear.

Bree's hair fell around her shoulders and she wore a pair of her work khakis and a green shirt. The color was an almost perfect match for her eyes. She held Charlie's hand as if she would never let him go.

Bree and her sisters, Ted, the man with Zoe, Charlie…they were all part of a circle. They supported one another, took care of one another.

Parker was on the outside. He'd always been. Until now, he'd preferred it that way. It took a lot less effort. It left him free to concentrate on his own needs and wants, without worrying about anyone else's.

But he now wanted to be inside that circle. He wanted the right to stand at Charlie's bedside and worry about him.

He wanted to be next to Bree, when she needed someone to lean on. Someone to hold on to.

The curtain rippled, and Bree glanced over her shoulder. When she saw him, she froze. Then she said something to Zoe and turned back to Charlie.

"You came," Zoe said as she stepped out of the cubicle and drew him farther into the hall.

"Of course I came. What happened? Is he okay?"

"He was hit by a car when he was out running. He was crouched by the side of the road and the driver never saw him. His arm is broken and he has a concussion. And a bad case of road rash." She wrapped her arms around herself. "But the E.R. doctor said he's going to be all right."

Parker's heart stopped. Had Charlie been looking at a snake? "Where was he?"

Zoe frowned. "What difference does it make?"

"It's important."

She fastened her gaze on Charlie. "He was on County U."

The road where he'd seen the snake. Parker grabbed the curtain and stared at the still figure on the bed. "Why is he unconscious?"

"He's not. The doctor gave him a painkiller. An orthopedic surgeon is coming in to set Charlie's arm, and it's going to hurt."

"How's Bree?"

"How do you think she is? Her son is in the emergency

room. A police officer came to the house to tell her he'd been hit by a car. She's a wreck."

"She probably doesn't want me here, but is it okay if I stay for a while?"

Zoe's expression softened. "Come on in."

Several wires snaked out from beneath the blanket covering Charlie, attaching him to various machines. One monitor showed a steady series of green blips that Parker assumed represented Charlie's heartbeats. On another machine, the number 98 glowed red. A bag of fluid was suspended from a hook above the bed, dripping slowly into a plastic tube. Charlie's left arm was covered wrist to shoulder in a thick bandage.

Without thinking, Parker moved next to Bree and put his arm around her. She tensed, but he didn't let go. Finally she relaxed, muscle by muscle, until she slumped against him, still holding Charlie's hand.

"Mom," Charlie said drowsily. "Can I have some water?"

Bree's arm curled around Parker's waist and she clutched his shirt. "Not yet, sweetheart. The doctor said you couldn't have anything to drink until the orthopedic surgeon gets here."

"How come? I'm thirsty."

Her hand trembled against Parker's side, and he covered it with his own. "In case you have to have surgery," she whispered. "You can't eat or drink anything."

Charlie slowly opened his eyes. "Why do I have to have surgery?" His words slurred, and Parker wanted to reassure him. Tell him everything was going to be fine.

But he had no rights in this room.

"Your arm is broken," Bree said.

Charlie scanned the people around his bed. "Ted? What are you doing here?"

The man's throat worked and he didn't speak for a

moment. Finally he said, "Your mom told me what happened. Of course I'm here."

Charlie's gaze skipped from Zoe to Fiona to Bree. Finally he looked at Parker. "Dr. Ellison?"

"Running buddies stick together," he said, although he had to struggle to dredge up a smile. "That includes when one of them gets into a fight with a car. What were you thinking, doofus?"

Someone gasped, but Charlie grinned weakly. "Yeah, kick me when I'm down."

"Just don't think you're going to use this as an excuse to quit training," Parker said.

"'Course not." Charlie's eyes drifted shut.

Someone elbowed Parker in the back. "Keep your mouth shut, Ellison," Fiona said.

"It's okay, Fee," Bree murmured.

The blue curtain was yanked open and a rangy blond man stood in the doorway. "Who are the parents?"

Bree let go of Parker and turned. "I'm his mother. Who are you?"

"Dr. Marek, the orthopedic surgeon. I need to examine your son, and I'm going to need some space. Everyone but you can go to the waiting room."

Bree nodded at Ted. "He's Charlie's father."

"He can stay, too. The rest of you, get out."

Parker let go of Bree reluctantly and followed her sisters and the other man out of the cubicle. He trailed them into the waiting room and hung back as they huddled together, talking in low tones. He'd been part of the circle for a few minutes. A very temporary part. Now he wasn't.

Had he left it too late? Would he get another chance?

CHAPTER TWENTY-THREE

BREE SANK INTO THE CHAIR in the hospital room and watched Charlie sleep. The right side of his face was covered with a square of gauze, stained yellow-brown by the disinfectant they'd used to clean his cheek. His left arm lay on top of the blanket, covered from his fingers almost to his shoulder in a bright green cast.

Her hand shook as she brushed a lock of his dark hair away from another scrape on his forehead. He'd been so lucky. If the car had been going faster, if Charlie had been another few inches onto the pavement...

She shuddered. She couldn't bear to think about the possibilities.

"Mind if I come in?"

Parker. Her heart leaped. She forced herself to glance over her shoulder. As if it didn't matter that he'd come to Charlie's room. He stood in the door, backlit by the light in the hall. She couldn't see his face.

"I thought everyone left a while ago," she said.

"Not everyone." He waited on the threshold. "I'm not going anywhere, Bree."

What was that supposed to mean? "Come in," she said wearily.

He stayed at the end of the bed, assessing Charlie. His gaze moved from the bandage on her son's cheek to his closed eyes to the cast on his arm. "I'm so sorry," he finally said.

"He'll be fine," she said. And when Charlie woke up and acted like himself, she might actually believe it.

"This is my fault," Parker said, reaching out to touch one of Charlie's toes beneath the blanket.

"How do you figure that?"

"He came to my office and asked me to go running with him." He touched Charlie again. "I got a phone call and blew him off." Parker clutched the rail at the end of the bed. "I'd told him about a snake I'd seen sunning itself on the road. He went to look for it. That's why he was hit."

"You're not responsible for my son," she said, struggling to keep her barriers up. All she wanted was to fall into Parker's arms and ask him to hold her. To have someone help her through this nightmare.

Foolish of her to wish it was Parker.

When he finally looked at her, his eyes were haunted. "I told him a while ago that he shouldn't run alone because it was dangerous out in the country by yourself. And then I sent him off."

Foolish of her to want to hold *him*. To comfort him. "Don't blame yourself," she said. "If it's anyone's fault, it's mine. We had a fight before he left. Maybe he was thinking about that and wasn't paying attention."

"It's not your fault, Bree." Parker shook his head. "Maybe it's not my fault, either. But I could have been with him so easily. I *would* have been, if I hadn't taken that phone call."

Parker sounded like a parent, assuming guilt after an accident, Bree thought uneasily. "You're doing my job," she said, trying to lighten the mood. "Blaming yourself when something happens to your kid is what mothers do. You're just his teacher."

Parker's hand whitened on the bed rail. "Was it horrible when they set his arm?"

"It was awful." She shifted her grip on her son's hand, only letting go when Charlie stirred restlessly. "Even with the drugs, it hurt him." She would hear him whimpering in her nightmares for a long, long time.

Before she realized he'd moved, Parker's hands were on her shoulders, massaging. Kneading her stiff, sore muscles. "It's better now," he said. "It likely aches, but the horrible pain is gone. And with the painkillers, he probably doesn't feel much."

She wanted to lean back against him, but held herself upright. "How do you know?"

"I broke my arm when I was a kid." He reached under her hair and rubbed her nape. "I was younger than Charlie, but I remember how much better it felt after it was immobilized.

"Why are you here, Parker?" she asked.

He dropped his hands. "Where else would I be?"

She kept her gaze on Charlie. "Talking to your donors. Planning your expedition. Doing the stuff you do."

"I want to speak to you about that. To try and explain."

She rounded on him. "Now? You bring this up while Charlie is lying in a hospital bed and I'm going out of my mind? My son could have died today, and you want me to listen to your lame excuses?"

"Get out, Ellison." Fiona stood in the doorway, holding a cellophane-covered sandwich and a cup of coffee. "She doesn't want you here. She has her family."

"I'll leave you alone. For now. But I'm not going away, Bree," he said.

THREE WEEKS LATER, Bree sat in the front seat of Zoe's car, heading toward Milwaukee. Zoe was behind the wheel and

Charlie was in the back seat, playing with the hand-held video game Parker had given him.

They were going to one of Fiona's jewelry shows. A high-end store in Milwaukee would be carrying her jewelry, and Fiona and the owner were going to announce it at a press conference. Zoe had said she wanted to see their sister in action, then decided she didn't want to drive there and back by herself. She'd offered to put Bree and Charlie up for the night if they'd go with her. After three weeks of inactivity, with Bree hovering over him and checking compulsively for signs that his concussion was getting better, Charlie was restless and surly. So Bree had halfheartedly agreed. Zoe had assured her she wouldn't have to do a thing except enjoy herself. She'd even packed her clothes for her.

Bree wished she hadn't come. The last time she'd been on this road, it had been with Parker. She wanted to banish those memories, but they jumped out at her everywhere. When she tried to sleep at night, she dreamed of him. When she went to work, she remembered how much she'd looked forward to seeing him every morning.

Parker himself had done nothing to banish those memories. That evening in the hospital, after Fee sent him away, he'd sat in a chair in the hall all night. He'd come over to the house to see Charlie almost every day since then.

He hadn't tried to get her alone to talk, hadn't touched her, hadn't said anything more personal than asking her where Charlie kept his video games. He was just there.

"Tell me about this jewelry show, Zo," Bree said, trying to drum up some enthusiasm for the event.

"It's a big deal," her sister answered. "It's important to Fee. Lots of swanky people, so I packed you a nice dress. All you have to do is have a good time."

"What about Charlie? What's a twelve-year-old going to do at a jewelry show?"

"Oh, I think he'll have fun. There'll be lots of stuff to see."

"Wake me up when we get there, okay?" She wouldn't be able to sleep, but if she pretended, she wouldn't have to talk to her sister. Or Charlie.

"I CAN'T BELIEVE YOU brought this outfit." Bree tossed the black skirt and tank top and the green jacket on the bed. "I'm not going to wear this."

"Why not? You look great in it."

"You know perfectly well why not." Bree's throat swelled as she gazed at the puddle of fabrics. The last time she'd worn those clothes, they'd ended up on the floor of the hotel room she'd shared with Parker.

"I'm sorry," Zoe said. She didn't seem a bit repentant. "But it's all I brought for you. Pretend it's something else."

"You wear it," Bree suggested. "I'll wear your outfit."

Zoe patted her still-flat abdomen and smiled. "Sorry, it wouldn't fit."

"Oh, come on. You're only a month along. Don't give me that."

"Hey, Mom, you dressed?" Charlie called from the bathroom. "Can I come out?"

"Damn you, Zo," Bree whispered. "Hold on," she called, grabbing the skirt and tank top and shimmying into them. At least the dry cleaning had gotten rid of Parker's scent. "Come on out."

Charlie wore slacks and a dress shirt with a badly knotted tie. "Come here, kid," Zoe said, grabbing the tie and tugging him toward her. "Let me show you how it's done."

Charlie's father should be showing him how to tie a

Windsor knot. Or his stepfather. Bree turned away. Ted would have to handle that stuff, because Charlie wasn't going to have a stepfather.

"You both look fantastic," Zoe said. "Let's head downstairs."

The jewelry show was being held in the same hotel. They rode the elevator in silence, then crossed the crowded lobby to a ballroom. When they walked in the door, Bree glanced around in confusion.

"We must have the wrong room," she said. "There's no jewelry here."

"We're in exactly the right spot." Zoe grabbed her hand and towed her along. "Come on over here."

The crowd of expensively dressed people parted for Zoe, and she and Bree emerged in front of a slightly raised platform. There was a lectern on it, and a table that held pictures of orchids.

Bree's heart slammed against her chest, and she yanked her sister to a stop. "Zoe, what have you done?"

"I didn't know any other way to get you here."

"I don't want to be here," Bree said, turning blindly to leave. Parker stood right behind her. He wore the same suit he'd worn the night in Chicago.

"Hello, Bree," he said. "Thanks for coming."

She rounded on Zoe. "Did you set this up?"

"It was Parker's idea." She grinned as she pried Bree's hand away from her wrist, and grabbed Charlie. "Have fun. We're going to a movie, then we're hitting the video arcade next to the hotel."

Fun? Her sister had tricked her, and now thought she'd have fun? Bree watched them leave, then turned to the man standing patiently beside her. "I'm going up to my room."

"Wait, Bree. Please. I want to talk to you, but I have to

make a speech first. These are some of my most important donors."

"That's exactly why I'm leaving," she said, her stomach churning. It was annoyance, she told herself. That was all. "You can talk to your donors for as long as you like."

"This won't take long. I'd like you to be here."

"Why? So I can be your rainmaker again? Not going to happen." She'd told herself the worst of the hurt was past. That she was getting over Parker.

She'd been so wrong.

She tried to move around him without touching him. "Get out of my way, Ellison."

Shelley and Jack Horton stood on the other side of the room, and they waved when they caught Bree's eye. "Stay right here, okay?" Parker said. "Please, Bree?"

"Why?" she asked wearily. "It's been three weeks. You say you want to talk to me, but even now your donors come first."

"Give me two minutes," he pleaded. "If you want to leave after that, go ahead. Just two minutes, Bree."

"All right. Two minutes." She didn't know why it mattered, but she'd give him that. "Then I'm out of here."

"If you want to leave after that, I won't stop you." Parker jumped onto the platform and went to the lectern. "Can I have your attention, everyone?"

The murmur of voices dropped off, and when everyone was quiet, Parker said, "I appreciate all of you coming to this event, especially at such short notice. I wanted you to be here because you've been my most reliable donors. You've come through for me time and again. You're the folks I count on when I'm planning my annual expeditions.

"That's why it's important that you hear what I have to say. Many of you met Bree McInnes at the Field Museum last month." He smiled at her as if she was the only person in the room. "I love Bree, and I'm going to ask her to marry me tonight."

Bree's heart stopped, then began pounding in a hard, heavy beat.

"But there's something I need to say first," he continued.

"No, Parker. Don't."

He put his hand over the microphone. "It's okay." Holding her gaze, he said into the mic, "Bree is a woman with a past. Just like all the rest of us. I should have told her it didn't matter. That it didn't change how I felt about her, because it didn't. But instead of thinking about her, I was focused on the bottom line. How it would affect my job."

He kept his gaze on Bree, and she couldn't breathe. She was torn between hope and fear.

"Like everyone else in this room, I've done some stupid things in my life." Parker gave her an almost imperceptible nod. "But this went beyond stupid. This was thoughtless and cruel. Once I realized what I'd done, I arranged for all of you to be here tonight so I could tell you that I don't care what you think of me or Bree."

Murmurs spread through the crowd. Bree covered her mouth with her hand, feeling both terrified and exhilarated.

"I'm not going to tell you about Bree's past. That's her business, and I won't break her confidence. But if she marries me, sooner or later it will come out. I needed you all to know that Bree is more important to me than my expeditions. I hope you'll all stick with me, but if you feel you can't, I understand. If marrying the woman I love costs me your support, so be it."

Parker took a deep breath. "Once again, thanks for coming tonight. Help yourself to the hors d'oeuvres and drinks. I'm going to be busy."

Laughter rippled through the room, and she knew everyone was staring at her. Wondering. Her palms were sweating.

Shelley and Jack Horton appeared next to her, one on either side. "We don't care what you've done, honey," Shelley said, hugging her. "That man loves you, and that's good enough for us."

Bree stared at her. "You're going to continue supporting Parker?"

"Of course. He's doing important work. And we like you a lot. We don't care what you did years ago. What difference does it make?"

"You don't know what it was," Bree muttered.

"No one is perfect." Shelley said gently. "If we judged people by their mistakes, we'd have to condemn everyone." She patted Bree's hand. "Parker told us what he did to you. He's a knucklehead, but he knows he made a mistake, Bree. Can you forgive him?"

"I can handle this myself, Shelley." Parker stood behind Bree, close enough that she could feel his breath on her neck. Close enough to feel the energy pouring off him. He didn't touch her, but her skin prickled.

"My two minutes are up, Bree," he said. "Are you leaving or staying?"

Her heart pounding, her stomach jumping, she turned to face him. "Why did you do this, Parker?"

"Would you have believed me if I came to you and said it didn't matter? That I didn't care if my donors left me?" When she didn't answer, he said, "I didn't think so. I'm desperate, Bree."

She looked around, and saw that no one was interested in the hors d'oeuvres. No one stood at the bar. Everyone in the room was watching them. "Do we have to do this in public?"

"If that's what it takes. Personally, I'd rather have the rest of this conversation in private. But if you want me to get down on one knee in front of everyone, I'll do it happily. As long as you say yes."

"No," she said. He flinched as if she'd struck him. "I mean, no, I don't want to stay here. Everyone's watching us."

Without another word, he hurried her out of the room. There was no one else in the elevator, and she couldn't help remembering the last time they'd taken an elevator up to a hotel room. Parker had to be thinking about it, too, because his hand tightened on hers.

They walked down a quiet, softly lit corridor, and he slipped his key card in a slot. When she'd stepped into his room, the door closed behind her with a solid clunk.

He was staying in a suite, with a sitting room and a separate bedroom. He led her to the sitting room, and began pacing. "I don't know where to begin, Bree. You were right. I was a jerk and a fool. It didn't take me long to realize what a mistake I'd made, but then Charlie got hurt. Waiting these three weeks while he recovered has been the hardest thing I've ever done."

Parker took her hand and brushed his lips across her palm, and she shivered. His mouth lingered and then he twined their fingers tightly together.

"All this time, I thought it was just sex for you," she said. "That's all you ever promised."

"I'm sorry I hurt you. That I let you think that. And it turns out I was wrong." He quirked an eyebrow. "Or are you saying I was your boy toy? That you were just using me?"

"You know I wasn't."

"Thank God." He drew her closer. "Although I've always wanted to be someone's boy toy. Are you sure?"

"Very sure."

"That's good, because I love you, Bree. It took me too damn long to figure it out, but I do. Completely. Nothing is more important than you."

She wanted to fall into his arms, to tell him that she loved him, too, but she couldn't. Not yet. "I'm part of a package deal," she said. "We're not just talking about the two of us. I have a son. I have two sisters and a brother-in-law." Her mouth curved. "A niece or nephew in eight months. Families can be difficult. I saw how uncomfortable complications made you."

"Because I was afraid of being left behind again. Afraid of letting myself care, then losing everybody. If no one was important, no one could hurt me. But I want to take the chance. I want the whole package. Charlie. Sisters and brothers-in-law. Nieces and nephews." He drew her closer. "I want to be part of a family. With you at the center.

"You're the most important thing in my world. Nothing else matters without you. I don't give a damn about going on my expeditions if I can't have you in my life. I've had plenty of time to think recently, and I know what I want. Will you forgive me? Will you marry me?"

He'd said in the ballroom he was going to ask her to marry him. But she still couldn't quite believe it. "You want to get married?"

"Isn't that what you do when you can't imagine life without the person you love? When nothing matters but her? I want to wake up with you every morning for the rest of my life. I want to make love with you, fight with you, make a family with you. You're everything to me, Bree."

He swept her hair away from her face. "I've been doing a lot of talking here, but you haven't said much. I thought you loved me. Was I wrong?" He gripped her shoulders. "Did I blow it? Have you decided you don't love me after all?"

"I love you, Parker. I've been calling myself all kinds of a fool for the past few weeks, but I couldn't get you out of my heart."

"Okay. Decision time. Will you marry me?"

"I want to marry you." Reality elbowed happiness out of the way. "But it's not that easy. What about your expeditions? You're gone for half the year. I don't want a part-time marriage. Or a part-time husband."

"Neither do I, sweetheart, so I have a plan." He skimmed his hands down her arms, then up to her shoulders. "First, tell me again that you love me, Bree."

"I do love you," she said, finally allowing herself to wrap her arms around him. "Completely. I've been so sad these past weeks."

"I've been the most miserable human being on the face of the earth. We've gone through two assistants since you left. Chuck Boehmer has threatened to banish me to the basement of the science building if I don't get you back."

She clung to Parker, unable to let him go. "So what's your plan?"

"I'll tell you the details later. Right now there's something much more important to talk about. Like boy toys," he said, drawing a finger lightly down the center of her chest. "And dancing lessons."

Desire hummed along her nerves and raced through her blood. "What are a boy toy's duties?"

"Hmm. I have a few ideas about that." He slid his hands beneath her silk jacket and spread his palms on her bare back.

"What about Charlie and Zoe?" she said.

"We have two hours before they'll be back."

"You planned this to the last detail, didn't you?" she asked, locking her arms around his neck and pulling him close.

"You bet I did. I wasn't leaving anything to chance."

She smiled. "I like a man who pays attention to details."

THEY MANAGED TO MAKE IT to the hotel lobby, clothing on right side out, just as Charlie and Zoe were walking in.

"How was the movie?" Bree asked brightly.

"Awesome." Charlie looked from her to Parker. "Hey, Professor. What are you doing here?"

He was just a little too casual, a little too innocent, and Bree narrowed her eyes. "I know that tone of voice, bud. Were you in on this, too?"

Charlie spread his hands and widened his eyes. "Geez, Mom, why are you so suspicious?"

"Because I know my kid." She turned to Parker. "Did you plan this with Charlie, behind my back?"

He spread his hands just like Charlie had done. "Geez, Bree, why are you so suspicious?"

Biting her lip to keep from laughing, she said, "So. A conspiracy in my own family."

Out of the corner of her eye, she saw Charlie grin and give Parker a double thumbs-up, despite the green cast he was wearing. Parker clapped him on the back. "We have stuff to talk about, kid. You want to come up to my room for a while?"

Zoe hugged her sister. "I'm beat, Bree. I'm going to bed."

"Thanks, Zo," Bree whispered as she hugged her back.

"What do we need to talk about?" Charlie asked as soon as they got off the elevator.

"Hold your pants on," Parker said as he ushered them into his suite. They'd made the bed in the other room, and Bree had tugged the door closed before they'd gone down to the lobby.

Parker slipped into the bedroom now, rummaged in his suitcase and returned with a paper grocery sack, which he handed to Charlie. "Here you go."

Parker sat down beside Bree, who leaned against him. "What's going on?" she murmured.

"Are you always this impatient?" he whispered. "Oh, wait. You are." He nuzzled her neck. "But I'm not complaining."

"That's the kind of attitude I like in my boy toys."

He tightened his grip on her waist. "You better watch it, or Charlie's going to get a show."

Ignoring the adults, Charlie opened the bag and pulled out a book and a small square box with a picture of a light on it.

"Reptiles of South America," he read, then looked at Parker, a question in his eyes.

"I figure you're going to need a reference book next summer. When we all go down to South America for my annual expedition."

"We're going with you?" He looked from Parker to Bree.

"We are?" she asked.

"You don't think I'm leaving you two behind, do you?" Parker shook his head. "Not a chance. I didn't think Charlie would want to miss school, so I thought we could spend our summers in South America."

"Sweet!" Charlie exclaimed.

"Parker and I are getting married, Charlie," Bree told him. But Charlie wasn't paying attention, he was flipping the pages of his new reptile book. Parker was, though.

"Finally I get a yes out of you," he murmured into her ear.

"You got more than one yes out of me a little while ago," she whispered, grinning.

Charlie looked up from the book. "You're getting married? Cool." He set the book on the couch and opened the box, taking out a round, red light attached to a piece of Velcro. "What's this for?"

"That's to wrap around your arm when you're running. It flashes, even in bright daylight. You need a keeper when you run, Charlie. In case I can't go with you, you can use the light."

"Awesome." He wrapped the strap around his arm and fiddled with the switch. Bree watched, amazed at how easily he'd accepted the news.

Parker put his arm around her shoulder. "You look pretty tired, Charlie. Why don't you head on down to your room? Your mom is going to stay up here for a while longer." He dropped a kiss on her head. "She's teaching me to dance, and it looks like I'm going to need a lot of lessons."

* * * * *

Silhouette Desire kicks off 2009 with
MAN OF THE MONTH, *a yearlong program*
featuring incredible heroes by stellar authors.

When navy SEAL Hunter Cabot returns home for some
much-needed R & R, he discovers he's a married man.
There's just one problem: he's never met his "bride."

Enjoy this sneak peek at Maureen Child's
AN OFFICER AND A MILLIONAIRE.
Available January 2009 from Silhouette Desire.

One

Hunter Cabot, Navy SEAL, had a healing bullet wound in his side, thirty days' leave and, apparently, a wife he'd never met.

On the drive into his hometown of Springville, California, he stopped for gas at Charlie Evans's service station. That's where the trouble started.

"Hunter! Man, it's good to see you! Margie didn't tell us you were coming home."

"Margie?" Hunter leaned back against the front fender of his black pickup truck and winced as his side gave a small twinge of pain. Silently then, he watched as the man he'd known since high school filled his tank.

Charlie grinned, shook his head and pumped gas. "Guess your wife was lookin' for a little 'alone' time with you, huh?"

"My—" Hunter couldn't even say the word. *Wife?* He didn't have a wife. "Look, Charlie..."

"Don't blame her, of course," his friend said with a wink

as he finished up and put the gas cap back on. "You being gone all the time with the SEALs must be hard on the ol' love life."

He'd never had any complaints, Hunter thought, frowning at the man still talking a mile a minute. "What're you—"

"Bet Margie's anxious to see you. She told us all about that R & R trip you two took to Bali." Charlie's dark brown eyebrows lifted and wiggled.

"Charlie..."

"Hey, it's okay, you don't have to say a thing, man."

What the hell could he say? Hunter shook his head, paid for his gas and as he left, told himself Charlie was just losing it. Maybe the guy had been smelling gas fumes too long.

But as it turned out, it wasn't just Charlie. Stopped at a red light on Main Street, Hunter glanced out his window to smile at Mrs. Harker, his second-grade teacher who was now at least a hundred years old. In the middle of the crosswalk, the old lady stopped and shouted, "Hunter Cabot, you've got yourself a wonderful wife. I hope you appreciate her."

Scowling now, he only nodded at the old woman—the only teacher who'd ever scared the crap out of him. What the hell was going on here? Was everyone but him nuts?

His temper beginning to boil, he put up with a few more comments about his "wife" on the drive through town before finally pulling into the wide, circular drive leading to the Cabot mansion. Hunter didn't have a clue what was going on, but he planned to get to the bottom of it. Fast.

He grabbed his duffel bag, stalked into the house and paid no attention to the housekeeper, who ran at him, fluttering both hands. "Mr. Hunter!"

"Sorry, Sophie," he called out over his shoulder as he took the stairs two at a time. "Need a shower, then we'll talk."

He marched down the long, carpeted hallway to the rooms that were always kept ready for him. In his suite, Hunter tossed the duffel down and stopped dead. The shower in his bathroom was running. His *wife?*

Anger and curiosity boiled in his gut, creating a churning mass that had him moving forward without even thinking about it. He opened the bathroom door to a wall of steam and the sound of a woman singing—off-key. Margie, no doubt.

Well, if she was his wife...Hunter walked across the room, yanked the shower door open and stared in at a curvy, naked, temptingly wet woman.

She whirled to face him, slapping her arms across her naked body while she gave a short, terrified scream.

Hunter smiled. "Hi, honey. I'm home."

* * * * *

Be sure to look for
AN OFFICER AND A MILLIONAIRE
by USA TODAY *bestselling author Maureen Child.*
Available January 2009 from Silhouette Desire.

CELEBRATE
60 YEARS
OF PURE READING PLEASURE
WITH **HARLEQUIN**®!

We'll be spotlighting a different series
every month throughout 2009
to celebrate our 60th anniversary.
Look for Silhouette Desire® in January!

Collect all 12 books in the Silhouette Desire®
Man of the Month continuity, starting in
January 2009 with *An Officer and a Millionaire*
by *USA TODAY* bestselling author
Maureen Child.

*Look for one new Man of the Month title
every month in 2009!*

REQUEST YOUR FREE BOOKS!

2 FREE NOVELS PLUS 2 FREE GIFTS!

HARLEQUIN®

Super Romance®

Exciting, emotional, unexpected!

YES! Please send me 2 FREE Harlequin Superromance® novels and my 2 FREE gifts (gifts are worth about $10). After receiving them, if I don't wish to receive any more books, I can return the shipping statement marked "cancel." If I don't cancel, I will receive 6 brand-new novels every month and be billed just $4.69 per book in the U.S. or $5.24 per book in Canada, plus 25¢ shipping and handling per book and applicable taxes, if any*. That's a savings of close to 15% off the cover price! I understand that accepting the 2 free books and gifts places me under no obligation to buy anything. I can always return a shipment and cancel at any time. Even if I never buy another book from Harlequin, the two free books and gifts are mine to keep forever.

135 HDN EEX7   336 HDN EEYK

Name	(PLEASE PRINT)	
Address		Apt. #
City	State/Prov.	Zip/Postal Code

Signature (if under 18, a parent or guardian must sign)

Mail to the **Harlequin Reader Service:**
IN U.S.A.: P.O. Box 1867, Buffalo, NY 14240-1867
IN CANADA: P.O. Box 609, Fort Erie, Ontario L2A 5X3

Not valid to current subscribers of Harlequin Superromance books.

Want to try two free books from another line?
Call 1-800-873-8635 or visit www.morefreebooks.com.

* Terms and prices subject to change without notice. N.Y. residents add applicable sales tax. Canadian residents will be charged applicable provincial taxes and GST. Offer not valid in Quebec. This offer is limited to one order per household. All orders subject to approval. Credit or debit balances in a customer's account(s) may be offset by any other outstanding balance owed by or to the customer. Please allow 4 to 6 weeks for delivery. Offer available while quantities last.

Your Privacy: Harlequin is committed to protecting your privacy. Our Privacy Policy is available online at www.eHarlequin.com or upon request from the Reader Service. From time to time we make our lists of customers available to reputable third parties who may have a product or service of interest to you. If you would prefer we not share your name and address, please check here. ☐

HSR08R

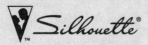

Silhouette® Romantic SUSPENSE

Sparked by Danger, Fueled by Passion.

Justine Davis
Baby's Watch

Former bad boy Ryder Colton has never felt a connection to much, so he's shocked when he feels one to the baby he helps deliver, and her mother. Ana Morales doesn't quite trust this stranger, but when her daughter is taken by a smuggling ring, she teams up with him in the hope of rescuing her baby. With nowhere to turn she has no choice but to trust Ryder with her life...and her heart.

Available January 2009 wherever books are sold.

Look for the final installment of
the Coltons: Family First miniseries,
A Hero of Her Own by Carla Cassidy in February 2009.

Silhouette®

SPECIAL EDITION™

USA TODAY bestselling author
MARIE FERRARELLA

FORTUNES OF TEXAS: RETURN TO RED ROCK

PLAIN JANE AND THE PLAYBOY

To kill time at a New Year's party, playboy
Jorge Mendoza shows the host's teenage son
how to woo the ladies. The random target of
Jorge's charms: wallflower Jane Gilliam. But
with one kiss at midnight, introverted Jane
turns the tables on this would-be Casanova,
as the commitment-phobe falls for her hook,
line and sinker!

*Available January 2009
wherever you buy books.*

Visit Silhouette Books at www.eHarlequin.com SSE65428

COMING NEXT MONTH

#1536 A FOREVER FAMILY • Jamie Sobrato
Going Back
He's not part of her plans. So why can't single mom Emmy Van Amsted stop thinking about her college sweetheart Aidan Caldwell? She's returned to this town to start over, not revisit history. Still, Aidan's presence is making her rethink her plans.

#1537 THE SECRET SHE KEPT • Amy Knupp
A Little Secret
Jake had blown out of town so fast—and so angry at his dad—Savannah Salinger had no clue how to find him, let alone tell him she was pregnant. And she's kept her secret for so long...what's she going to do now that Jake Barnes is back?

#1538 A MAN SHE COULDN'T FORGET • Kathryn Shay
Clare Boneil has stepped into a life she can't remember. That's especially so for the two men pursuing her. She cares for both, but only one makes her feel alive, feel like herself. Until her memory returns, can she trust her heart to lead her to the one she loves?

#1539 THE GROOM CAME BACK • Abby Gaines
Marriage of Inconvenience
It's past time Dr. Jack Mitchell divorced Callie Summers. Rumors of their marriage are beginning to affect his reputation as a star neurosurgeon—not to mention his love life. But returning home for the first time in years, Jack doesn't even recognize the knockout woman she's become. And she's not letting him leave home again without a fight.

#1540 DADDY BY SURPRISE • Debra Salonen
Spotlight on Sentinel Pass
Jackson Treadwell is proving he's got a wild side. Clad in leather astride his motorcycle, wild he is. He so doesn't expect to meet a woman who makes him want to settle down—let alone settle with kids! But he's never met anyone as persuasive as Kat Petroski.

#1541 PICTURES OF US • Amy Garvey
Everlasting Love
The photographs that line the mantel of the Butterfield home celebrate every highlight of Michael and Tess's life together—from sweethearts to marriage to parenthood. But when crisis strikes, can these same images guide them back to each other?